An Omega's Choice:
Predators and Prey

The Omegas of The New South Book 4

by

Sharilyn Skye

Copyright 2021 by Sharilyn Skye
All Rights Reserved
Paperback: 9781736133750
EBook ISBN: 9781736133743
First Edition: December 2021 update 02/17/26
Cover Design: PaigeLCro Photography
Cover Photo Credit: Kevron2001

Quotes:

It's natural. Nature is dark and light, birth and death. Everything and its opposite. And in nature, there are predators and prey. The hunters and the hunted. The heartbreakers and the heartbroken. The beautiful thing is that nature lets us choose which we want to be.

~Lynn Weingarten

She had never been so close to anybody. It was as if they were one being, together, not predator and prey, but partners in a dance.

~LJ Smith

Prologue

After decades of uncertainty and strife, in 2072, the Great War finally happened. As the victor often writes history, no one knows what precipitated the warheads flying from continent to continent, but the truth is that they did. The entire west coast of the United States disappeared within minutes, as did choice targets on the eastern seaboard. The missile defense network saved parts of the country, but not all. The areas not destroyed by bombs were altered forever by the fallout.

In retaliation, any place suspected of launching those warheads was turned to ash, glass, or rock, depending on its original landmass's makeup. The last order from the dying central government was to push every button on every missile silo in existence.

No winner was declared.

Afterward, the United States fell upon itself, ripping and tearing apart what remained. Factions split the remainder of the country into three areas containing a few hundred thousand residents each. The New North, The New South, and Middle West's total population is estimated at less than two million souls.

Deep divisions within the military began the split, and civil war finalized it. The Army ruled the West, the Navy the North, and the Marines the South. The Air Force as an entity did not survive the Great War, and the remaining members chose which country they wanted to call home. Most of those individuals settled into post-military life without looking back. An uneasy peace followed.

It took decades to rebuild the power grids and a century for technology to begin to recover. Due to the atmosphere's damage, air travel was restricted to three thousand feet or less and limited to smaller shuttlecrafts or helicopters.

High walls separate the three new countries, and their cities are encapsulated by smaller, less ominous walls in an attempt to keep citizens safe from the wild things unleashed during this troubled time. Although life outside the walls was viewed as impossible by those living within them, it does go on.

Everything changed.

Exposure to unknown agents caused a shift in the human genome. From a population comprised of what would become genetic Betas, came Alphas and Omegas. The pre-war world had used the term Alpha Male like they knew what it was all about.

They did not.

Not that all alphas are male. Alpha females are known to be particularly vicious and wickedly smart. The rarest of all creatures is the Omega. Small of frame and gentle of spirit, they bear the burden of creating more Alphas and Omegas. Their bodies call specifically to the Alpha, each providing something to the other that is not only necessary for them, but for all that remain as well. Fertility rates among all the dynamics are abysmal. Still, enough are born to keep the wheels turning, even if just barely.

The Alphas rule, omegas shoulder the burden, and Betas keep the status quo, and everyone is grateful for that if nothing else.

Chapter One

Bala

The ancient, rusted-out shitbox clattered down the sand road toward camp. High winds made a washboard of it as they often did, and the bumps made the old truck groan. Between Jah and me sat the Omega we'd met just a week before, after a short battle with The Alpha for the right to claim her. Our joining ceremony was this morning, as his wife, Eve, and our new bride insisted. Not that we cared or would've refused. We were in it for the long haul, and with an omega we'd both wanted to claim, how could we not be?

Tosha Randolf was a wild card from a faraway place up north in the Seventh District. It was the most beautifully wild place I'd ever seen, but it was also deadly unpredictable, making me wonder what kind of omega survived there unmated. Jah and I participated in the short, bloody skirmish in the Seventh, helping crush a rebellion against The Alpha and The New South.

Our Omega had been part of a particularly vicious group of fighters, made up of mostly women and all Omegas. Such a thing had never been heard of before. As they came to be known, the Omega Force decimated the rebels with little help from the trained marines trailing behind them like lost dogs.

If I hadn't been there, I wouldn't believe the tales that sprang like seagrass as word spread. Glancing at the head of the silent

Omega next to me, I wondered, not for the first time, what role she played in that victory.

Jah and I were relegated to mountaintops and high vantage points, acting as scouts and sharpshooters as was our job most days. Rarely do we kill up close and personal, at least not in our official roles as killers for The New South. Now personally? Well, unless our contracts specify how the killing must be carried out, we do what we want.

Sun reflected off the untamed honey-gold hair that hung to the waist of the woman next to me, making me blink. It was so odd to see that bright shade on a human that it was confusing. It was almost unnatural. As if feeling my eyes on her, she turned her face upward, pinning me with her strange eyes. We'd never seen anything like her.

When we went to The Alpha to ask for an Omega female who might allow two mates, Lukas balked. We'd presented our arguments because, for us, it was imperative that we not divide our focus. Having separate mates would cause conflict, and we couldn't afford that. We functioned as a team, and any threats to that were avoided at all costs. After a while, Lukas had come back with a name and his grudging consent.

According to her file, Tosha came from a place so treacherous that more than one mate was needed to keep families safe. She agreed to our request after meeting us just once instead of three times as NS304 requires.

She blinked her violet eyes before looking away. She hadn't said a word since the joining ceremony was over, and I wondered what this day might bring. I wasn't used to quiet women.

Jah and I are Gullah or Geechee. Our women are boisterous and loud. They sing, laugh, and talk from morning to night as they care for our small community on the edge of the sea. In as much as anything is old-fashioned in this new world, we are. The women build the home, and men fish and hunt for food.

There are Omegas. There are even single Omegas in our community, but it is not their tradition to be shared, so we'd looked to the strange, exotic females instead. But her silence concerned me. I looked to find my brother watching. He quirked one eyebrow in question, and I shrugged my shoulder in response. We didn't need words to communicate, and I understood that he was just as confused as I was.

"We won't hurt you," I started, thinking she was concerned about the upcoming hunt. I kept my voice low and spoke slowly as she fought to understand our accent. "It is an old tradition that is played out to ensure a fruitful union. It's nothing serious," I added, thinking she was scared about being alone in the woods with us.

After the Great War, when females were scarce, men raided local towns to steal brides. Gran'maamy said that this custom goes further back to when we came from faraway places. But I don't know nothing 'bout dat. I thought, forcing my internal dialogue to correct. When we'd been recruited to join the Marines, we'd barely spoken English. Our town, and many others that survived along the strange, new coastline, had reverted to the lost dialect of our people. Neither of us had gone to school beyond what was required and struggled to communicate with outsiders.

"It's fine," she said, but added nothing more.

My eyes narrowed, and I again looked toward Jah. This female was confusing. Fine never meant fine; I didn't need a college education to know that. He raised his brow and gave one sharp shake of his head, but added nothing meaningful to the conversation.

The post-war truck rumbled to a stop, and Jah cut the ignition before opening the door with a screech of rusty hinges. We'd picked the northernmost section of our lands for this hunting farce as there were pines, grasses, and thick undergrowth for cover. We owned hundreds of acres near our small town, and this section was perfect. We'd brought down many a deer to fill our freezer here. We hadn't intended on going through with this crazy tradition, but our Gram had insisted.

Jah unfolded himself from the truck, stretching after the long ride from the Capital. I opened my door, sliding out and doing the same. Tosha sat a moment longer, her head swiveling to take in the surroundings. Finally, she slid out the driver's side, her eyes constantly moving. She looked from the tops of the trees to the edges of the scrub, missing nothing.

"We should skip this, Bal. It's dumb," Jah said, finally breaking his silence. "We could go to Gram's for supper instead."

"The hunt is never dumb," Tosha whispered, continuing her slow assessment of her environment. "There are always questions and answers to be found there." She looked up at both of us, her eyes rounded with what I took as fear.

"We won't hurt you," I tried again.

"I know," she answered, looking away.

She was so small. Thin, tan exercise pants covered the fawn-colored skin on her shapely thighs, accentuating the round bubble of her ass. Her waist was so tiny I could span my hand across it. Still, curves exploded from there, making my mouth water. Her scent was intoxicating, and the early spring warmth made it more intense. She wasn't in estrous, or even near it, but she was mouthwatering all the same.

I glanced at my brother. The gleam in his eye had turned feral, and I knew he was thinking the same thing. Tosha was right about the hunt. Maybe I was glad we hadn't skipped it after all.

"You'll get a ten-minute head start," Jah said, his accent as deep as I'd ever heard it. Lifting his head, he scented the air and checked the direction of the wind. He was getting a baseline of her scent and the scents around us. "Nothing in these woods is dangerous," he added, and I smiled at his lie. There were dangerous things in these woods, and the golden-colored omega was looking at two of them.

She turned to face us, her huge, purple eyes round as she backed away, and I felt a tingle of excitement from her fear. Then she tilted her head, narrowing her eyes as a feral smile spread across her features. She raised an eyebrow and shook her head in what I took to be disbelief. She took three more backward steps and then completely disappeared.

Chapter Two

Jah

What the actual fuck? The woman was in front of me. She was right fucking in front of me, and then she was gone. It's black magic. She must be a cunning woman. I inhaled, catching her sweet scent on the breeze before I lost it to the wind. Not a twig snapped, and not a blade of grass moved.

"Damn, her profile said she liked to hunt. I didn't take it literally." Bal chuckled beside me, and I knew his tone for what it was. Excitement. Nothing got our blood moving more than stalking prey, and the omega was tempting fate to even try hiding from us. I'd assumed she'd find a clearing and carry through with the tradition in its vaguest form, sitting and waiting for us to come across her. Surely she didn't mean to really hide from us. Did she?

And that smile.

I recognized it for what it was. I looked at my ComLink, checking the time before walking to the bed of the old truck we shared. I'd packed a cooler of drinks and a few snacks in case the piece of shit broke down. Pulling out supplies we kept handy, I poured chilled water into a canteen and shoved some jerky and nuts into a pack. The omega didn't know the territory, and as we hadn't stopped to feed her on the way, she'd be hungry when we found her. Bal did the same, and neither of us said anything.

I'd known these women were fighters, but I discounted it. I'd seen them in combat and ignored all that. Hell, I'd known they were killers and forgotten that, too. That smile. I knew that smile. I felt my cock harden. I hope she hid well.

I rechecked my ComLink and saw that eleven minutes had passed. With a look between us, Bal and I headed into the woods to claim our mate. We crossed the sandy clearing soundlessly, stepping into the shadowed pines. The faint trace of her scent was gone, though the breeze wasn't strong enough to carry it away. It should have lingered. No broken twigs or turned leaves showed her path. I nodded to the right, and Bal immediately split from me, walking a short distance away but keeping pace as we threaded through the trees, looking for a sign of where our mate hid.

She'd dressed in dull browns and tans to meet us. At the time, I thought it an odd choice. Gullah women are colorful. They peacock around town loud in body and spirit. Tosha had downplayed her clothes, and I saw it for what it was- camouflage. We had told her about this tradition before she'd agreed to bind with us, not wanting to surprise or frighten her. Turns out the joke was on us. I remembered how the New South's drones struggled to find the Omega Force in the mountains of the Seventh. They blended with their surroundings perfectly. Our golden-haired, tan-skinned, earthen-dressed omega had taken very, very thorough advantage of our stupidity. I'd mistaken her quiet for fear or unease; it turns out she was planning.

Silently we prowled the woods, moving further and further from the truck. We knew these woods like the back of our hands, and no place would fit an omega that we did not check. We fanned out, each knowing our role. The only scent on the air was salt, and that was no help. This close to the ocean, everything smelled of salt, sand, or pines. Long ago, this area would have been miles inland. Time and the War changed the landscape, bringing water levels higher, making coastal properties of inland homes. Not many of those old homes remained. Climate change made the storms that hit the area ten times stronger, and folks brave enough to stay as near to their homelands as they could had to adapt. Our islands disappeared long ago, and the small villages that popped up on the higher stretches of land contained buildings on stilts strong enough to withstand tidal surges not seen in the old world.

An hour or more passed with no sign of the omega. I could feel Bal's frustration growing. Tosha was beating us at our own game, and it was beginning to wear. We'd circled back, rechecked the groundcover, and checked again.

We'd rounded the corner into a thicker section of woods when we got our first break. Fresh wood shavings lay scattered along the pine needle covered ground. I picked one up, bringing it to my nose. The scent of pine was sharp, and the wood still a little damp from being shaved off. I looked up for the first time, chastising myself for not doing it sooner. It was a rookie mistake I wouldn't have made it had I been hunting a wanted man or anything else for that matter. Tosha was clearly taking this game more seriously than Bal and I had.

Turned leaves and a missing branch told me something important. Two things, really. One, my mate is playing me, and two, she had made herself a weapon.

Chapter Three

Tosh

I love it when people underestimate me. Seriously, my favorite thing ever; no sarcasm intended. I watch my Alphas from behind the branches of a nearby tree. As good as these men are at hunting prey, and I've seen their statistics, they are excellent. They missed the mark this time. I threw them off balance with my silence, preyed upon their alpha instincts with my pretend unease, and ripped the wound wide open by disappearing. They didn't see it coming until it was too late. An hour in, they were finally getting it.

They picked up the slivers of wood I left scattered in a sunlit spot. Any hunter worth a damn would have found them, and Bala and Jah did not disappoint.

When Eve and Lukas came to me with the brothers' proposal, I'd been intrigued enough to research them. It hadn't taken long to realize that it was a perfect match. I'd spent years in the woods hunting anything that could be eaten for food. Soon after turning twenty, I'd started hunting a different kind of prey.

I came from a little town called Cameron in a forgotten section of West Virginia, or the Seventh District as we're supposed to call it. Cameron was close enough to the New North and the Middle West that you could hit both with a rock. It wasn't uncommon for skirmishes with both sides to happen. I'd hunted many a stolen sister, car, cow, or other assets, making myself a nice nest egg in the process.

I'd been lost since Eve's fight for change was won. The Alpha now paid more attention to the Seventh, and I wasn't needed to help keep my hometown safe anymore. At least for now. For now, New South Marines scoured the area looking for insurgents and strengthening the borders, and, now, I was bored. When presented with the opportunity to mate with two strong Alphas who were not at all unlike me, I jumped at it. We'd make a good team. I got them, and in time, they would get me too.

They might think I was a sweet little omega happy to sit in a nest all day. Though I was little, and I do like to nest, there was nothing sweet about me. I'd fit with these men like a puzzle piece they didn't know they were missing.

As they searched, they hadn't spoken a word, not that I could understand them. Bala and Jah spoke with deep accents, often using a dialect of English I'd never heard. More often, they didn't use words at all to communicate. Looks, nods, and slants of the eyes conveyed conversations I had no hope of keeping up with.

Now they stood, glancing at the clues I left and finally at the treetops above where I hid. It had taken them long enough. Humans rarely look up. As a species that can be either predator or prey, humans adapt to whichever role they choose. As an omega, I was natural prey, but I'd learned to be a predator. Say what you will about the mountains of the Seventh District. They are lovely.

They protected an endemic population from the worst of the Great War's fallout. They sustain many people that, to this day, the government knows little about, but they are wild.

While exploring the border between The Seventh and The Middle West, my sister and I unearthed an old metal sign. It had been buried under the debris of a collapsed, pre-war roadway. After scraping the dirt off and running some water over it, we'd been able to make out the words "Welcome to West Virginia" scrawled across the top, and at the bottom, it read "Wild and Wonderful." My ancestors weren't wrong. It was that untamed place that turned traditionally soft, pampered omegas into hunters; they made prey into predators. Those mountains made survivors out of everyone who survived there. It was the nature of that beautiful beast. Had those hundred or so Omegas I fought beside been born anywhere else, there would have been no Omega Force. What astounded outsiders made perfect sense to me because I'd grown up there.

Those rough mountains were the reason I watched them soundlessly from my perch. They split, circling below me as they looked to the sky. I'd chosen my clothes carefully, knowing what they had planned. On top of that, I'd taken advantage of the ten-minute lead and the salt marsh to the east, covering my scent and adding an additional layer of muddy cover. I blended so perfectly with the surroundings that both of them looked right at me before turning and sliding away through the woods.

Unfortunately for my Alphas, there was a custom from my community that they were unaware of. Due to the location of my small town, the frequent raids, and the lack of females, it became necessary for men to share a mate. More than that, males proved themselves worthy of that mate by stealing her from her family or other well-guarded places. It was all consensual, of course, in that the males asked for permission in advance, but beyond that, nothing was scripted. This supposed game my boys called an old play on tradition, was a way of life for those in my tiny strip of land between countries. Capturing a female proved that you were capable. Females in that area are strong, independent, and wily. We do not make easy prey. Add in my training, and I was chuckling high above the men below.

I'd been hunted numerous times and never been caught. I smiled to myself at the thought. None of those alphas had been worthy, but Jah and Bala were, and even though we'd already had a claiming ceremony, I wasn't going to make this easy for them. My genetics wouldn't let me. How could they keep an omega safe if they couldn't find her hidden in territory she was unfamiliar with? Some part of me demanded they prove themselves.

When they were gone, I slipped down the tree like a silent squirrel. Only those assholes are never quiet. Sleeping in a tree stand waiting on a big deer? To be sure, a squirrel will wake you. You'll think it's a giant buck too. Moving without making a sound, I trailed my boys deeper into the woods. Using trees for cover and climbing them when necessary, I followed them until the smell of their frustration reached me high in the trees. Then I shimmied down, darting away. In a clearing far from my alphas, I began my own hunt.

It was there that I made my first mistake.

Chapter Four

Bal

My gaze snapped to Jah's, and his eyes met mine, narrowing instantly. Tipping my nose up, I turned slowly. The scent of blood carried on a southeastern breeze. Sharp and fresh, it was uncommon enough to cause a smile to spread across my face.

We'd so grossly underestimated our omega that it was laughable. We'd stopped treating this as a play on tradition and started hunting Tosha in earnest hours ago. There'd been no trace of her until that faint scent of blood on the air. The land's two best scavengers, hunters, and killers hadn't found so much as a stray hair from their mate, and it was sobering. But that blood? That blood was a definite sign.

There'd been no screams, so it wasn't a rabbit caught in the talons of an eagle. There'd been no grunts or squeals, so it wasn't a wild hog caught in a trap. I hoped it wasn't Tosh bleeding, but dismissed that immediately. Anyone who could avoid us on the trail for this long would not bleed easily. We turned as one, heading to the marsh along the border of our land.

Finally, we began to see signs we could track. An overturned rock here and a broken leaf there led us to a small clearing of mostly sand and some scattered grasses. A skinned and dressed sika deer hung from a tree by thickly braided grasses, the entrails left by the marsh's edge for the gators, and the hide was missing.

Our hunting cabin stood not even a hundred yards away, the windows darkened, and shutters closed.

It was at that moment that our plans changed. We'd thought to catch our prey within minutes, not hours. Tosha had proven to be slick and smart like a fox, forcing us to change our course. Jah might think she was a witch or a cunning woman, but her cunning was of a different kind of magic. Jah took the deer, slinging it over his shoulder, and we walked to the cabin together. I didn't think we'd find our mate sprawled out and waiting, but we had to check.

The cabin was an old, low-slung design like many left standing in modern times. As we walked up, we froze, heads swiveling to the edge of the small clearing where we stretched hides to cure. The sika deer hide hung, pulled tight on the cords set up for that purpose. A note that read 'needs salted' was pinned to the fur with a large sewing needle that had to come from inside the cabin. Jah stomped up wooden steps to the swaybacked porch, practically kicking the door open. His growl was deep, and I could see the hairs standing on his neck. He was as frustrated as I'd ever seen, maybe even more so. I moved to light lanterns and the logs in the fireplace. It would be chilly tonight, and as the day was getting away from us, we'd made the unconscious decision to stay here.

"I can't think straight, Bala," he said, running his hands through his dark shock of loose waves. "Where the fuck is she?"

"Each minute from the claiming ceremony that we don't actually claim her is making me crazier. Maybe we shouldn't have done this. If we got called in for a job right now, I couldn't do it," he finished, voicing our worst fears.

"Eh, brother. We set the game; she's simply outplaying us. The only job we have now is to find her, and we will." I opened my pack, took out my canteen, and emptied it. Somewhere out there, Tosha had to be getting tired, hungry, cold, and thirsty. She'd had nothing with her, and the brackish water wasn't fit to drink. It wasn't good for her or us for this to continue. The only good thing is that she might start making mistakes. I didn't think we would find her if she didn't.

"Should I start the generator?" I asked.

"I guess," he answered, tearing into the jerky he'd brought as he stewed. "How the fuck is she doing it?" he asked.

"She's good. We discounted that." I went through the small kitchen toward the back door.

"Never again," he said, moving to light the old meat smoker.

He was right about that. We would never again underestimate our omega.

Out back, I started the generator, allowing the well pump and water heater to function. Jah had cut up the small deer our mate had killed for us and placed it in the smoker. Within a few minutes, we closed the cabin door, crossed the porch, and went back to our hunt.

We picked up her trail in the clearing where she'd left the deer. She was less careful now, and I felt like I was being remediated by some of the clues she left. Like maybe we weren't smart enough to find her at her best. Some of them were obvious and others not, but we were getting a better picture of her movements. She'd taken off her boots, and we'd found them under some dense vegetation. Our omega was running barefoot among snakes and sand spurs, and still, she never left a footprint. We found the impression of her right little toe by a small stream and went the way the toe pointed.

She didn't leave us much. We found a creased leaf and, based on the direction of the crease, thought she might be heading toward the river. A single long hair waved from a low hanging branch, and we continued forward, feeling better about the situation. We separated again, moving apart in a wide circle but working together to make sure we didn't miss anything. If we caught her at the river, we could trap her. While it was possible to swim, the water was high this time of year. It moved fast and would be hard for even an expert swimmer to navigate.

We picked up our pace. I caught the first trace of her scent since she'd left us at the truck. A twig snapped in the distance, and we broke into a crouched run, ducking silently through the Sawgrass and pine trees. We moved silently, and as a team, we created a bottleneck that Tosha couldn't escape. Then I realized that there was something special about this hunt. It was primal. The urge I had to grab Tosha and claim her immediately upon finding her was so strong that my cock leaked through the restraints of my pants.

This is how our forefathers did it. I doubt very seriously that the women they hunted had been easy prey either. A low growl escaped my lips, and I found that my brother had bared his teeth as well. His nose tipped up as he scented the wind, and I watched as he flexed his fingers.

We hadn't talked about this part. We hadn't even thought about what would happen when we caught Tosha. I think we both thought we'd have a nice, tame walk through the woods and end the night peacefully at our grandmother's house, eating supper. Not now. Now my blood ran hot, and I needed to feel my omega beneath me. The anticipation was killing me, and each minute that passed fueled the flames higher. The little omega had pushed us past our breaking point by evading us so perfectly. Mix the thrill of the hunt with fear over having her running unprotected in wildlands she was unfamiliar with, and she'd lit the fuse to two ruthless predators. Now it was time for the explosion.

The woods thinned as we got within a mile or so of the river. The current was so fast that I could hear it, even from this distance. Fueled by recent rains, it rolled and crashed against its banks. My worry increased, Tosha may know the Appalachians like the back of her hand, but this place wasn't nearly as stable. The banks of the old Edisto could crash into the torrent of water with no warning. I hoped she didn't take the game too far.

The ruins of a once sprawling town slowed us, forcing us to pause and search for more potential hiding places. This area had once been heavily populated, but only the bones of old homes remained. Storms weren't the only thing that had grown stronger since the War. The river took no prisoners when it ran at its worst. Anything in the floodplain of the twisting banks was flattened and carried away to the sea. Heavy rains had made the area muddy, and I quickly scanned for more prints.

I found a heel impression that hadn't yet filled with water and knew she was close. Whether she knew we were hot on her trail or not, she was moving fast now, not caring about the little clues she left behind.

In a thicker grove of trees, we lost her again, but we'd tracked her enough that we picked up some of her tricks. We looked up. She wasn't there, but the evidence that she had been was clear. Bent branches and crumpled leaves highlighted the path she had taken as she moved through the trees like a squirrel. We stared at her path, astounded by the agility required to do such a thing. It was absurd. At that moment, I realized she had probably done this all along. We rarely found a trace of her on the ground because she hadn't been there. I growled, tipping my nose up and catching her scent. It was strong now, musky, sweet, and filled with omega need.

Beside me, Jah groaned, reaching to adjust his pants. His pupils were nearly blown as he glanced over before taking off in a loping run. We'd spent so much time together that he didn't need words to tell me how this was going to end. Our omega was going to get taken where we found her.

Chapter Five

Tosh

An inhuman growl came to me, vibrating on the wind, and I knew the time to run was over. These Alphas had dogged my tail since the chase began. It. Was. Glorious. I'd never been so thoroughly hounded in my life. Eve had been right; these men were a perfect match. Smiling, I turned, bracing my feet wide and twirling my makeshift bo staff. I'd done the best I could with the switchblade wedged between my breasts. It wasn't a perfect weapon, but it would do. The river at my back sounded like the purest form of violence. Slick trickled down my leg as arousal reached a crescendo mirrored by the raging waters beyond. I shook my head to clear the haze it formed.

This wasn't estrous, not at all. This was something baser and more primal. A growl slipped from my lips as I scanned my surroundings, looking for a fighting edge. The hunt may be over, but there was still one more test for them to pass. I had high hopes that the fight would be epic.

They came around the corner, their growls sending shivers down my spine and raising goose flesh on my arms. Bala's amber eyes were obliterated by the black of his pupils, and his breathing was fast and hard. I didn't think that had anything to do with exertion and everything to do with the stiff rod tenting the front of his pants. Jah's loose waves were a frenzied mess, and only a rim of his hazel iris remained. My grin spread as I took in their wildness. They will make excellent mates indeed.

I gave the staff another twirl, testing the weight and balance. Widening my stance, I waited for them to make up their minds on how to end this.

Bala's growl deepened as he prowled toward me, all alpha and all male. "It's over," he said, his words barely discernible from the sound of gravel being ground into smaller pieces. "Yield," he finished as he advanced.

I set my feet and pointed the tip of my staff at him. "Make me," I said, my voice barely a whisper.

Jah cocked his head, looking nothing like a man and everything like an animal. He tipped his nose, scenting the air rapidly, in, in, in out. In, in, in, out. His eyes zeroed in on the trail of hot slick flowing down my legs, and his growl elevated to a howl. He broke into a run, outpacing his brother. I brought my staff up, countering his hands as they reached for me. He looked confused as he circled, splitting my focus between them.

Like wolves, they worked to bring me down. I fought as best I could. I'm far deadlier with a long-range rifle or throwing knives than I am the staff, but I could fight with anything if needed. Where alphas have brute strength, omegas have speed, and I used every ounce of that advantage to keep their hands from touching me. I knew I wasn't going to win. Hell, I didn't want to win, but I did want to make them work for it. They needed to prove their strength, and I needed to prove mine. I wasn't an omega who was willing to sit out a fight. They needed to know that. Plus, this? This fight? I'd never been hotter in my life.

Oh, I'd had a man. To survive, you had to accept that your virginity wasn't going to last long past your first estrous unless you were crazy or suicidal. I was neither. I'd made the standard contract and been served through every estrous since I was nineteen, and that was two years ago. This was something else. These men were my mates, and I'd never wanted any alpha more, estrous or not. My grin grew into a happy smile as I lunged to the side, quickly escaping Jah's big hands.

Rough fingers scraped my skin as I dodged, twirled, and struck at them. Each time their flesh touched mine, I became more frantic to have them, but they hadn't won yet. I landed a hard blow on Bala's shoulder, sending him roaring backward. His arms were covered in raised welts from my strikes, but it didn't slow him for long.

Jah went low, charging at my legs, forcing me to jump and tuck to avoid being tackled. I landed and cartwheeled away, leaning back as another swipe missed. Heart pounding in my throat and echoing low in my core, I rolled away from a kick that would've taken me to the ground. I extended my bo, bringing it down on Jah's thigh as it straightened toward me.

I sprang away toward the roaring river, losing my footing in the mud. My staff went flying, and I reached for it, only to be grabbed by an ankle and pulled roughly away from the raging water. Above me, Bala breathed heavily and pinned me under him, caging me with his body.

"Enough," he roared, bringing his nose the hollow behind my ear and growling low. My chest arched into him, and I whimpered, turning my head on instinct and offering him my throat. His ragged breathing was even louder than the raging water. He pulled in my scent, the rumble in his chest evening out at my response. I was done fighting, too.

My thin pants were ripped from my hips, and another pair of hands spread my legs in the muddy grass. I'd had men, but I'd never had two men. An omega only needed multiple mates when it came to lifelong protection. One was enough to see her through an estrous, and this next part would be a mystery to me until it was done.

Fingers sought my core, flicking my clit and making me moan. Bala's lips fell onto mine, devouring my mouth in a fevered kiss. We'd never kissed or touched before, and the feeling of his tongue on mine and Jah working me had me coming already. I clenched around his fingers as I cried out for more.

"Move," Jah said, and Bala did. His weight was replaced immediately, and Jah wasted no time before entering me to his balls. I cried out at the force of it, whimpering as I curled into his chest. He was big, like all alphas, and hadn't given my body time to adjust to his size. He arched away from me, needing room to leverage himself deeper. My head was twisted to the side by my hair, and Bala's cock pressed against my lips. "Open," he said.

I took him in, tasting the sweat from our hunt and the sweetness of his pre-cum on my tongue. I smiled around his cock as he forced it all the way in. His balls hit my chin, and I groaned as he wrapped my hair around his hand and began fucking my mouth in earnest. None of that halfway shit for him. No, Jah drove in and out of my mouth until I almost gagged, which is a feat since omegas don't have a gag reflex.

My body stopped belonging to me as they took me from both ends, causing me to jolt with the force of their impacts. I screamed another orgasm as it began to rain. Bala growled, causing more slick to flow as I clamped down on his cock, begging for his seed. And still, they fucked me. At the moment, I couldn't see it for what it was, a thing of beauty. Afterward, I would marvel at how well they worked together and understand why separate mates wouldn't have worked for them.

Their hands were everywhere. I'd guessed when the chase started that it would end this way. It's hard to take time and learn your mate's body when you've been pushed beyond your limits. Jah's movements stuttered, and he reached down, gripping the base of his cock hard before unleashing a torrent of cum down my throat. His face tilted into the falling rain, he grunted his release, refusing to allow his knot to expand.

When the last stream of cum disappeared down my throat, he pulled me from under Bala like I was a doll and settled me on his still hard cock. Rain pelted my shoulders, and the angry river grew louder. Soaking wet, my hair streamed into my eyes, blocking my view. I could see flashes of Jah's toffee-colored skin as he thrust up into me, but then my body was pushed flat against his by a hand in the center of my back.

A bent knee appeared beside me, trapping me, and Bala's tip pressed against my ass. Using slick and other fluids, he worked a finger into my ass and then another. I'd never been fucked there, but I knew it was part and parcel with having more than one man. An omega's body was built differently, simply put. We have more pleasure receptors and can accommodate the larger-sized alphas in any hole, including that one.

Without preamble, I felt him push inside me. He wasn't as quick to push in as he had been the first time. He stroked my back and massaged my shoulders while his brother continued to fuck me from below. But even Jah's thrusts slowed, allowing his brother to be gentler. Jah's mouth found my throat and his tongue licked the sweat and rain from my skin. Teeth grazed my neck, and I shuddered at the feel of them.

Bala took his time, crooning and purring as he worked his way in. He tugged at the strands of my hair until I was limp, allowing the last few inches of his cock to slide home. I shuddered again, breathing deep. I was so full that my body spasmed, trying to push them out. As one, they groaned.

Bala's hands encircled my waist. He manipulated my body into a better position before pulling out and pressing back in. I cried out, unable to stop myself. Bala fucked me harder, forcing my body onto Jah's until the fullness intensified to the point of being uncomfortable. I cried out again, and Jah growled for me, releasing more slick and easing the feeling.

Hands found my breasts. Fingers pinched my nipples. I was pulled up so that Jah could bend his head to one. Bala pinched again, harder this time, and Jah soothed the pain away with his deft tongue. I tried to pull back and ease the pressure further but was stopped. Bala blocked the movement with his big body, bringing his nose to my ear and breathing in deeply.

"Be still, little wife," he growled. "You can take this and more. You will take this and more. You bested us, and this is the first part of your punishment," he thrust deeper into me, and I felt his balls slapping against the empty space between my legs.

Only I couldn't take it. It was too much. The feeling of fullness and their tandem movements had me falling over the edge. The orgasm started deep in my body. Like an earthquake, it moved out, causing ripples of pleasure and pain with its intensity. I came with guttural noises and the complete loss of sensation in my body. Slick squirted out of my body in hot torrents. I went limp between them as my epicenter quaked, kneading their bodies and trying to force their own orgasms. Bala caved first, pushing deeper into me as he shouted his orgasm to the sky. I screamed as his knot expanded. I hadn't expected that to happen. Jah came a split second later, and both of their mouths met my flesh. One on the left and one on the right, they bit hard enough to mark me as theirs and seal the alpha bond for life.

Their knots kept their cum from seeping out, and I felt impossibly and uncomfortably full. It was the kind of discomfort that reminded you that you had done something pleasant but entirely too much of it.

I lay pressed between them, surrounded by their smell and filled with their essence. Their scent imprinted on my brain, and I'd forever know them anywhere. My body registered all parts of them as belonging to it, and never again would another man be able to please me. The mate bond snapped into place, and I felt their peace through it. I felt their satiation. Their bodies vibrated together as they purred for me, not offering to move. And the rain fell.

We lay like this, their knots pinning me perfectly between them. They could undoubtedly feel each other through the thin barrier between them and seemed unbothered by any of it. Their knots abated simultaneously, letting the mix of our fluids pour between us all. We lay a while longer.

Eventually, Bala rose, throwing aside his ruined clothes and standing naked in the rain. He pulled me from Jah, ripping the remainder of my soaked clothes off before offering Bala a hand up. Jah cast the rest of his clothes aside, too. It was crazy how in tune they were with each other as they pressed me between them and checked for injuries. Rain had washed most of the mud from my skin, but they examined every inch to ensure I was okay.

Bala scooped me up and cradled me gently in his arms, beginning the long walk back to the cabin I had assumed was theirs. Jah followed, keeping an eye out for danger. In my travels today, I'd seen many deer, a ton of alligators, a few wild hogs, and one panther. I didn't think the area was overly dangerous, but it was getting dark, and I didn't know the terrain or wildlife.

Once we crossed the flood plain and headed into slightly higher ground, Bala handed me to Jah. I could have walked, but I knew they needed this. They needed to care for and protect me like I needed to breathe, and I wouldn't fight them on that. They were alphas, and this is what alphas did. I didn't care about being completely independent as long as they understood that I could be if needed. I snuggled into Jah's arm, appreciating his warmth as the temperature began to drop. He purred louder, using one hand to tug at the tips of my hair and sending me into a blissed-out coma. I'd never been so satisfied in my life, even though I wanted more of them.

It didn't take us long to get to the cabin. My alphas hadn't said a word to each other, but the silence was companionable. Sunset came quickly as there were no mountains to slow it, and the air grew almost cold.

The cabin was warm when we entered, and the smell of cooking meat made my mouth water. I'd eaten a few nuts and berries I knew to be safe, so I wasn't starved, but the smell made my mouth water all the same. Despite my wet skin, Jah set me on the couch and wrapped a fur around me before going to the fire and filling it with wood.

Bala moved to the kitchen, and I watched his muscles flex as he peeled some type of root vegetable and set it to boil. Jah moved about, arranging furs and pulling out dishes. Both worked naked.

The cabin was nice. It was one large room with a bed in the corner by the fireplace and the kitchen directly opposite. The couch was covered with pillows and furs and smelled strongly like Jah. The bed was large enough for both of them, but I didn't get the feeling that they shared it. It was perfect for hunting trips or short stays, and I already felt comfortable.

"Come here," Jah said, sitting on the edge of the bed. They hadn't spoken on the way to the cabin, and the sound of his voice startled me.

Pulling the ends of the furs together, I stood up and walked to him. Bala left the stove, rustling around in a chest of drawers, looking for something.

"Drop the fur," Bala said from behind me. Because of his thick accent, I didn't understand the words immediately and didn't respond. The fur was ripped from my body, and I gave a startled shout, turning on the alpha with a glare. His eyes scanned my body, noting every curve and lingering on an old scar on my thigh. "What is that scar?" he asked, speaking slowly, so that I understood him.

"I fell out of a tree and broke my femur as a child. I had surgery.

"Surgery?" Jah asked, seemingly confused by my answer.

"Yeah, they had to align the bones and put a plate on it." I reached for the blanket, but Bala kicked it away.

"You're not to run from us," Jah said from behind me. "No running and no hiding." It sounded like run'n and hide'n, but I understood what he meant.

"This isn't a safe place," Bala picked up. "Maybe you're safe from men, but not nature. Stay out of the treetops," he said, and I narrowed my eyes at him. I was perfectly safe in any treetop. I opened my mouth to tell him, but he stopped me by saying Jah's name.

I was pulled backward and turned over Jah's knees. His cock was hard and pressed against my stomach. "What the fuck?" I yelled, kicking to get up. Steel arms banded around me, and I was pinned with my ass in the air.

I heard the sound of something moving through the air before I felt the crack of leather against the flesh on my ass. I screamed, bucking hard to get away.

"Stop now, wife. This is your punishment for running from us." Another crack of leather landed on my ass, then fingers reached between my legs, pinching my clit. My hips bucked again, trying to evade the fingers touching my sore flesh.

"And no foul language," Jah added, rubbing his rough hands over the stinging skin.

"You have got to be kidding me," I yelled, trying to twist on his lap. "The tradition is to run. I just did what you told me." My voice rose to a shout, and the belt fell again in three consecutive strikes before fingers found my clit again, rubbing and pinching until slick flowed freely.

I howled in outrage, fighting with everything I had to get away from them. How dare they? What the actual fuck? I didn't know these men, and they didn't know me. Maybe this had been a colossal mistake.

"Settle, Tosh," Jah said, soothing the skin again. "The tradition is to run, yes. Then it is tradition to punish you for that. You must always listen to your alphas. It's our job to keep you safe."

"I did fucking listen!" I snarled, and the belt fell again, hitting the tops of my thighs. Hot slick flowed faster, and my face grew hot from embarrassment. My mind might hate what they did, but my body did not. My body was thinking that they were indeed the perfect mates. What weird-ass medieval shit was that?

Fingers caressed my slit, and a wide thumb penetrated me, making me groan and writhe against the hands that held me. A harsh slap to my clit made me see stars, and the belt fell again on the round flesh of my ass. Another slap followed by two strikes from the belt, and I was panting. "Please," I begged, not knowing what I was asking for. Did I want them to stop? Did I want them to keep going? I wanted to cum; I was desperate for it. "Please," I whimpered.

"Not yet," Jah said. "You were a very bad omega. You put yourself in incredible danger when it was supposed to be a game. You can't be doing that," he said, his accent growing thicker. I strained to get the gist of what he said. His cock was so hard that it hurt where it pressed into my gut.

I heard the belt drop and Bala's rough hands smoothed over the welted skin. "Brother, 'dis ass is marked beautifully. I don wanna mess it up," he added, his words ending in a growl. I turned my head in his direction and saw that his pupils were blown.

He walked behind me and buried his face between my butt cheeks, finding my clit with his tongue. I gasped, pulling away. I was a mess of tears, old cum, and sweat, and his face there shocked me. I heard the belt being dragged across the floor, and he stood again, placing three quick strikes to the tops of my thighs.

Jah finally moved his hand, soothing the skin and circling my clit slowly. "That's a good girl," he said. "Almost done." He slapped my clit again, and my body clenched around nothing, needing to be filled. I didn't understand any of it.

The belt fell twice more, followed by a pinch to my clit. Bala held it hard between his fingers, and I came so hard the edges of my vision went dark.

"Now, now. That's good. You're okay," Jah said, and I started sobbing. I cried so hard that my body shook.

Bala scooped me up, and I fought him, hitting his chest and trying to push away from him. "It's for your own good," he said, raining kisses on my head and ignoring my slaps and scratches. "You're fine. You're perfect," he crooned, rocking me side to side until the sobs turned into shuddering breaths. He sat on the couch, and Jah tossed him the fur they'd taken from me.

Jah moved to the stove, finishing whatever dish Bala started. Bala rocked me, purring and pulling at the long strands of hair. He massaged my scalp, and I melted into him, the mate bond washing my anger away like that river washed wreckage.

I felt his contentment through the bond like this was standard everyday stuff. I knew women who enjoyed that kind of thing but never considered myself to be one of them. But I had enjoyed it; I'd come harder than I ever had. They hadn't hurt me, not really. Everything they'd done felt good. It was very confusing. I sniffled as tears continued to fall, running down Bala's chest. I curled around myself, and his purr grew louder, the vibrations of his chest soothing me. My eyes grew heavy, and I let myself fall asleep.

Chapter Six

Jah

The sight of Tosh's violet eyes, rounded in fear of us, hurt my soul on a level I didn't think possible. I never dreamed that a simple behavior correction would cause that response. We knew nothing about the omegas from the northern lands, but we learned something today. So did she.

Omegas can't hesitate to follow their alpha's commands. One tiny bit of resistance can mean the difference between life and death for them. Between rivers turned into wild killing waters, hurricanes, panthers, alligators, and raids by other towns, a one-second delay can mean the difference between escape and death.

It is customary to punish your bride on your wedding night. I think that's why the stupid tradition of having them hide was started. Your omega should never hide from you, and they shouldn't feel the need to. But they should understand that it is now your role as their alpha to hand down any punishment. They learn to look to you, not their father, for guidance. Tosh didn't understand that, and I hope that we didn't make a fatal mistake.

The sound of her sobs as Bal comforted her turned my stomach, and, not for the first time, I worried that I wasn't cut out for this.

Yes, she enjoyed it in the end, as many omegas do. My father had warned me to be careful and not to let her feel only pain. Then he'd given me a wink like I should understand what he meant. Bal and I talked to a cousin who suggested we tease her and make her come. Bal dated an alpha for a few months who liked to be spanked and said he would volunteer for that part. I'd shaken my head, hoping we wouldn't go too far with it. The signal from Bal had squashed that hope.

Her soft cries had stopped, but Bal's purr hadn't. Neither of us had made that sound before today; funny how instinct works. My brother's head was tilted down, his nose planted on Tosh's soft hair.

Yesterday, we were bachelors without a care in the world, and today, we are mated to the same omega. Not only was she a fierce creature, but she was so beautiful that it made my heart ache to look at her. It was like looking at the sun; everything about her was touched by its brightness. I'd never seen purple eyes on any creature, wild or not. I was proud to have her.

I gave the paolos a final stir. Radiation from the bombs had changed so many things, including the food we ate. While you could still grow regular potatoes, paolos were more common in the deep, deep south. They were a cross between a turnip and a potato and were uncommonly good when salted and buttered. I hoped Tosh liked them.

I pulled the tender meat from the smoker and arranged it on a large platter before placing it on the small table by the fire. I brought the paolos over and a bowl of apples from the fridge. It wasn't much, but it would do for now. I sat, leaving plenty of room.

I cleared my throat, giving Bal a nod when he looked over at me. He rose smoothly, cradling Tosh in one arm and wrapping the fur around her with the other. She whimpered in her sleep, not wanting to rouse, but she needed to eat. He bent his mouth to her ear and whispered for her to wake up. She stirred then stilled as he walked forward, settling her on my lap. I positioned her upright, tugging her fur tighter so that she didn't get chilled.

This area we'd chosen to call home was as close to our origins as we could get. Before the War, our people had come from the small barrier islands off the coast, spreading to the mainland when crowding became an issue. Buried by time and the War, then destroyed by the sea, those islands were gone.

There was nothing left of the lands to the east of the old roadway they called I-95. We'd settled as close as we could to the sea and still be safe. We lived in a town called Cope, and that is what we had done. Cope. The sea was a short drive away, but it wasn't what it once was. My Gran'maamy had a picture book of where her great-grandparents were born, and it was nothing like what is there today.

People once bathed in the ocean, wearing thin scraps of clothing. Children made castles, and men fished by the shore.

Women talked and swam in gentle Atlantic coast waves under clear blue skies.

That was then. Now? Sometimes, the skies were reddish, sometimes orange, and sometimes a pale blue, almost white. Gone were the brilliant blues. The bombs had changed all that.

The days would be brutally hot with humidity that would curl the straightest hair and make stones sweat. At night, the air would grow so cold that you couldn't sleep under the stars without a fire and many blankets. This is why we had to be harsher with our wife than we would've liked. Her birthplace may have been wild, but it was likely more predictable and, most definitely, safer than her new home. If nothing else, she knew it better and needed to rely on us and not herself until she got her sea legs.

I tucked the stray hairs of her honey-colored curls behind her ear, noting that she had lighter highlights scattered among the dark strands. The contrast between dark and light made her golden skin stand out more. She opened her eyes, stopping my heart with their brilliance.

I propped her higher on my lap, bringing a piece of meat to her lips as Bal set a glass of our homemade beer by my plate. She took the meat, chewing slowly, then closing her eyes with a low groan of pleasure. Smoked sika was fantastic and well worth the wait. I offered her a paolo. She brought her button of a nose down, sniffing the light pink vegetable before curling her generous lips around my fingers to take it. Humming, she nodded her head.

As much as behavior correction seemed a foreign idea to her, this did not, causing me to wonder if another alpha had ever fed her. I growled, clutching her small frame to me in a show of typical alpha assholery.

She blinked wide eyes at me, looking up but saying nothing. Sighing, I took another bite of meat to her lips, watching in fascination as she took it.

These omegas were strange to us southern folks. Technically, they were also southern folks, but their customs were far different from those of the New South proper. Omegas were often contracted for as babies. Alliances were forged at their birth between families for wealth, power, food, or any number of reasons. They would come to their alpha at or right before their first estrous, and she would know only him.

Yes, there are omega houses where scattered omegas choose to sell their services. There, an alpha paid for the right to serve an omega through estrous. An alpha could also pay to be served through his rut. As there were more alphas than omegas, this wasn't uncommon. These omegas either survived the death of their mate and refused to be remated, or they escaped notice until later and sold their first estrous to the highest bidder. Either way, they made money and lots of it.

A few of the omegas in the seventh had insisted on the right to choose their mate later in life. They did things differently there, and it was allowed. The idea spread in the Seventh, and instead of arranging bonds at birth, some waited. They contracted with alphas on an estrous-by-estrous basis and survived using males until they found one they liked. Only a few of the younger omegas from the area had been virgins. Most of those had returned to their families after the troubles with the rebels were over and NS304 the law.

The Alpha's wife, Eve, had blazed a trail through the New South. She used her knowledge of a coming insurrection and herself as bait, snagging the land's strongest alpha as her own. Now every omega had a choice, and contracts could not be entered into until the omega came of age. Not that there weren't backroom deals and shady goings-on. No doubt there were, but now an omega had recourse. The punishment for violating NS304 was death. And if the government didn't get you, the Omega Force would. They did not play.

We'd known Tosh had other alphas before us, but that hadn't mattered. It still didn't, but now that we were bonded, I planned to find out who they were and kill them. It was that simple. It was a visceral type of pain thinking about it.

Picking up another paolo, I let her bring her mouth to my fingers and take it. She hadn't said a word since waking. She really hadn't said a word since we captured her by the river; begging for us to stop punishing her didn't count, and I felt terrible about that.

She ate until she was full, and when her bites slowed, I offered her a drink from my cup, loving the way her throat moved as she swallowed. She gulped several mouthfuls, and when she was done, she curled into my side, hiding her face in my neck as I finished the plate.

I met Bal's eyes over the table and saw his concern. Nothing had gone as planned, and maybe if she hadn't given us a run for our money, we would have skipped that last bit. But we'd been pushed, and this was the end result. Tosh sat still and unmoving, but her body was wire tight like she was ready to bolt if need be.

I sat back, bringing one arm around her as I finished my beer. Bal watched through hooded eyes, his need for her resurfacing with claws and teeth. I buried my nose in her hair, inhaling her scent of thunderstorms and lightning strikes to let it soothe my worry over the girl.

"Let's get you into the tub," I said. "Tomorrow, we'll go home and have a good shower, but this will do for tonight." I stood, propping her on my hip with her legs on either side. She kept her nose buried, hiding her face from me, and I hated it.

Bal rose, clearing the table and starting dishes. He was usually the calm, soothing one. There was not much gentleness in either of us, but he didn't often go over the edge. The hunt had triggered something for him, leaving me to care for her while he struggled to get his shit together. It was usually the other way around, but I wasn't complaining. Tosh made the hardness in my core soften instinctively.

The only private area in the cabin was the bathroom. It was small but clean. We washed in one of the streams that ran behind the property during hunting season and didn't use it much. A porcelain clawfoot tub sat in one corner next to a sink and toilet. There was no shower, and neither of us would have fit into the old thing. It would swallow Tosh, making me realize just how small she was. Fierce things often look larger when fighting with their backs against a wall.

I turned on the radiant heater, listening as it clanged to life. After sitting Tosh on the closed toilet, I ran the water until it was clear and hot, then plugged the drain. While the tub filled, I dug through the cabinet on the wall for soap, finding a few bottles with labels too old to read. I stripped her of her fur, she grabbed at it, but I tossed it to the side then scooped her up, putting her slowly into the water against her protests. She tried curling into a ball and turning her back to me, which hurt more than it should.

"Don't hide from me," I said when she looked away. Taking her chin in my hands, I pulled her face to me. "Did Bal hurt you?" I asked, not understanding her reaction. I had expected this ritual to be easy and natural. I hadn't expected the minefield of emotions I would endure during the process. The need to make her feel better rode me harder than anything I'd ever felt. My alpha instincts screamed at me to fix her. To fix this.

She hesitated, then shook her head, still not meeting my eyes. I kneeled on the floor, tucking my legs behind me before sifting through the bottles to find one for her hair. Leaves and dirt floated as the water rose, coming to her chin before I turned it off. "We care for you," I tried, feeling the truth of the words in my gut.

"You don't know me," she hissed, finally meeting my eyes. A storm raged across her violet seas, and I knew that had been what she was hiding. She wasn't hurt; she was pissed.

"Tosh. It doesn't matter. The minute we bonded, that stopped mattering. You know that."

She sighed, tucking her knees to her chin and curling around herself. Picking up a plastic cup from the side of the sink, I filled it, gently pouring it over her head. "Look up, baby." She tilted her head toward the ceiling, and I soaked her hair, careful not to get it in her eyes. "You evaded us very well, little squirrel," I said, massaging the soap into her hair and building it into a rich lather. "You were tough to find."

"I wasn't even trying. If I didn't want you to find me, you wouldn't have," she said, giving me the cut of her eyes. Every southern man knows there is more danger there than anywhere else.

"I believe you," I said, working the shampoo to the ends of her hair and letting it sit while I soaped a rag.

"I can do that myself," she huffed, reaching for it.

"I believe that too, but I want to do it. It makes me feel better." I pulled one of her arms from the tight ball of her body and began to wash it.

"It makes you feel better about beating me? Is that how it's going to be? Beatings and apologies?" she asked, accusation oozing out of every pore in her body. My heart sank at the hint of pain I caught hiding behind her bravado.

"Tosh. That wasn't…we didn't beat you. That's not what that was about," I sighed, rinsing her arm and taking up the other one.

"It wasn't?" she snapped, pulling her arm from my hands and rinsing it off herself before ducking under the water and swishing her hair around like a mermaid.

When she surfaced, it was slicked back from her face, highlighting its fragile heart shape. But looks are deceiving, as there wasn't anything fragile about Tosh. She held my eyes, daring me to disagree. I accepted her challenge, saying, "It wasn't a beating. We would never do that. It's, I don't know, cultural because nothing is safe here. There are wild cats bigger than you that would drag you into the marshes. The weather changes on a grain of rice, and there are bogs and quicksand pits that would swallow you before we could move a finger in your direction. The wild boars are vicious. It's like nature took steroids, illegal drugs, and radiation and made the worst of things, not the best. I've heard a lot about the Seventh. Hell, I spent a few weeks there helping to quell the insurrection. It's beautiful and wild. It's undoubtedly untamed, but it isn't nearly as deadly as these lowlands, Tosh. Our omegas learn from the beginning to look to their fathers for safety.

The wedding spanking ritual is supposed to, you know, pass the torch to an omega's mate."

"So, fathers spank their omega children to teach them to listen," she said, cutting her eyes at me again.

"Yes," I said, finally feeling like we were getting somewhere.

"And then the goal of that little ritual is to transfer that duty from father to mate," she said calmly, watching me.

"Exactly." I felt confident she was getting it, so I poured some conditioner into my palm. I began massaging into Tosh's long strands so they'd be easier to comb. She hummed her approval, tipping her head back and closing her eyes. Her wet hair hung to her waist, the tips floating on the top of the water around her.

"And alpha fathers spank their omega children as you spanked me." She quirked an eyebrow.

And here is where I saw the trap she set for me. "Not exactly like that, no." I began to get nervous about where this was going.

"So, you idiot alphas devised this little ritual where you chase down a frightened, undersized, traditionally weaker person, who, let's face it, is usually female. After she does precisely what you've asked her by running away from your dumb asses, you proceed to turn her over your knee and punish her for it?"

"Uh. Yeah, but the orgasm," I tried.

"Not gonna lie; it was a good orgasm," she started, a smile curving on her lips. "In fairness, if you try that stunt again, I'm not sure you'll walk away from it. Just warning you. I'm on the fence about how I feel, Jah. Maybe it'll be the most fun we ever have, and maybe I'll feed you to the alligators. You'd better make sure whatever made-up infraction is worth it."

The look on her face was priceless, and I wanted to laugh but choked it back. "Noted," I said instead, dropping my voice to let her know I took her seriously. "But it's not a no," I added on impulse, laughing when she swung her arm through the water and soaked me completely. "Tosh!"

"You deserved it," she laughed, shaking her head and ducking under the water to rinse the conditioner. She looked comfortable in the water, and I hoped she could swim. That would make days at the lake a little more fun.

"You've had a long day; let's get you into bed." I plucked her from the tub, wrapping her in a towel and drying her off.

Bal had dragged her small suitcase from the truck, and she went to it and began digging around. She pulled out creams and lotions, dropping the towel and rubbing them into her skin in some process only she understood. Then she pulled a long gown from the bottom of the bag, dragging it over her head with a sigh. She took her comb, moved to the corner of the mattress closest to the fire, and combed through her curls. I watched them spring back in fascination.

Bal finished cleaning up from supper and sat in a rocker on the opposite side of the room, watching her. I moved the suitcase from the couch and stretched my full length out on it. This place was never intended to house a woman. Bal always slept in the small bed while I took the couch. Neither were particularly comfortable. We hadn't planned on spending our first night together so spread out, but Tosh's insistence of taking the old tradition seriously had changed all that.

When she was satisfied her curls were where they should be, she went to stand by the fire; the flames creating a dark shadow of her body through the sheer material. No one said anything; we just watched each other from our corners. It wasn't uncomfortable. In fact, it was peaceful despite the distance. The bond sang happily, weaving in and out between us.

Tosh turned, facing the fire. Bal growled low at the sight of her rounded ass through the gown. She took her hair, fluffing it and scrunching the curls tighter. "You shouldn't comb curls," she said. "But they were full of leaves and tangles, leaving me no other choice. The only hope for them is to dry before I sleep on them and make things worse," she said, almost to herself.

Outside, the sky was dark, and the chill from the night moved into the cabin as the moon rose. In the distance, a panther screamed, and a wild hog squealed. Tosh didn't jump at the sound, only turned a little more to dry another section of her riotous curls. They hadn't seemed so untamed earlier, but southern humidity will do that. If you think it can't be cold and humid, you've never been to the true south.

Finally, she went to the bed, pulling back the covers and tucking under them. I smiled as Bal pushed off of the chair, gliding toward the bed. I'd wondered where she would land, this little bird of ours. Though I took up most of the couch, she could've chosen to squeeze in with me. Instead, she picked Bal's spot. Maybe it was a diplomatic move on her part, maybe not, but I felt some of Bal's tension ease.

I'd never considered that I'd get even more insight into his feelings once we shared a bond with an omega. We were already so in tune that I never dreamed we could be even closer, yet there we were. Her choosing his bed calmed his frayed nerves, settling him. I smiled, watching as he stoked the fire and turned off the lights before sliding under the covers with her. He pulled her to him, tucking her under the wing of his arm with a sigh.

I turned on my side, facing them and the fire, letting my eyes fall closed. I would have loved to have my wife under me again, and, no doubt, Bal felt the same way. But it had been a more demanding day for all of us than we thought it would, and my brother's soft snores filled the air almost immediately. I met Tosh's eyes over the protective hold of his arm, giving her a slow wink. I watched until her eyes closed too, before letting sleep take me.

Chapter Seven

Bala

I needed to bury my cock into the little squirrel nestling her ass against it. Her gown had ridden up to her hips in the night, and the silk of her skin on mine set my teeth grinding as my cock twitched. Before I could think not to, I had impaled her from behind, eliciting a loud squeal from her sassy lips. The noise went straight to my hindbrain, making me harder as I waited for her tight sheath to accommodate my size. My heart pounded in my chest, fueled by a deep desire I'd never felt before.

My hands traveled higher under the gown, cupping her breasts and sliding over the flat planes of her stomach. She sighed, relaxing into me as she grew more awake. I found her clit, rubbing it lazily before stroking into her again. We lay on our sides, facing the same direction. Jah slept on the couch, stirring when a soft moan escaped Tosh's lips.

Burying my nose in her neck, I inhaled. Never had anything smelled so good, and I found it odd that a creature from the mountains could smell so much like home. My teeth traveled the column of her neck, nipping lightly along the path to her shoulder. The one I marked was up, and I ran my tongue over the savaged flesh. Tosh moaned again, pushing herself lower onto my cock.

I moved my hands, gripping her hips tightly, noting how my fingers met around the tiny curve of her waist. Holding her in place, I pushed the last of myself inside of her, letting out a long and pleasured sigh when I slipped behind her cervix to the extra space made just for me. Her body gripped mine, causing a louder moan to fall from her. I felt goosebumps rise on the skin under my hands when I clasped onto her shoulder gently with my teeth, not biting, simply holding her in place.

With one hand, I worked her clit slowly, loving the way it hardened to my touch. Between us, the bond sang, and I'd never felt more complete in my life. I didn't need to move my hips; her body massaging my cock had me ready to cum in seconds. Each flutter of her walls got me closer to orgasm than an hour fucking a woman ever had. I slid out, loving the feel of her slick as it chased my cock, urging it back with its warmth.

She groaned louder, her hips bucking into me so that I slid into place again. With a sigh, she arched her hips away, then back again, fucking me. I used my palm, trying to hold her still while I worked her clit faster, wanting to feel her orgasm before she took me too far with her hips. There would be time for fucking her all night, but Jah and I had abstained for long enough, so that time wasn't now. I surged into her as she cried out, waking Jah. He watched as she shuddered on my cock, her body clamping down. She forced my orgasm with hers, and my knot expanded as I filled her. Aftershocks from her orgasm pulled more seed from me. Her body gripped and fluttered around mine, almost to the point of pain.

I remembered this from yesterday, but thought that it was a fluke. Having never knotted an omega, I hadn't known that it would be that way. My knot may have held us together, but it was her body that kept mine prisoner as it pulled so hard on my cock that I saw stars before she made me cum again. She demanded, I gave. When the second orgasm was finished, I lay spent. A puddle. My body felt light, and spots swam behind my closed eyes as I fought to catch my breath. Never had anything felt so good.

I understood genetics. I hadn't gone to college, but I understood the difference between the dynamics and how our bodies were made to respond together. Still, I never dreamed that it could be this way. I watched Jah's eyes skim over the heaving form of our mate. He met my eyes with a smile, and I knew he felt it too. Contentment. Peace. Joy.

This is why we chose one female. Should we feel this way with another, bond to another, we would lose the connection between us. Sharing Tosh made our natural tie so much more than it had been, and together, we were something new.

I felt Tosh's stuttered breath under my palms and pulled her tighter, crushing her to me. My scent on her soothed any remaining rough spots the day before had left. I watched as Jah rose, moving to fill the fireplace with the remaining wood.

Soon, the heat would be oppressive, but we would be home with central heat and air conditioning by then. Yesterday, I bemoaned this pit stop, but today I was glad for it. Cope was small. Small southern towns were built on a foundation of gossip, prejudice, and treachery. Tosh would not fit in, and we'd known that. We hadn't cared, but these few precious hours alone with her were priceless to me. I knew Jah felt the same, even if the little squirrel ran much too fast for my liking.

When the knot loosened, I released Tosh from my crushing grip, loving the little growl she gave at being moved. I kissed her cheek, nuzzled the base of her neck, and jumped to my feet, not bothering to cover myself. "We'll get breakfast on the way," I said. "The cabin isn't stocked this time of year."

I took a towel from the kitchen and used it to wipe the mess from between Tosh's legs, grabbing her ankles and holding her when she tried to twist away.

She rose with a grumble when I finished, settling her long gown over her hips as she glared at me. Jah shook his head, finishing straightening the cabin and getting it ready to close up until hunting season. Tosh disappeared into the bathroom, and I went to pee off the front porch.

The day was already warming. The sun had risen over the tree line, and if I listened, I could hear the rush of the river to the east. An alligator crawled through the long grasses to the north, making an unmistakable shushing sound as its belly dragged the ground.

Somewhere in the distance, A wild boar dug into rain-softened ground, its soft grunts reaching my ears. My wife and brother rustled in the cabin, their voices low behind the closed door. I took a minute to let it roll through me. The sights, smells, and sounds of this place soothed some of the anxiety growing at taking Tosh home.

The psychological change from bachelor to mated alpha was more abrupt than I dreamed it would be. My instincts were screaming at me to protect her and keep her from what I knew would be a difficult transition. I hadn't counted on that. I thought that the bond would strengthen over time, allowing the change to be gradual. I hadn't known it would snap like a rubber band on my soul, allowing no time for adjustment.

I'd dated girls. I imagined bonding with Tosh would be something like that. It was so far from those experiences that I was taken aback. The first person who cocked an eyebrow at my omega would meet my bad temper head-on. Jah and I weren't known for subtlety. We weren't known for kindness. We were known as what we were, stone-cold killers. I didn't envy the population of Cope one bit. They knew us as hunters and marines, but they didn't know the specifics of what we did, and for a good reason. They would need to adjust, too, unless they wanted to see who we truly were.

A bark of laughter drew me from the rabbit hole of worry I'd fallen down. Fast, light footsteps sounded across the wooden floors, followed by heavier ones, which were given away by the louder creaking of wood. Shaking my head, I took another look at the deep woods before opening the door and heading inside.

Tosha was crouched behind one end of the couch, bracing her arms for a quick bolt in either direction. Jah towered over the other end. Both wore wicked smiles.

Jah feinted left, but Tosh didn't bite. Too late, Jah realized she'd read him perfectly, and she sprinted away, heading straight for me. Laughing, she ducked behind my back, spinning me to face my brother. He tried to reach behind me and snatch her up, but I stepped forward, blocking his reach when I spread my arms wide. Behind me, Tosh giggled when Jah failed to grab her.

Jah's frustrated roar turned to laughter. He threw up his hands, shaking his head as he retreated across the room. "She needs a bell around her neck, brother. She's a crafty mink," he said, grabbing her suitcases and trying to slide behind me to the door. The thought of Tosh in a collar made my cock twitch.

She edged around me, keeping me between them, her laughter tickling along my spine. Jah feinted left again, dodged her strike, and scooped her up, flipping her over his shoulder and popping her pert ass lightly as she wiggled and screamed. Pinching the bridge of my nose, I looked toward the long-dead gods for patience. "Ladies," I sighed. "We need to get going. I'd like a hot shower, lunch, and some of Gran'maamy's sweet potato pie," I finished, double-checking the room to make sure the cabin was ready to close up.

Tosha looked at me from her upside-down position like I had two heads, her head cocking to the side. I didn't think she understood a word we said most of the time and just went along with us for grins and giggles.

Jah left the squealing omega where she was, grabbing up her suitcase and changing direction to the door. Shaking my head, I grabbed the rest and locked the door behind me.

Tosh sat in the middle as the truck bounced down the rutted road toward the two-lane. From there, it was a quick ride to Cope. Our mate sat forward as we approached the small town that clung to its past in hopes of never forgetting where it came from.

A few old buildings remained, though they were ravaged by time and the weather. Newer structures stood tall on pylons in hopes of keeping the water from dragging them into the sea. We drove down Main street, sand pelting the truck, blown on a stiff breeze from the east. By nightfall, it would threaten to cover the old, worn bricks, and street sweepers work to keep it at bay one more day. And isn't all that any of us can ask for?

Heads turned as we drove, tracking the truck's progress. Jah had grown quiet. I could feel his mind tripping and falling down the same rabbit hole of worry I'd dug myself from earlier. The stiff slant to Tosh's shoulder told me she was feeling our unease.

How do you tell your mate that she will struggle to fit in among your people? You don't. You hope for the best. You hope they will rise up and accept your choices, even if they disagree with them. They are southern, after all. Grace being a signature southern trait bred into the bones of its infants by generations, even the Gullah people. It would be okay.

I pulled the truck in front of the low-slung concrete building with a bright red-and-white awning to shield customers from the sun's brutality. Metal tables and chairs painted white and covered with red fabric huddled under the shade, offering outdoor seating for any crazy enough to brave it. Jah opened the door for Tosh, giving her first access to the artificially cold air of the diner.

"Boy, look'a here," my grandmother said, pushing her bulk from the counter to walk around. "Lawd, she beautiful," she said as she ambled forward to pull Tosh into a crushing hug.

Tosh disappeared into the old Alpha's mass until all I could see was the bright yellow of her sundress.

"Now, Gran'maamy, that's enough. Let the girl breathe," Jah said, taking his life into his own hands.

Our grandmother is a force of nature. As an Alpha female, she didn't take kindly to anyone telling her what to do. She'd managed to slap dynamics in the face and birth three children, who in turn had birthed a passel more. She did what she wanted when she wanted. If she could thwart the laws of dynamics, you were no problem, b'leve dat. I shook my head, smoothing out my thoughts.

I walked forward, gently extracting Tosh from the older woman's embrace. "Tosh, this is Beulah Dawn O'Day," I started. "Grandmother, this is Tosha."

"Tosh," the omega interrupted, giving Gran a shy smile and offering her hand, which Gran took.

"Mm, Tosh O'Day. You are a fine thing, aren't you?" my Gran said, walking around my mate like the predator she was.

"Thank you, ma'am," Tosh answered, keeping her eye on the alpha female that stalked around her.

"Call me ma'am again and see what happens," growled Gran. She'd been around omegas all her life, but something about mine had her ears pricked. "You boys keep an eye on her, hear? Don' want no trouble. And you, young lady. You call me Miss Beulah or Gran; none'a dis ma'am business. You dem boys' wife, ain't no formalities here. Now come on and sit a spell; I'll get you some breakfast cooking on the griddle."

Chapter Eight

Tosh

Beulah Dawn O'Day is a force of nature. I'd never seen a woman so big, and not just in size. Her personality filled the diner she lorded over like someone had emptied an entire bottle of perfume in the place. It wasn't unpleasant; it was just a lot.

Dark as a mountain night and just as intense, when she wrapped me in her arms, I thought I was a goner. I struggled to understand her version of English, but in some ways, it was easier than when Jah and Bala spoke. I got the gist of it, and that's all that mattered.

My mates had been quiet on the ride to the town called Cope, buried in the depths of the Sixth District, causing me to wonder. Their tension radiated across every line of them, and even if the bond hadn't been screaming that something was wrong, I would have known.

The townsfolk turned to watch as we drove through, their faces closed and suspicious. The only thing shining bright about them was their curiosity, but I could sense their disapproval through the steel doors in the truck.

It didn't bother me. As an omega of a certain age deep in the bowels of the Seventh, I was no stranger to disapproval. I was long past the age when I should be mated, and with no children or male to care for, I was considered an anomaly until I met Eve and Lorelei. They'd shown me that there was another way if I wanted to take it. I had, and it had brought me to this strange new place where greenery threatened human life daily. I swear the plants had grown an inch during the ride to town.

Bala touched the small of my back, guiding me past the upturned faces of other patrons and to an L-shaped booth in the back of the diner. Men's eyes lingered, and women's narrowed as I was escorted by them, and I ignored them all. When it came to what others thought about me, I had zero fucks to give. I wasn't as brash as my omega sisters, but I wasn't shy either. The people of this town could try me all they wanted. I would meet like with like.

A low growl sounded in Jah's throat as he slid by a table of men who had already taken my dress off with their eyes. Their glances dropped immediately to their plates and did not look my way again.

Alphas in the seventh are distinctive. Broad-shouldered and narrow-hipped, they remind me of the football players of old pasted across the tavern walls back home. The alphas here were leaner, no less tall but trimmer of build. More like swimmers, their muscles popped across their reedy frames, except for Jah and Bala, that is. They were a cross between the two types and much larger-framed than the others in the room. I wondered if it was geography or genetics that caused the difference. Either way, I doubted any of the alphas in the room were a match, and no one seemed willing to test them. Still, my thin-strapped sundress left my claiming marks bare, leaving no question as to whom I belonged.

We hadn't made it to the table when a young girl of no more than ten placed a basket of hot biscuits and a plate filled with butter and jam there before scurrying away. Jah sat me down, sliding me over with his hips while Bala went to the other end, keeping me between them. Their eyes scanned the diner, and I couldn't help but notice that our backs were to the wall. We are all predators and prey.

The girl returned, sliding three tall glasses of iced tea that I assumed was sweet on the table, as there is no other kind in The New South. She set a pitcher of water at my elbow, along with an extra glass of the same. I smiled, shaking my head a little.

I drained the glass of water first before testing the tea. Naturally, it was a prescription for diabetes, but I drained it as well. Jah refilled both glasses, and Bala put a jam-covered biscuit to my lips. I took a bite, groaning as the taste of peach jam hit my tongue, causing Bala's chest to vibrate with a growl.

Another biscuit appeared in Jah's hand when the first was gone. With a chuckle, I ate from his hand too. Plates appeared from nowhere. Mine was filled with eggs, hash browns, bacon, and sausage. A bowl of creamy grits drowning in salt and butter sat to my left, and before I could spoon any in my mouth, Bala beat me to it. The taste of real, slow-cooked grits made me hum with pleasure. Jah's jaw ticked as he filled my water glass again. Their singular focus had me fed, watered, and yawning before they'd ever touched their plates. I'd drunk the entire pitcher and cleaned my plate before I noted my mates' distress over my nutritional state, or lack thereof, at any rate.

I offered Bal a piece of bacon, but he growled and, instead of taking it, pulled me onto his lap, where he tucked my head under his chin. He ate while he held me to his chest, whispering with Jah in a language I didn't understand.

People came up and spoke with them, wandering away with news of their bonding ceremony and our claiming. They fielded questions from other diners, and I knew that the population of Cope would know every detail about me within the hour. They'd probably make up a few they hadn't been told for good measure. That's just how small towns were.

My eyes grew heavy as they held court, eating slowly and talking when needed. When left alone, both men purred softly for me, their chests rumbling low so only I could hear. My thoughts sailed like birds on the wind as I half-slept and half soared. I couldn't help but wonder about this new place and the things that it might bring.

Halfway through their third plates, I roused, lifting my head and yawning wide. The water I'd drunk sat heavy in my bladder, and I looked around for a place to tackle that problem.

"Bathroom?" I asked, blinking my eyes in an attempt to wake up.

"Past the counter to the left, little squirrel." Bal's eyebrows sank, and he looked around the diner for trouble before he released me from his lap. I shook my head as he lifted me and set me on my feet like a child. It was no effort for him at all; the muscles on his arms didn't even strain.

I walked away from them, needing to go worse now that I'd thought about it. The restaurant had all but emptied, and I caught Ms. Beulah's eyes as she headed to her grandsons' table. She gave a warm smile as she padded past but switched to the same slow, accented language the men spoke, and I worried I was missing something.

Fighting the feeling in the pit of my stomach, I took care of my bladder. The door to the bathroom opened and shut, only to be followed by silence. The stall next to me remained empty, and the faucet didn't turn on either. The hairs on the back of my neck stood at attention, and I knew that my paranoia was not unfounded.

Straightening, I slid my sundress into place, then opened the stall door to find I wasn't alone. Two women blocked the door, arms crossed and eyes narrowed. The glint in their eye was unmistakable, and I recognized it for what it was: fury.

"Mm, mm, Mm," one said, letting her arms fall loose to her sides. She shook her hands out, limbering up for the violence hanging in the air between us. "So this chit of a girl be da one that took our men, no?"

"We'll see 'bout dat," the other answered.

68

I stepped back, leaving myself room to work. The bathroom wasn't tiny; there was ample room to maneuver if you were small.

"Scared, girl?" the first one laughed. "You should be. Dat's my man you sittin' on out 'dere, and I'm about to get him back."

I let my eyes scan her. She was pretty. She'd have been prettier if her eyes weren't so hard. Like me, she was an omega, and her rich scent filled the room. But unlike me, she was big. Not tall, just thick and not in a bad way. Luscious curves tracked her frame, and long, black hair fell to her waist. Her skin was dark and flawless; its creamy perfection looked touchable, and my gut roared. She'd touched my mate. In my mind, I could smell him on her. Jah. Jah had known this omega. I don't know how I knew, but I did.

"What's da matter, bitch? Cat got your tongue?" the second one said. "Those bites on your shoulder were for us. We're going to go ahead and remove them for you." She stood to her full height, flexing the muscles in her arms.

The growl started in my soul and worked its way out. I didn't know who these bitches were, but I knew who they'd been. They'd been my mates' girls.

Mine.

They were mine. The growl deepened, and the women looked at each other. I didn't need to say a word to telegraph my displeasure.

My eyes swung to the beta woman in front of me. She was much bigger than her omega friend, and her sturdy frame rippled with muscle. Maybe she was beautiful, maybe not. All I could see was red when I looked at her.

Omegas may be soft. An omega's body is made to tame the extreme wildness of an alpha. It's the crux of the way dynamics work. But the other side of an omega is not soft. There is nothing more dangerous than a pissed-off, cornered, protective omega, and these women were about to find that out. Stories were written, and legends passed down. And there was about to be another one.

Whatever these women had been to my men, it was over. Right fucking now. I launched myself at them, my filed nails extended into the claws they were meant to be. I took the omega down first, slamming her head onto the tile repeatedly when she fell to my attack. I landed three punches to her face before the larger one pulled me off, throwing me into the wall. I bounced back at her, not registering the hit. Using her size and momentum against her, I took her to the ground. Following her down, I attempted to knock her out with a flurry of punches to the side of her head.

It didn't matter that all they'd done was monologue. They not only stood between me and the door but between my boys and me. I couldn't allow that. I wouldn't. They'd chosen me, and I'd accepted; they were mine now.

I was yanked up by my shoulders and pinned against a broad chest. My growl turned into a high-pitched roar as I fought the arms holding me, straining to get to the downed women. I wanted to paint the walls red with their blood; my honor demanded it.

But I'm not dumb.

I went limp, letting my weight sag in my captor's arms. When they loosened, I dropped to a low crouch. It didn't matter who I was fighting. All that mattered was that they tried to keep me from my prize.

I slashed out at the closest woman with my fingers, causing blood to spray across the wall. My spirit hummed with satisfaction at the sight. I was scooped up again and fought wildly until an exaggerated purr filled my ears. The tips of my hair were pulled rhythmically, causing me to go limp like a goddamned animal. "It's okay, little fox," Jah said. "I've got you."

A screech like I'd never made before came from my throat, and I turned on him. Growling louder, I sniffed along his jaw and down his neck, looking for even a hint of another on his skin. He froze. The violence in the air thickened, despite his purr.

I nuzzled first one side of my face against his neck and then the other, marking him. Climbing him like one of my favorite trees, I continued the process on his face and down the other side of his neck. He stood unmoving, even when I buried my nose in the pit of his arm, daring a foreign scent to be there.

Once satisfied, I leaped to Bala, as my nickname suggested. He caught me with one arm, and I couldn't stop myself from repeating the process with him. I nipped and growled at him when he dared try to fend me off. It was instinct. I couldn't have stopped myself if I tried, though I didn't. I learned long ago never to doubt instincts.

Instinct is the thing that keeps you from the darkened Appalachian woods on a moonless night. Instinct is the thing that makes you avoid a particular part of town without understanding why; only later do you learn there was some sort of violence there. Instinct is what drove most of us in the Seventh to survive. Instinct made us hunker down in valleys and old coal mines when the bombs flew, and that's why we outnumbered the rest of The New South three to one. I'd never discount it.

I found no other scent on my men and allowed Bala to pull me to him. I curled into a ball in his arms, growling quietly in warning when he attempted to straighten me out. Instinct told him there would be no reasoning with me until I was away from this place.

"Get her on home, boys," Ms. Beulah said from the door. "And watch dat one. She ain't like dese girls you been messing wit. She far deadlier," the old alpha paused. "Don' worry 'bout dis. I'll take out da trash."

I growled louder, threatening to do that last part myself. Bala pulled me tighter, grabbing the back of my neck like I was a kitten and purring louder. The rumble in his chest satisfied my need for more violence, and we left the diner immediately.

A silent conversation flew over my head as Jah and Bala walked with me to the truck. Though I missed the finer points, I

72

understood the totality of it. The feeling of their worry slid down their spines and through our bond. I bet they thought this had been a monumental mistake.

I wondered if I'd killed either woman and felt a thrum of satisfaction at the thought. I didn't consider myself a bloodthirsty person, but the bond brought that out. One little-known aspect of omegas is just how vicious they can be when challenged. I hoped both of them were dead. I purred at the thought, causing Jah to chuckle.

Bala drove. He shifted me to his brother's lap, and I swiped at him in anger over the disruption. He grabbed my hand before it could cause any damage and firmly said, "No."

My purr turned into a shrill cry at the challenge, and I launched myself at him. Jah pulled me back, unfolding my stiff limbs around his body so he could hug me. "Hush, little fox. He's yours. It's okay; we belong to you. No fighting." His hands rubbed my spine, sending soothing energy into me.

Mollified, I rubbed my cheek across his before settling my head under his head and purring softly for him as the truck sped through the quiet streets.

Chapter Nine

Bala

Holy. Fucking. Shit. I'd been warned. My Gran'pappy had told me plenty of times never to get between an omega and something she wanted. I'd heard the stories. I still never believed that the sweet bundle of curves and softness I'd mated could ever, no, would ever be so vicious.

I wasn't sure if the girls we left behind were alive or dead, not that I cared. Akari and Moesh had been distractions, not girlfriends. Moesh could have been Jah's mate had she not refused to mate with me, too. We always wanted one mate; it had never been a question for us. We'd never lied to them or been scoundrels about it. Akari was a beta and had known all along that there was no future for her in my life. Jah had never knotted Moesh, and I'd never promised Akari anything.

We'd stopped seeing them months before we asked The Alpha for an omega to mate with. They were just being catty and trying to intimidate our wife. Interesting how it turned out for them. I would never doubt that Tosha could take care of herself again, not that she'd have to. That was my job. Mine and Jah's.

The omega in question purred softly to Jah, her head resting on the curve of his throat. He pulled the tips of her hair, keeping her calm and pliant when the hint of violence still radiated off her.

His eyes were closed against the unfriendly faces we passed as we drove to our cottage at the edge of Cope.

I'd never heard of an omega purring, and it thrilled me on a level I didn't understand. In theory, it was possible, but it was so rare. Tosh had purred many times for us. These omegas from the Seventh were something else entirely. It made me want to go there and see what had made them so true to their dynamic when the rest of The New South had failed them.

It was hard to take my eyes off her. Randomly, she would raise her face and rub her cheeks along Jah's neck to mark him. She was running on instinct and not even trying to fight it, and I didn't care. Fuck this town. They would accept her, or we'd burn it down. This had been our choice. They'd made theirs.

In their eyes, we'd turned away from our people and heritage. They thought we'd snubbed our own blood for the exotic, pale-skinned creature. In our eyes, they'd refused to meet our needs. The offer had been out there for years, but every available omega thought she was too good to be shared. I didn't understand it. In Tosh's hometown, the best omegas were shared by many. Not that we would agree to share with anyone else, but the point is, how can populations be so different?

We didn't give a rat's ass what color Tosh's skin was as long as she willingly accepted both of us. That she was the most beautiful thing I'd ever seen was just a bonus. It wasn't about heritage or hate for us; it was about the dynamics of our relationship with each other. We needed to be united in all things.

Our house was right off the road and as near to the water as it could be. I pulled the truck into the shade the parking pad provided and opened the door. Before Jah could get out, I walked to the passenger side and took the omega from him, ignoring her growl of disapproval. She breathed in my scent and snuggled closer to me, nuzzling the side of my neck. She hadn't spoken a word since the diner. She was still in that place between human and beast, and I left her there, not caring.

She purred into my chest, and the tiny vibrations made my dick so hard I thought it would burst, but I ignored it. I climbed the steps to the cottage, noting that sand had made them shorter. It was a constant battle to keep the sea from claiming this place, but it was worth it to be closer to the rough, wild shoreline. When things settled, we would dig the pylons holding our house up, once again taking a stand against nature.

Though the sea was several miles away, the unmistakable sound of waves crashing was music to my ears, and even Tosh seemed to grow limper. The ocean must be raging for us to hear it, and I wondered if a storm was brewing.

Inside, the house was blissfully cool. Drawn blinds and the low hum of the air conditioning chased away the heat of the day. The relative darkness in the house hit me, and I relaxed immediately.

This place was a fortress. We'd made it that way. In our line of business, we took safety seriously, and this place was as safe as they came. I felt ten pounds of stress leave my shoulders just from walking through the door.

We'd made some adjustments for Tosh, and I hoped that she would like them. "Baby," I said, running my hands down her back. "We're home. Let us show you around."

Her head lifted from under my chin and swiveled as she took in the house. She straightened in my arms, sighing as she slid down my body and onto her feet. She went through the large, open living room, taking in everything from the pictures on the walls to the furniture. The room was done in dove grays and whites. Sheer white curtains covered the blinds and softened the look of them. Gray tiles led to the white kitchen, and her hand drifted over the marble countertop. Soft gray veins broke up the white, and it was one of my favorite finds during the remodel.

We'd taken two of the four bedrooms and made a large master suite we'd planned to share once she moved in. She walked into it, smiling. The color scheme didn't change, and the room was cool, dark, and comfortable. If the blinds were open, you could catch a hint of the sea beyond the trees. The extra space was used to add a bigger bed and a small sitting area in the corner. There was more than enough space for two alphas and one omega to move around in. The ensuite bathroom had a giant tub, separate shower, and triple sinks so we could all get ready together if needed.

Down the hall were two smaller bedrooms we hoped would someday hold children, even though the birthrate was abysmal. Still, the northern omegas were batting a thousand in that department, so there was hope. I wasn't in a hurry for that. Tosh examined everything from the bedrooms down the hall to the Jack-and-Jill bathroom they would share. She said nothing as she went, but shared a soft smile when she was done.

"Would you like to clean up?" Jah asked, setting her suitcase down.

Tosh looked at her blood-splattered dress and the dried spray on her arms and nodded.

My brother placed his hand on the small of her back and led her back to our room. As he passed me, he arced his eyebrow in question. I lifted one shoulder in response and followed them down the hall. The peace of the house was absolute, and the chill of the AC felt amazing after yesterday. I stripped off my clothes, intending to shower as well. Jah glared at me. I shrugged my shoulders and walked around them to warm the water for my mate.

"We can take you shopping after lunch, you don't have nearly enough clothes, and your shampoo bottle is almost empty," he finished. I gave him a sharp look, wondering when the hell he noticed her shampoo bottle was almost empty.

Tosh didn't say anything as she stripped off her dress and walked under the strong spray of hot water, but she did let out a relieved groan that made my cock twitch. It reminded me that I didn't want to go shopping. We'd bought some things before we picked her up, and we had more than enough to make do. The refrigerator was full, the bar stocked, and the house clean. The last thing I wanted was to take her back into the wilds of Cope so that she could have more interactions with its people.

While Jah stood watching, I slid into the shower and soaped the new body sponge we'd bought. I kneeled behind her, and while hot water rained down her front, I cleaned her back and massaged out the knots of worry I found there.

"Will there be others?" she asked, her voice barely above a whisper. She didn't turn to me and seemed smaller with her back turned.

"There are others," I answered, unwilling to lie. "There is no one who meant anything to either of us, Tosh. You're here now; there will only ever be you."

Her back straightened as if pulled taut by a string. She nodded once and turned to me, stunning me with the golden hue of her beauty. Jah still leaned by the wall watching, though there was plenty of room for him. His arms were crossed, and his jaw tight. Ignoring him, I began to wash her front, keeping my attention clinical. I hated the smears of blood that dotted her flesh, even though the reason they were there thrilled me. I moved to her hair, cleaning and conditioning it like I'd done it a thousand times when it was a first for me.

Tosh had defended her claim on us. She'd taken on another pissed off omega and an oversized beta to do it, and I was proud to belong to her. She really was one of us. She was bold and fierce, yet soft and sweet. The dichotomy was not lost on me.

"I understand need," she started. The tone of her voice, more than the words, sent a chill up my spine. "Of course, I do. Every three months, I suffer from a need that will kill me eventually if not sated. I understand that. I used an alpha before you, obviously. I am not Eve and could never torture myself like that."

At her words, a growl spilled from Jah's lips, and his knuckles went white where he clutched his arms. "You knew this," Tosh snapped, silencing his growl with a glare. Jah looked away first. "I'm sorry. We both knew it. I've only ever been with one other person, alpha or otherwise, and he was gay. He was also my best friend, and we turned to each other only when need demanded it. He couldn't deny his rut any more than I could my estrous. There weren't any omega males in our community, and he had to turn somewhere. Same as me. It filled a need safely, but we'd usually cry the whole time. We didn't want it to be that way," she said, letting out a strangled laugh. "I have no right to be mad about those women; they just surprised me. I'm not going to apologize for attacking them. They came after me and mine; they deserved it," she finished, her eyes hardening into stones of violet.

"We wouldn't want you to apologize." And we wouldn't allow it. Those girls would've kept coming if Tosh hadn't shown them who she was right off the bat. Then I'd have had to step in, and that wouldn't be good. I'd never hurt a woman in my life, but that didn't mean I wasn't capable. I'd hurt anyone, male or female, that came after my mate. It was just that simple.

With apologies in mind, I sank lower, cupping her pretty pussy in my hand. "This belongs to us," I said, swiping my tongue down her slit and loving the way her hands buried in my hair. I looked up her body and watched her head tilt back. Long hair the color of black gold brushed her waist, and I'd never seen anything more beautiful in my life. "This belongs to us the same way we belong to you. Body, mind, and soul, little squirrel. I can't apologize for my past either. I can only promise that you are our future," I finished as I swirled my tongue around her clit, eliciting an indecent moan that went straight to my balls.

I caught Jah's eyes and saw them heavy with need.

"You could cheat. Some Alphas do," she said, watching me with guarded eyes as she spoke.

Jah's growl grew louder, raising the hair on Tosh's body. Instinctively, she understood that she'd angered the bigger predator in the room and gone from hunter to hunted. He grabbed her throat, not putting too much pressure on it but forcing her to look at him. His thumb ran over the racing pulse in her neck, soothing any hurt he inflicted. "Never," he said, his voice cracking with anger. His lips crushed hers, not caring that he knocked her back and exposed more of her for me to dive into. "Never say that again," he demanded as she whimpered into his mouth.

I lashed her clit with the flat of my tongue before pulling back to slap her pussy as an accent to his threat. Wetness poured from her, and I sucked her until she came, covering my face with slick. I lapped it up with a groan as her knees buckled. I lowered her onto the bench along the shower wall and stood in front of her as I pulled on my cock. She reached for me, but I slapped her hand away. We should've done this immediately. Honestly, we should've waited for her estrous to claim her, but we had wanted her right away.

Had we waited, some of this would have been avoided. Our bond would've been rock solid, and there'd have been no doubts as to our claim over her. I jerked my cock viciously, not delaying the stream of cum that erupted from me and onto her chest. Once the spasms stopped, I sank to my knees again, rubbing it into her skin. Jah took my place, emptying himself on her seconds after. We rubbed our essence into every part of her.

Our scent filled the small space. As much as I would've loved to be clean, I reached to turn the shower off. Tosh needed our mark. Our smell should've been etched on her skin already, and that was our oversight. With that problem solved, Jah wrapped her in a towel, drying her skin without removing our cum. She sank into him, more relaxed than she'd been since I'd met her.

Omegas are the most exotic of the dynamics. They require specialized care. Being mated to two alphas and not one would increase her dynamic-driven need to feel safe and comfortable. I didn't have a college education or any formal training but what I had was a grandmother who is whip-smart.

Ms. Beulah knew more about dynamics than any college professor and had been very firm in her teachings. She'd had two omega daughters and insisted she help them blossom. Jah and I were experts despite our lack of experience. This was also the reason he'd never been serious with Moesh. He hadn't wanted to lead her on.

Jah sat Tosh on the bed and tried to move away from her. She gripped his hips, pulling her face into his groin and nuzzling him as she marked him with her scent. He smiled at her indulgently, knowing she was feeling a little fragile and that she would hate it if she realized. When she stilled, he pulled away, going to the closet to pull out another sundress. He draped it over her head, pulling her limp arms through.

"As much as I'd love to stay here all day with you, little fox, I want to show you something more," he said, settling the long dress over her short legs.

I went to the closet and pulled out a clean pair of jeans only to have the little squirrel land on my back and sink her teeth into my shoulder. Laughing, I swept her forward. "Tosh, it's okay," I said, bringing my nose to the hollow of her neck and inhaling the scent of my brother and me on her. Okay, I admitted to myself. Marking her had helped us all.

She rubbed her cheeks on me and ran her tongue up my neck, making me shake my head. "Come on, kitten. You'll want to see it too."

Tosh hopped down, landing on the balls of her feet and shaking out her hands. "Okay," she said, speaking her first words in a long time. She hadn't said much since we picked her up, and I wondered if it was her nature to be quiet. If she ever officially claimed us, we wouldn't need words to communicate. Jah and I could already do this, and it would be nice to include Tosh as well.

Tosh stood, the sapphire blue dress ghosting the tops of her feet. It looked gorgeous against the buckwheat-honey of her hair. She was striking. You might miss it at first glance, but the longer you look at her, the more beautiful she becomes. The look of her flowed from one stunning feature to the next, and when she shocked you with her violet eyes, it was almost too much. Add in her scent of thunderstorms and ozone, and I'd been gone from minute one. I was fucked, and I knew it.

Jah and I dressed quickly while Tosh wandered into the kitchen and grabbed a bottled water from the fridge. Passing one to each of us, she followed us out the door, down the steps, and across the small backyard. I opened the small in the white picket fence for her, allowing her to step through. Jah led the way through the deep sand of the path that wove between sand dunes.

It was a long walk. Holding hands with Tosh in the middle, we wove through dunes, pampas grass, and scrub until the sound of waves crashing on the shore was deafening.

As much as anyone can, we owned this land. The house sat on the extreme western edge of the property to be safer from the tumultuous sea. Seven hundred acres separated it from the shoreline. It was untouched. Most of the debris of the past had been washed away in the storms since. Only a few posts, pylons, and cement slabs remained, and they'd be gone, eventually.

The detritus and dunes protected the once inland town, but eventually, we'd be pushed back. Some day, Columbia would be on the coast if the experts were to be believed. I wondered if any of it would be left when Mother Nature avenged her losses, and maybe it would be better if it wasn't. Humans had gotten better since the war, but there was still an innate sickness in us all that wasn't seen in nature.

We rounded the last corner of the path, and I smiled as Tosh stopped in her tracks. I smiled at her face, thrilled that I got to see this look for myself. Her mouth was open, and her jaw slack. Wide violet eyes skipped from the ocean to the beach and to the wild horses lounging in the sand. She dropped our hands and strolled away.

Then I was the one who was speechless as I watched her walk forward. The sun glinted off her curls, casting golden highlights that shimmered. Ignoring us, she walked toward the waves. The beach was wide, and the horses barely raised their heads as she approached. They were so unused to humanity that they didn't know to be afraid. No one came to the section of the beach. It was rare that anyone went to the beach at all. It was no longer a place for family vacations; most believed it was dangerous and unpredictable. Jah and I would never tell that it was also a place of unrivaled beauty.

Tosh approached the small herd's stallion, her fist outstretched. Her voice softened, and she spoke to the creature watching her warily. He rose to his feet and shook the sand from his hide, and I rushed forward. She stopped me with a quick glare and a wave of her arm.

The stallion sniffed her hand then squealed, darting away. The rest of the herd rose, and he rounded them into a tight knot and moved them to a far corner. They watched her as she made her way across the stretch of sand and to the water's edge.

"Tosh, wait," Jah yelled, running after her. "You have to be careful. The tides can be vicious."

Tosh threw her head back, laughing as she picked up her hem and waded knee-deep into the surf. I caught up with them in time to hear her say, "And that's where life is lived, Jah. Between pleasure and danger is where we make a stand." She ripped her dress off, tossed it onto the sand, and dove naked under a wave as it crashed onto the shore.

"Tosh, no!" I yelled, wading in after her.

She surfaced ten feet away and swam toward me with lazy strokes. I plunged forward, cursing as I plucked her from the water and put her on my shoulder, and delivered three sharp smacks to her ass. Of course, she could swim; she really was a little fox. She just laughed and smacked me back. No, not a fox; she is a mink. Minks are far more dangerous. And a brat. She's most definitely a brat.

Jah stole her from me and dashed away through the waves. The one difference between us is that he loves the ocean, and I do not. Laughing, he stiffened his body and planked into an oncoming wave. Tosh slapped at him, sputtering when they broke the surface.

"Let me teach you something, little fox," he started.

"Mink," I interrupted.

Jah tilted his head in thought, rubbing his finger across his chin. "You're right, Bal. Okay, little mink, put your feet down."

Tosh stood beside him, her face upturned to his. A wide smile graced her lips, and she looked happier than I'd ever seen her.

"The ocean is dangerous," he started again.

"The mountains are dangerous, the river is dangerous; everything is dangerous," she chuckled.

"That's true. Then let's say that the ocean is vicious. Some currents will rip you from the shallows and drag you to the depths. It happens before you know it. When it does, don't fight. Let the current take you, then swim parallel to the shoreline until the current stops pulling. You should be able to swim in from there."

She looked thoughtful for a moment before saying, "Okay."

I shook my head at her fearlessness.

"There are sharks," I added.

She pursed her lips, nodding at my statement.

"They are huge things with endless rows of sharp teeth," I offered, looking down at her upturned lips.

"They don't usually come in this far, Bala," Jah growled.

"Sometimes they do," I said helpfully, wishing to scare my little mink to dry land.

"If a shark fin approaches, punch at its nose and zig-zag to shore," Jah laughed out.

"Okay," Tosh said a bit too gleefully for my liking.

"Now, focus on the pull of the sea," Jah said, glaring me to silence from under his dark lashes.

It made me wish we'd never brought her, but he was right. She'd have found the place and been unprepared. The most beautiful things in nature are usually the most deadly. Take the blue-ringed octopus or the black widow spider. Both are mesmerisingly beautiful but can kill you with the smallest of bites. I had a feeling Tosh had more similarities to them than I'd thought, and she'd have discovered this beach and explored it on her own.

"Did you feel that?" Jah asked, steadying her as the pull of the sea took her legs.

"Yeah?" she answered, her puzzled voice soft.

"That means there is a giant wave coming. The stronger the pull, the bigger the wave. The bigger the wave, the harder it will recede. That's when you are at the greatest risk of being pulled out to sea. Never go beyond where the waves break unless the ocean looks like glass. Those days are rare, and there is still a risk, but you can play farther out if you are careful on those days."

The smile on her face was brighter than the sun as she agreed to listen to his warnings.

The giant wave he spoke of curled in the distance. It was a monster at twelve to fifteen feet high, making me wonder again if a storm approached. I'd check so that we could be ready, but in the meantime, I watched it crash not ten feet from my mate. Its frothy-white remains rolled around her to the sand beyond. Jah steadied her again as she hadn't found her sea legs before walking her back to the shore. "From time to time, pools of water will be trapped by dips in the sand. Those are safe to swim in, but watch out for jellyfish; they sting."

Nodding her head, Tosh scooped her dress up and slipped it over her head. Pert nipples hardened under the fabric, clinging to her wet skin. She pulled her hair out, letting it drip down her back. I'd never dated a woman who would've willingly walked into the sea the way Tosh did. She was fearless, and I loved that about her, even if I didn't want her playing in the ocean.

"One more thing," Jah said, making me laugh. He started to sound like an old schoolteacher, and I laughed even harder when

Tosh rolled her eyes. He pinned me with another glare, and I looked away before I lost it. "You can certainly come here while we're gone, but be very careful and don't wade out too far," he finished, looking proud of himself.

"Wait, what?" Tosh asked, turning to him and pinning him with a look of her own.

I took a step back. We hadn't planned on saying anything about leaving so soon. In Jah's excitement over teaching her, he must've forgotten.

"Where will you be going?" she said, turning her head to me.

"Uh. We have missions we do, you know. Jobs that we take." Jah answered, speaking slowly so she could understand him better, which seemed to piss her off more.

"And you think I'll be okay to just hang out in a town full of ex-girlfriends and assholes while you're gone?" she said, her inviting tone more dangerous than that aforementioned spider. She was luring him in, but he couldn't see it coming.

"I mean, yeah?" he answered. "They'll accept you as our mate, and Gran'maamy will look after you.

She launched herself at him. I paddled backward, watching the train wreck from a distance. "If you think for one minute that you are leaving me in some godforsaken town while you run off on secret missions, you have another thing coming." She boxed his ear and scrabbled after him as he tried to get away from her.

I'd warned him. He is my brother, and I love him, but I had.

"Tosha," Jah yelled, back-peddling from her flurry of strikes.

"What if my estrous comes? Huh? What if more of your girlfriends jump me? I'm going, and that's final. I'm an asset to the team, not a liability. I won't be left behind." She landed a remarkably accurate hit, and I hid a smile behind my hand as I tried to school my face to firmness.

"Do you think for one second that yesterday's little game was a one-shot? I'm good. You might not know you need me, but you do." She stopped her attack, dropping into a crouch before straightening.

"Tosha," Jah tried, reaching for her as she backed away from him.

"No. Don't Tosha me, fuck that. Bring it," she said, shaking her arms out and moving into a fighting stance. "Whoever goes down first wins, Jah." She wiggled her fingers in a beckoning gesture, and I lost my battle with laughter.

It boomed loudly, creating a momentary break in the tension between my two partners. Jah looked at me for help, his eyes wide and panicked. I don't think he was worried for his safety but looking for a way to get out of the mess he created. The plan had been to sex her up real good and break the news when she was soft and pliant. Well, he'd fucked that up, so he was on his own. I doubted the plan would've worked anyway; I didn't think Tosh was ever that pliant. I shook my head, raised my hands, and backed away.

Jah looked skyward, pinching the bridge of his nose as he prayed to long-dead gods on his behalf. Tosh chuckled, then quick as a panther, she struck out, sweeping his legs from under him with a freakish dance move I saw in a movie once.

"That's bullshit," he roared. "I wasn't ready."

"Ready or not, asshole," she glared, moving back into her fighting stance.

"Best two out of three then," he growled, pouncing forward like an oversized gorilla. He dwarfed her by three times, and she evaded him easily. His long monkey arms swung, trying to catch the little mink on her retreat, but she ducked. His balance faltered, and he nearly went down again, making the fight moot.

He caught himself, rebounding nicely. He stopped, and I watched him get his shit together. Sighing, he took a deep breath and centered himself on his feet. Of course, we were trained. We were highly trained. He'd let his emotions guide his movements, and I watched him shut them down. When he opened his eyes, I saw Jah the hunter, Jah the assassin, and Jah the warrior, not Jah, the mate to Tosh. She noticed the change and cracked her neck with a side-to-side motion. A wicked smile spread across her face, and I saw what she'd been trying to show us all along: Tosh, the hunter; Tosh, the assassin; and Tosh, the warrior. She really was the same as us.

In one swift move, Jah surged forward. Like the fox she was, Tosh was no longer there. She leaped to the side, ducked, and struck Jah in the solar plexus before he could react. He struck again, landing a blow to her shoulder. And her smile grew. A nervous tingle went up my spine, and I worried this was going too far.

Tosh threw herself backward, landing on her hands and kicking upward into Jah's face, since it was the only way to reach it. She backflipped backward, finishing the maneuver. Blood ran from Jah's nose, and it was likely broken.

"Stop!" I roared.

Jah and Tosh froze. The chirping birds and singing insects silenced too, and the breeze seemed to go still around us. "Enough," I said more quietly. "We're not going to fight each other to decide this. Sit down, both of you."

Jah closed his eyes and took a deep breath. I saw the fight drain out of him as he took off his wet shirt, wiping the blood from his face and holding it to his bleeding nose. Folding his knees under him, he sat at the edge of the dune to which their fight had brought them. Keeping back, Tosh followed. I stepped between them to discourage more violence and sat near him in the shade of the tall seagrass.

"Listen," I started, laying my head in my hands. "Tosh, you first. You need to understand that there are times that you won't be able to go with us. No," I said, brokering no argument when she started to object. "I'm serious. Any job we do for The New South that is confidential in nature, you'll have to stay behind in either a hotel room near our location or here." I stopped, letting her realize that I wasn't saying no to her going with us some of the time.

"And, Jah," I continued, spreading my hands out palm up and trying to soothe the feelings between them. "She's right. What if she does go into estrous? We don't know her schedule, and being with us may trigger her sooner rather than later. We can't leave her alone until we get a better handle on things." Jah growled, his jaw set in a stubborn line. His eyes flashed with violence, his alpha nature fighting him every step of the way.

I got it. I did. Our lives have been in grave danger while working. Our jobs are not easy and certainly not safe. If not for our strength and training, we'd have been killed many times over. It's not a place for Tosh, but we'd figure it out. Eventually, things would settle, and we'd make better arrangements, but in the meantime, she'd need to stay with us, or one of us would have to stay home. I didn't consider the last option viable, and I told them so. Jah and I were better together. That's why we'd wanted one omega. Maybe we didn't think this through, but we were together now, and we'd stay that way.

"Tosh, you are a well-trained fighter, I see that. Jah sees that, too. But you're still an omega, and more importantly, you are our omega, and the bond demands that we care for you. You understand that; I know you do." I watched her eyes drop and knew that she did, in fact, understand what I said.

"Jah," I continued. "You're feeling threatened by your own omega in regards to her safety. I understand that, and she understands that, but you've got to get it together. Physically fighting with your wife is not the way to go here," I finished with a chuckle. "We'll figure it out."

"Sorry," she said, not sorry at all. Glancing up at him, she gave a sickly sweet smile. "I'd have kicked your ass," she murmured so low I almost didn't hear.

"Yeah, sorry," he returned, the steel rod he had up his ass not bending at all.

"Right. Well," I sighed again, wondering when I got elected mediator of this little group. Jah and I rarely fought, but when we did, I usually settled it. I guess that did make me the leader, but I didn't have to like it. "It's almost three miles to home. Let's get started. I can hear Tosh's stomach growling from here."

I popped up, helping Tosh to her feet. I kept my fingers twined in hers as we slugged our way through the deep sand to the trailhead that led home. Other, smaller trails lead to other places on the property. Someday we'd take the time to explore them with her, but today had been rocky from start to finish, and all I wanted was a hot shower, Tosh, and bed. Maybe not in that order.

Chapter Ten

Tosh

If I had to recap the lecture I just endured from my new husband, I don't think I could. But I'm pretty sure Bala said that I could go with them on their missions. He was talking so fast, and his accent was so deep that he could've been reciting the price of beef on the hoof at the latest auction, for all I know. I needed an interpreter. How can we be from the same country and not speak the same language? It made me wonder if they had problems understanding me. I mean, I didn't think so since I spoke actual English. My friends said I was the one with the accent, but if they ever met these two, they'd be dumbfounded. Like me. Current situation. Color me confused.

I replayed the conversation in my head, breaking it down into simple parts and slowing the words. He definitely said something about danger and missions and sometimes. I was okay with that. I knew it would be a hard-won battle to go everywhere with them and would settle for that. He was right; I did get it.

The surprised look on both of their faces when I backflip kicked Jah into the Middle West was priceless, and I'd cherish it forever. They needed to understand I wasn't a shrinking flower. If I established my lack of damsel in distress syndrome early, we should all be okay.

After the first few hundred yards, Jah caught up to us and gripped my fingers. He nursed his pride but held my hand anyway for the rest of the trip home. I reminded myself to reward him for that later; he was trying. Any other alphas would've probably waited until I was comatose from orgasms to pull the disappearing rabbit out of the hat trick, but not these two, and I appreciated that.

As we approached the house, I noticed something I'd missed before. On the side facing east, a giant deck jutted from the wall. No stairs were leading to it, which is why I hadn't noticed. My safety-conscious men probably didn't want another access to the house, but it would be an excellent place to sit and take in the sunsets. The railing was a little tall, but it would make a nice gun rest too. I nodded my approval of their design as we walked into the shade under the house to the centralized stairs leading up.

I hadn't looked before, but a variety of toys were housed in the makeshift garage. A flat bottomed boat, two kayaks, and myriad fishing gear rested against the lattice in the far corner. An assortment of paddles and other accessories were there too, and I thought maybe it would be nice to have the time to play with them.

After the long walk from the beach, the air in the house was almost cold, and chill bumps covered my arms as we went deeper inside. I grabbed water from the fridge and chugged it before taking another. I'd never seen the ocean. I'd seen beaches along the slow-flowing rivers of the Seventh, but never anything like the vast spread of sand here. It was incredible. Back home, the beaches were narrow, half sand, half mud hybrids of the pure sand beaches here. I could imagine hordes of people bathing in the calm sea or lying on the sand to catch the sun's rays, and it saddened me that those days were long behind us.

Bala was right; I'd felt the danger in the current and the unpredictable nature of the moving sand as I'd played just feet from the shoreline. Something had slithered between my legs, making me want to scream, but I hadn't. I hadn't wanted to seem afraid of something Jah so obviously loved. Nothing happened, and the thing swam away. I was a strong swimmer, but even I had limits. It was lovely, though, but I imagined it would be. Dangerous things usually are.

Back home, there is a snake that can kill you with one bite. It may not be colorful, but there is beauty in the patterns on its skin and the way it hides in nature. It's the stealthiest of killers in the Seventh, and I even I was afraid of it.

Bala pulled meat from the refrigerator and ingredients from the cabinets, combining them in a butter-filled skillet. Jah cut fresh broccoli. Without a word, they moved around the kitchen, making supper. I studied them closely. They had a deeper bond than I imagined and needed no words to accomplish this task. Glances, gestures, and head nods did what paragraphs would do with others, and it was humbling to watch.

Jah was shirtless, and his muscles rippled and flexed as he moved. The vee of his waist and light dusting of hair leading down caught my attention. He was a perfect alpha specimen. Beauty and grace wrapped around power and strength, and I hummed with pleasure just looking at him. Bal's white shirt hid the muscles underneath, but shorts showcased the herculean nature of his thighs, making me wonder if my estrous was closer than I thought. My mouth salivated, and pussy dripped as I looked them over.

Jah glanced over his shoulder with a smirk, the fucker. Amusement filtered through our bond, and peace settled over us like a dusting of snow. Bal caught me looking and grinned as he plated our meal. I almost felt bad about doing nothing- almost, but not quite. A formal dining area was set up on the far side of the house, but the men put the deep-fried chicken, broccoli, and buttered paolos on the island instead. They stood shoulder to shoulder, waiting for me to fill my plate. Their looks were expectant as they visually demanded that I eat.

That first bite? If I hadn't already married them, I would have dragged them to the altar with a shotgun over my shoulder. There is no doubt about that. My groans were unseemly as I ate first one plate and then another. They smiled, shaking their heads knowingly. Bastards.

Supper was followed by apple pie and sweet tea, guaranteeing I'd be in a coma before nightfall. I cleaned up the kitchen while my boys separated to shower the sand and sweat off. We hadn't said anything to each other since the beach, but it was the most comfortable I'd been in ages. I couldn't remember ever feeling so at home with silence.

When the dishes were done and the counters clean, I headed to the bedroom, hoping to have a shower myself. Jah and Bala sat on the balcony, speaking softly in that melodic language they shared. The words ebbed and flowed lyrically and not at all unlike the tides. There was a magical quality to it that was stunning, despite not knowing the meaning of their words. They stopped speaking, watching me walk toward them.

"What language is that?" I asked, leaning against the open double doors. I'd never heard it before meeting them. In fact, the only language that was supposed to be spoken in The New South was English. Though I'd certainly heard of Spanish and French, I'd never known anyone to speak them.

"It's Gullah," Bal said, patting his legs for me to sit on his lap. "It's the indigenous language of our people."

"Your people?" I asked, staying where I was.

"Many hundreds of years ago, our ancestors were brought to this country as slaves. It was long before the Great War and the great war before that one. They were eventually freed but stayed clustered along the coast. Even though we are all mostly mixed heritage now, I guess the Gullah pass on those traditions in hopes they won't be lost." Bal shrugged his shoulder, watching me.

"Like everything else has been," Jah added with a sigh.

"Is that why the town doesn't like me?" I asked, knowing I'd nailed it. "They don't like me because I'm an outsider?"

The men looked at each other, sharing a silent conversation. "For the most part, yes," Jah answered, finally looking my way.

I looked between them, then down as I realized something else. "Is it because I'm lighter-skinned than you?"

Bal burst out laughing. Jah smacked him on the back of his head before rising and walking to me. "You're lighter-skinned than just about everyone in the New South. But yeah, they were angry that we went outside of our community for a mate. They didn't want us, though, not on our terms. They have no right to hold it against any of us that you accepted us as yours. They knew, and they made a choice. Don't worry, Tosh. It doesn't matter what any of them think." Jah wrapped his arms around me, silencing the thread of doubt roiling in my gut.

"Doesn't it?" I asked.

Jah's intense hazel eyes bore into mine. "No. It doesn't. Not even a little bit, little squirrel. We belong to you in a way we never belonged to them."

I nodded at him. "I'm going to hop in the shower," I said, stepping back from him.

"Need help?" Bala offered, giving me a wink.

"I think I actually want a shower this time," I laughed, feeling some of the tension drain away.

"Fine," Jah huffed. "We're going to ruin it anyway." The smile he gave as he backed away to his chair on the deck melted the panties right off me, and I realized for the first time that I was in deep, deep trouble with these two. How I hadn't realized it before that moment, I don't know. It was short-sighted of me.

With a tingle deep in my core, I showered, washing away stale sweat and saltwater. My hair had been wrecked by the ocean, and I washed it too, finger-combing conditioner through it, so the curls rebounded. It felt amazing to be clean, but Jah's threat had me moving faster, wanting to be with them.

It was unusual to claim a mate outside of estrous. Even though it was illegal to claim a mate during estrous unless it was planned ahead of time and consensual, it was still mostly done during that time. My mother said the bonds were stronger that way. Jah and Bala hadn't wanted to wait. I'd just finished my estrous when they'd asked for me, and none of us wanted to wait three months.

Why had I agreed to mate with them? They were incredibly handsome, but they were also nice and respectful. They didn't see me as a liability, and I liked that about them. I'd been courted before, but none of them had struck the chord that Bala and Jah had. They'd been the most potent alphas I'd ever been around. Yet, there'd been no chest puffing, preening, or shows of blatant masculinity when I met them. They were secure enough in who they were to actually be fun. I'd liked that about them. Being with them felt like home, but I'd be lying if I said I wasn't intrigued by their exotic nature. Their accents, their customs, and their utter foreignness were intoxicating. I'd known from the moment they introduced themselves that I'd say yes. Add in their jobs and the subtle nature of the danger they presented, and I was lost to them.

But it was still an adjustment.

If we'd waited, we would have emerged from estrous bound tighter than denim. As it was, we were still getting to know each other. That was okay, but it wouldn't have mattered if we'd gone straight in estrous as we were designed to do.

I turned off the shower, toweling my body and hair. After massaging lotion into my skin, I pulled a long tee-shirt over my head and walked into the bedroom. Jah and Bala still sat on the deck. Beyond them, the sky was crimson, orange, and yellow as the sun lowered onto the horizon to the west. It took my breath. Moving forward, I stood at the railing. My mouth dropped open at the beautiful display of nature. We had pretty sunsets in the Seventh, but I'd never seen anything like this. The wide swath of ocean visible from the deck soaked up the colors of the sky, reflecting them upward. It was stunning, and I was speechless.

I stood until the sun dipped below the horizon, listening to the sound of waves pounding the sand. I'd been at peace before that moment, but it solidified in my soul, pounded deep by the ocean beyond my view. With a sigh, I turned when the last of the sun's rays extinguished. Jah and Bala stared at me like they'd been staring forever.

"Take dat shirt off an lay on da'bed, little mink," Bal said, his accent thickening as he rose from his chair and stalked toward me.

My eyes swept to Jah. The wicked tilt of his lips and the hungry look in his eyes told me he was of the same mind as his brother, and there would be no quarter there. I stripped the shirt over my head, dropping it on the floor before crawling up the oversized bed and lying down.

My heartbeat was like a rabbit's, fast and erratic as they walked to the edge of the bed and stared at me with predatory eyes. Their eyes skimmed my body, catching on my pebbled nipples and glistening lower lips.

As a unit, they stepped out of their clothes, and the darkening sky was still light enough to catch the hollows and peaks of their musculature. Jah leaned over the bed, grabbed my ankle and pulled me to the edge. I let out a squeak of surprise and flushed red when his soft chuckle raised the hairs on my arms. The chuckle changed to a moan when he sank to his knees and licked up my lips teasingly. My breath caught.

The light in the bathroom came on, casting the room in shadows but allowing me to see. Bala climbed onto the bed, taking first one nipple in his mouth and then the other. My heart fluttered as a brief moment of flight or fright came and went. They'd said nothing to me or each other. Jah's tongue circled my clit, causing slick to flow unabated. My core clenched with need, and suddenly they were the only things I could think about. Not the sunset, not the sound of waves crashing, and not the unfriendly town of Cope.

No, all I could think about was the dangerous beauty Jah and Bala possessed as they licked and sucked me.

My back arched into Bala as he pulled my nipples into his mouth. Jah's forearms wrapped around my thighs, and his wide palms pressed my hipbones into the bed. All I could feel was them. Bala's mouth hovered over mine, breathing in my moans and whimpers before his tongue licked between my lips, coaxing my tongue to join his. His mouth was hot and tasted sweet like the tea he'd been sipping on the deck.

Jah's tongue ran up my seam again, lapping up what my body gave him. Then he latched onto my clit, and the tidal wave of pleasure I'd been floating on came crashing down. I cried out, arching to force myself fully onto his face. I clenched around nothing, coming so hard that I saw floaters. Bala palmed my breast, taking my cries into his mouth and demanding my tongue dance with his.

My thighs shook, and breaths came hard and fast. As soon as my heart slowed, Jah licked my clit again. "Little mink, you taste like heaven," he said before moving away.

"My turn," Bala said, trailing his hands down my abdomen and over my thighs.

I reached for him as he sank between my legs. "Bala, no. I can't take anymore."

Jah grabbed my wrists with one hand, pinning them above my head and stretching my body tight. He skimmed the fingers of his other hand over my nipples and up to my throat, gripping it and saying, "Shhh, squirrel. Let us have you." He mounted my chest, straddling my breasts and gripping the back of my head. He brought his cock to my lips, pushing through to the back of my throat.

His head fell back as he fucked my mouth hard and fast, holding my head tight to his body. I struggled to accommodate him, but he used my lips roughly, never slowing. "I've needed this all day," he groaned. "I need to cum, fuck," he said. His hips stuttered as he pushed his cock past the threshold of my throat and came in a violent spasm, his body shaking.

While his brother's cock was still emptying into me, Bala vibrated his tongue on my clit, making me scream against the flesh in my mouth. Painful spasms in my core made me ache until Bala's cock slammed home, filling the emptiness there. He stilled in me, letting my body relax around him. When I caught my breath, he began to move.

Jah's cock hardened again, but he pulled it free with a loud pop of my lips. He staggered back to sit on the side of the bed and watch his brother fuck me. Bal's back bent with each thrust, the muscles straining. He fucked me slowly, watching my face and occasionally lowering his body to kiss me. Jah watched it all with desperate eyes. His cock grew harder, grazing the skin of his abdomen as he leaned down to kiss me too.

"She can take it," Bala said, glancing up at his brother with a nod.

"We'll take care of you, mink," he said, flipping so that I was on top of him. He gripped my hips, pounding into me hard enough to make my head fall back, and a groan of pleasure came from the deepest parts of my soul. He flicked my clit as he pistoned in and out of me, and slick flowed freely, making a mess between us.

He stopped playing with me right before I came again, and I let out a whimper of frustration as I twisted my hips, chasing the orgasm he stole. Hands from behind stilled me as they pushed my chest down to Bala, who stopped moving inside of me.

Jah kissed up my spine, sending shivers of need through me. I felt a second head nudge my entrance and froze, sucking in a ragged breath. "You can take it, baby," Jah said, his hot breath in my ear. His tongue traced the shell of it as his cock nudged deeper.

It hurt. It hurt a lot. One alpha cock is one thing, but two is something else entirely. I gasped as Jah worked himself into me, my body tightening and clenching at the added invasion. When he'd pushed beyond the resistance, he paused, sighing as he kissed my neck and his claiming mark there. I took a steadying breath, letting my body relax around them as they both penetrated me to the roots of their cocks. I was full beyond comfort, and my body tried to fight theirs. Whether it wanted them out or deeper, I couldn't say. With a shared look, they began to move, their timing perfect. I screamed, unable to stop myself. It was too much.

Bala's fingers found my clit as their synchronized rhythm worked me perfectly, and the pain of their cocks turned into something else. My head dropped to Bal's shoulder, and he kissed his claiming mark as he fucked me. Pressure built in my core, and I felt the beginnings of something life-changing.

Sweat rolled between us as they took me how they wanted: together. Like everything they did, their movements were perfectly timed and executed. I sang the song of the omega between them as they obliterated thoughts of anything but them and us. They switched it up, going off rhythm so that one moved into me and one moved out. I was constantly full. The change brought me closer to the cataclysmic end I felt building. If I went off that cliff with them, I felt there was a strong possibility I might die from the fall. But it would be a good way to go.

I'd never felt anything like it before. Being surrounded on all sides by a wall of sweat-soaked muscle and filled with the hardness of their bodies was transcendent. I was literally a changed person. Had this happened during estrous, I would have missed the nuances of the experience. The memory would have been hazy, at best. Instead, every sensation etched across my brain, branding me with my alphas. Everything I breathed was them. Everything I felt was them. They were everything.

They worked me until I couldn't even moan from the pleasures they gave, then with a final flick of Bala's fingers, I shattered, screaming their names. I whipped my head around, clamping my teeth into Jah's shoulder and ripping away his flesh with a warrior's cry. Then I turned my teeth to Bala, sinking them into his neck low enough so as not to destroy his jugular. A primal thought, not a coherent one, kept me from killing him. I savaged his flesh, sending blood flying. It dripped from Jah's shoulder onto my back, and I came again as the final element of the bond snapped into place, clamping down on their cocks so tightly they couldn't move. They bloomed inside of me, their knots sealing me tight as they bathed my womb with their cum.

Jah roared behind me, his body shaking. Bala bit me again, covering his prior teeth marks with new ones, and we all bled for each other. Their cocks spasming was the last thing I felt before I blacked out.

Chapter Eleven

Jah

We'd made a deadly mistake. There is no possible way pleasure at this level is survivable. Can you fuck to death? I'm pretty sure you can. I'm pretty sure we just about did.

Tosh lay smashed between us, her breathing slow and steady. Her heart rate had finally calmed, and the frenetic pulse was no longer visible in her neck. She'd claimed us. Her eyes had been wide and electric when she'd whipped her head around to clamp down on the only part of my body she could reach. My shoulder ached and pounded to the beat of my heart, but I didn't care. She'd savaged my flesh, and it was a mark I'd proudly wear.

Our knots held us in place. I could feel Bala's cock against mine. We'd never done anything like this with another woman, but I wasn't disgusted by the feel of his flesh touching me. It was just another thing we shared. The pressure of our cum locked behind our knots had to be intense, but Tosh hadn't complained. No, she'd blacked right the fuck out. We'd positioned ourselves on our sides with her in between, knees drawn to her chest to accommodate us. Her belly was so full it was rounded, and I'd never been more satisfied in my life.

"Fuck," Bala said in Gullah. "If we die from fucking is it an accident, suicide, or murder?" he added in the old language.

"All three? None of them?" I answered in English, "I don't think she likes it when we speak Gullah," I said, brushing the hair from her sweaty face.

"I don't think she understands half of what we say regardless of the language," he chuckled, but switched to English.

It was a pivotal moment in our lives, having Tosh pinned on our knots and sleeping from pleasure overload. "I think she liked it," I said, smiling over her head at Bal. "I know I did."

"Like isn't a word I would ever attach to this experience. It's not even in the right family of words. I can't think of a word in either language that actually fits." Bal smiled back, and I knew we had made the right choice.

The mating bond sang between us, and I felt Tosh so strongly that I wondered if it was normal.

"Is this normal?" I asked, voicing my concern.

"Of course," he answered right away. "This is how it should be. I can feel her satisfaction. She's happy. She knows she made the right choice. I love that there is no more doubt between us. We'll always know what the other is thinking," he finished in Gullah, not realizing the switch. He placed a kiss on her shoulder.

Bala wasn't actually my brother. He was a distant cousin whose mother had died during his birth. We'd been raised like twins, and we looked enough alike that people always thought we were. We were born a few days apart, but we had shared a birthday, a crib, parents, and now a mate since the beginning. We shared a house, a job, and a purpose. It's who we were. We never considered ourselves anything but brothers.

Tosh sighed, and Bala's amber eyes snapped to mine as our knots deflated simultaneously. Hot cum rushed out, soaking everything in its path, and I made a mental note to buy sheets in bulk. There was a closet full of nesting material, but it was mostly blankets and furs of different textures. No sheets. We really hoped Tosh was a nester. Her profile said she liked to nest, but we'd been with her two nights and had yet to see that behavior.

She sighed again, her eyes opening like a kitten's for the first time. Her focus was soft; then, she lasered in on Bal's neck. She gasped, bringing her face up to his. "Are you all right?" she asked, worrying over his wound.

I could've answered the question for him, but he beat me to it. "I'm fine, little mink. Your mark feels perfect on my skin."

"I feel," she started, shaking her head. "I feel that. I can tell that you don't mind it. That's weird. I didn't feel you like this before," she finished, tilting her head and looking at him.

Her hand reached out to touch the deep bite mark on the side of his neck. She'd placed it a little low, but it would be visible no matter what he wore. I was a little jealous. My mark would be covered by anything but a tank.

"The bond goes both ways, Tosha," he explained, his voice holding a quality I hadn't heard before. His gaze upon her was reverent. "It wasn't complete until you marked us in return."

"Oh," she said. "I'm not sure what came over me; it just felt right at the time." She laid her head on his chest, purring softly for us. Her tranquility spread through our bond like smoke.

"It was right, little fox. You did it because it's natural."

Tosh nodded, seeming shy for the first time ever. Not all omegas marked their mates, and it was considered a high honor if they did. Couples could be bonded for years before it happened. More often, the omega never did it. These northern omegas were on to something when they pushed NS304 into existence. All the alphas they chose had been marked as if having a choice was the key. Maybe it was. We hadn't chosen Tosh; The Alpha's mate, Eve, had. We'd read her file and accepted, but this was basically an arranged marriage by tacit agreement. Yet, here we were, happily bonded and freshly claimed by the sweet, violet-eyed omega from the northernmost reaches of the New South. And all within a few days. It was humbling, really.

"I'm thirsty and swimming in a sea of cum," she laughed, pushing away from Bala and into my chest. My dick twitched, and we both groaned, making me laugh too. I have no doubt we groaned for different reasons. "Put that thing away, Jah. I think you broke my vagina," she groaned again, pulling herself up. She walked to the bathroom with a limp, making me almost feel bad. But not quite.

Bala and I rose too, stripping the sheets from the bed since she wasn't wrong. I grabbed the other sheet set we had for the oversized king we'd bought while he picked up the woven grass baskets filled with nesting material. My Great Gran'maamy had made them using the traditional methods of our people. It had been her wedding gift. Old and ageless as time itself, she'd talked about teaching Tosh to weave baskets as she'd worked. As unaccepting of our choice in mates as the community had been, our family stood behind us like a wall, solid and impenetrable.

I carried them to the side of the bed as Bal finished tucking in the sheets and pulling up the ancient handmade quilts to cover them. The water in the bathroom turned off, and a wet, sleepy Tosh walked past us to the bed. Her eyes caught on the baskets, and her hands twitched, but she didn't pick up anything, choosing instead to climb under the covers and make herself into a small ball.

I turned off the lights, snuggling in behind her while Bal closed the drapes and followed. Tosh alternated between us during the night, snuggling into either of us as she turned in her sleep. I would like to say I slept like the dead, but I'd never actually slept overnight with another human, and now I had two moving about. It kept me up, but I didn't mind. Had I slept well, I would have missed the sight of the moon's rays kissing Tosh's skin like a jealous lover. I would've missed the little smiles she gave in her sleep. And I would miss the sight of Bala's face, utterly relaxed and completely at peace. I don't think I'd ever seen that face before, not even in childhood.

Bala and I chose the lives we have, and we wouldn't change them. Still, at our core, we were not good men. Between us, we'd killed dozens, if not hundreds, of people. We think we'd done so for the right reasons, but that doesn't mean everyone agreed. There was most certainly darkness in our souls, and we'd given up pieces of ourselves along the way.

We always looked over our shoulders. In our line of work, we had to. Yet, Tosh had taken some of that from him, and the look on his sleeping face was worth more to me than anything. In the wee hours of the morning, I'd thought all I could about my new situation. Wrapping my arms around both of them, I finally fell asleep.

Bala's ComLink sounding woke us all. With a groan, he rolled away from us to ignore the call. It rang again immediately, letting us know something needed our attention.

"O'Day," Bala growled our last name when he finally answered.

I recognized The Alpha's voice growling back, "I need you and your brother in my office immediately."

"Sir," Bala responded, modulating his voice to sound less irritated than I knew he was. "We are newly mated and on our honeymoon. Can it wait?" he added.

"If it could wait, I would have waited," Lukas growled, sounding not at all happy at Bal's resistance.

The Alpha seldom called us directly. We had contacts and handlers who gave us assignments. Yes, they originated from The Alpha, but he'd only called a handful of times himself when the mission was serious or personal. For him to be calling so soon after the bonding ceremony he'd attended, it was likely both.

The Alpha gave a resigned sigh before adding, "I'll send a shuttlecraft. I need to speak with you in person, but I can have you home tonight to arrange for your omega."

Tosh's head popped between Jah and me; her teeth bared as she growled. The Alpha just laughed when he heard it. "How's it going, boys?" he said, sounding smug. I wanted to see him so that I could wipe the knowing smile off his face. So he and Eve had been right, more Eve than Lukas, as he'd fought us until she'd made him change his mind. Whatever. I guess I did owe him a debt anyway.

Tosh growled harder, pushing her nude ass into me. My groan added to the mixture of sounds in the room, and Lukas's booming laugh came through the ComLink because he heard it all.

"Two hours," he said, his voice softer. "They'll land on the beach if the winds are right. Be ready."

The ComLink clicked off, and Bala rolled onto his back with a grumble. "Fuck," he said, shaking his head and bringing his hands to cover his face.

"I'm going," Tosh said, pushing her way to the end of the bed to hop off. Her arms crossed angrily, and she glared down at us.

The problem was that she was deliciously and gloriously naked. The tight tangle of dark honeyed curls accentuated her sex, making my mouth water. Her arms pushed her breasts up, and her little golden nipples pushed me over the edge.

"Tosh," Bal groaned, and I noted the hardened bulge under the quilts. He was as affected as I was, but her anger through the bond let me know now was not the time.

"Little squirrel," I interrupted. "We need to talk to the Alpha about involving you in our missions before we actually do it. We'll be home in a few hours. You could go with us and hang out with the other girls if you want. Remember, we have to do this on a case-by-case basis. I promise we won't leave you out."

Her arms fell to her side, and shoulders slumped. "Fine," she said, not showing any kind of fineness through the bond. She was still mad as hell, but she also understood.

This bond thing was pretty cool.

"I don't want to hang out with the other omegas," she said with a sigh. "I don't like being in the city anyway. It's suffocating." She turned her back to us, walking into the bathroom.

"I don't like this, Jah," Bala said, rising from the tangled sheets. "It's too soon."

"It was never going to be a good time, brother." I got up too, and together we straightened the bed and picked up the clothes abandoned on the floor. "We needed to talk to Lukas anyway. Now is as good a time as any."

Bala nodded, walking toward the bathroom where the shower had turned on. Tosh was still mad; I could feel her anger tweaking the lines between us. I could also tell Bala disagreed that she would be fine left by herself, but he declined to voice that fear.

I tried to look at the bright side. We'd see Lukas sooner rather than later. We could talk to him about Tosh and involving her in some of our missions. She was an asset. Just like Lukas's wife Eve, Tosh could help. In reality, she already had. The landscape of the New South would undeniably be different if the omegas hadn't alerted The Alpha about the insurrection in the north. The New South may have been lost had they not helped fight in those cavernous valleys and vast mountains. Lukas knew that. I didn't want Tosh out there on the front lines, but she could certainly help in some capacity.

Her back was to us when we walked into the steamy bathroom. Her motions were sharp and angry as she washed the remnants of our amazing, still not the right word, night down the drain. Bala purred for her as he entered the shower, grabbing the sponge from her hand. He pulled her into a hug and purred louder.

"I don't like being left behind," she said as her body went slack.

"And we don't like leaving you, little fox. You can still go. You can see your friends and spend time in the city if you want." Bala sponged her back as he held her, purring into the crown of her head.

I picked up the shampoo bottle and squirted some into my hand before massaging it into her scalp and down to the ends. I'd looked up how to care for a woman's curly hair when she agreed to bond with us and tried to remember all the steps to washing it. While she thought about Bal's offer, I finger-combed her tangled curls until they fell loosely down her back. My hair was curly too, but I used a three-in-one shampoo, not caring about it.

Finally, she said, "No. I'll stay. Maybe I'll move things around or just get used to being here. As you said, you'll be right back. I'm just silly. It's not like we can be together all the time; this will be good," she finished, moving away from Bala and ducking her head under the waterfall shower to rinse.

I growled, unable to stop myself. In my mind, we could be together all of the time, and saying otherwise was offensive. Tosh laughed, swatting my chest. "It's fine, Jah. Everything is new; we'll get used to it in time." Only I hoped we never did. I liked this crazed feeling and how much I needed her. I didn't want it to get old.

I hoped we never got to the phase where we watched TV in separate rooms or one of us slept on the couch. I always wanted it to feel this way, even if some of it was downright scary. I grabbed the mink and pulled her to me, finding her lips with mine. I sank into her mouth, loving the moan that slipped from her lips as I teased them with mine. I found her seam, and the hot feel of her slick drowning my fingers made my cock twitch.

"We're supposed to be cleaning up," she whispered, sinking onto my hand.

"Lukas gave us two hours for a reason. It's a quick flight via shuttlecraft," I answered. "It's his way of apologizing." I pinched her clit, and her body practically vibrated. "Come for me, little squirrel." And my omega did. Slick ran down my fingers, and she clutched me, her body shaking. Her orgasms seemed violent to the point of pain, her face twisted and tight with pleasure. I slid two fingers into her, and she clamped me tightly.

She rode out her orgasm on my hand, throwing her head back and twisting her hips until she was satisfied. The Bala took her from me and started the process again. I wanted to bury my cock in her, but we didn't have time. But we did have time to give her a few orgasms, and then maybe she'd sleep until we came back.

Bala pulled Tosh to him on shaky legs, sitting her on the bench. His face disappeared between her thighs, and her head fell back as he tongued her. She buried her hands in his hair and moaned. The bond vibrated with sheer happiness, and I was grateful to feel it. To think we wouldn't share this if we hadn't met Tosh.

I leaned against the shower wall, stroking myself as I watched Bala make Tosh cry out. It was so sexy to see them together. His back hunched, and her hands pulled at his hair violently. One hand reached down, and I saw he had the same idea as me. He made quick work of making her come, latching onto her clit and sucking her until she screamed his name. He stood, and I stepped next to him. We both came on her chest again, and her hands rose to rub it in. She smiled softly, drained of the anger she'd had a few minutes before.

"You're evil," she sighed, her lids heavy when she opened her eyes. "Terrible, awful creatures. Don't think I don't know what you did here," she finished, heaving herself up like it took all the strength she had.

Bala wrapped her in a towel, scooped her off her feet, and carried her to the bed. "Take a nap." He winked at her, flashing a smug smile. "We have time to whip up a quick breakfast. We'll leave it for you." He sank beside her, pulling her to him in a hug. After kissing the top of her head, he said, "We'll see you soon."

I dropped down next to her, tucking a wet curl behind her ear before booping her nose. "See you soon, mink. By the time you wake up, maybe we'll be home. It might storm later, so don't stray far from the house. Keep the doors locked," I added on a whim.

She yawned, rolling over and pulling the covers high. We hadn't slept much last night, so I knew she had to be tired. In the kitchen, Bal had bacon frying and coffee brewing. "Do you think she'll be okay?" I asked, frowning at the floor.

"She'll be fine, and we'll be fast, in and out of the capital like a surgical strike." He flipped the bacon and added eggs to the grease. It would heat up well, and Tosh wouldn't have to worry about making anything.

"Like that time in Columbia when we took out that gang leader?" I asked, thinking back on the shortest mission of our careers. We'd known exactly where this guy was and walked in the door, slit his throat, and walked right back out. We weren't there long enough for the helicopter blades to stop moving.

"Yes, exactly like that," Bal said, plating breakfast for Tosh and then us.

I wolfed it down, watching Bal walk into the guest room. When he came back, he held a few knives from the safe we had hidden in the floor there. Funny how her profile mentioned she loved them. He set the knives next to Tosh's plate, and instinct told me they would make her happy.

After he ate, we cleaned up the kitchen and checked on Tosh. She'd fallen asleep with her hands thrown over her head, her features arranged in ethereal beauty, and I knew I loved her. How could that happen so quickly? I wasn't sure, but there was no denying it. She was the center of our lives and the link to what souls we had left. I would hate any moment we were apart. I placed a kiss on her forehead, loving the soft sigh she gave before leaving her, closing the door.

We locked the front door behind us and jogged down the stairs before picking up our pace for the long run to the beach. I heard the shuttlecraft approach as we cleared the last of the dunes. It was just setting down, and the doors opened; we jumped in, circled over the sea, and headed west to The Alpha.

Chapter Twelve

Tosh

They left me knives. I grinned wildly as I tested their heft and balance in my hands. I'd never had a better gift in my life. Smiling, I tossed one at the dartboard on the wall, striking the bullseye. Before the handle stopped quivering, I'd thrown the second, third, fourth, and fifth. My grouping was nearly perfect, with only one outside the second-smallest circle on the board. I needed to practice.

They weren't just regular knives. They were antique Maxam Triple Threats, and they were almost as sexy as my men. Shorter than most knives, they were harder to control but fit my hands better than longer models. Made of graphite-colored stainless steel and sharpened to a spear point, they were incredibly sharp and wickedly dangerous. I was in love with them. The boys had left a sheath that held all six, but I clutched the last one to my chest instead of throwing it at the board. I smiled as I tossed the blade, catching the non-lethal end before tossing it again. It was perfect.

I scooped my reheated breakfast into my mouth before pulling the knives from the board and throwing them again. My grouping narrowed, and I felt a little better about myself.

After Jah and Bal left, I'd napped for hours, waking to find the sun long risen and my eggs cold. I gulped a large glass of ice water before refilling it and going onto the massive deck. The sun was high and hot when I settled onto a chair facing the sliver of water I could see. It felt amazing on my skin, even though I'd burn in no time if I stayed. I gave a contented sigh, the weight of the blades on my hip comfortable.

I'd had good days in my life. But I'd had bad ones too. I'd never had a string of good days like this, though. Until meeting my boys and bonding with them, there'd been a hole. That hole was filled to bursting now, no pun intended. I breathed deeply, loving the smell of the sea on the breeze. It ruffled my hair, lifting it and cooling my sun-warmed scalp.

The waves didn't sound as brutal as they crashed onto the sand, and I wondered if it was glassy enough for a quick swim. I didn't want to encounter any sea monsters, but if I stayed close to the shore, I might be able to avoid them. Gulls and other birds cried as they searched for lunch, and I was almost lulled to sleep again by the sound. The boys had taken excellent care of me this morning, and I was still riding the high left from their touch. Their scent mingled with the ocean's in the breeze, and it was incredible. As a perfume, it would be a best seller.

I almost missed the first hint of trouble. The noise of it was buried in the quiet sound of the waves and shrill cries of birds. Whispers in the distance carried in the brief lull of sound, and I tuned in to discern the words.

"There's only one way in and out. She's up there; can't be nowhere else," someone whispered from the carport below the house.

I sat stone-still, knowing they'd hear if I moved even a hair.

"You sure they left her?" another voice said.

"Yeah. The shuttle landed on the beach. They're off on some mission; they ain't going to take an omega for that." The voices were both male, and I worried about the thing women must always worry about. They wouldn't be here if they didn't want something.

"Think she'll answer if we knock?" the voice was deep and southern, though not as hard to understand as Jah and Bala. The cadence was slower too.

"No way. I'm sure they told her not to open the door, dumbass." They shuffled below like they were looking for something, and I knew I'd have to be quick. They were both dumbasses, but they would still be bigger than I was, and nothing good would come of them getting their hands on me.

That's when I heard the girl.

"Is she in there, Daddy? I want that bitch dead. She took my mate." I recognized Moesh's voice immediately, and the game changed. I wondered if her beta friend was down there, too. It was four on one if she was, and those aren't the best odds, especially in unknown territory.

"I think so. Stand back, honey, and we'll take care of this for you. On three, one, two." Bodies pounded against the door, but it

125

held. Jah and Bala weren't dumb. As safety-conscious as they were, I'm sure the door would hold for a little while. But it wouldn't hold forever, and I had no intention of being here when it came down.

They'd given up being quiet and were now speaking to one another at full volume while banding together to break down the door. Using the noise as cover, I crept to the edge of the deck furthest from where they worked. While they shouted at one another and slammed into the door, I climbed onto the railing and climbed down the support post hand over hand to the ground.

I heard the door give and sprinted along the path to the dunes, not bothering to cover my tracks. There was no time. The slider had been open to the deck, and in moments, they would know I'd been there.

"Daddy! There!" Moesh shouted as she caught sight of me from the higher vantage point as I ran through the dunes.

Shouts echoed as they pounded through the house, down the steps, and raced behind me. But I was used to running and was faster. Jumping from dune to dune, I stayed ahead of them, racing, not toward the beach as they probably thought, but to the trees edging the property.

Their shouts faded in and out as I lost them in the maze of Sawgrass and dunes. I placed my feet higher on their sandy sides, and my tracks were covered by natural filling as the sand shifted.

These weren't trackers or hunters. They were an angry family who thought I was the problem. They probably thought that if I were out of the way, Jah would take Moesh back. Maybe they just wanted to hurt him; I didn't know. Maybe it was a misplaced sense of honor. Regardless, when Jah and Bala found out, the family would be erased. I had zero doubts about that.

They reached the open expanse of the beach and shouted their frustration that I wasn't there. I ran faster, knowing they'd backtrack and come my way, and jumped on the first climbable tree, scurrying up in seconds. I'd always been a natural squirrel, and it was funny that my boys called me that nickname first. Though fox and mink both fit, squirrel was much more appropriate.

At the top, I jumped to the next tree. The branches were further than I would've liked, but I made the landing, scurrying to the other side. From tree to tree, I flew until I nestled in a thicker copse. Hidden from sight, I settled in for a long wait. It wasn't the first time I had taken to the air to hide from pursuers, and I knew the drill. Jah and Bala would be back, and if not, these fools would give up, and I'd come down. I wished I'd peed, though; those glasses of water were getting to me.

I heard them at the treeline, looking for a sign of where I'd gone. They crashed through the brush like elephants on parade, proving they were unskilled hunters.

"Where is she? What the fuck? Is she a conjure woman? You didn't say nothing about no conjure woman, Mo," I assumed her father said.

"She ain't no conjure woman, daddy. She's an omega, just like me. She's small. We just have to keep looking. Not like she'd get far," Moesh said.

"She could be anywhere, baby," the other man said.

I'd never heard a fourth voice and was glad. My odds improved without the lean, muscled beta woman in the mix.

"We should go back. This isn't going to work, anyway. You said she had claiming bites on her. Killing her could kill them." The other man added.

"No, Uncle George. She took him from me, and I want him back. The only reason he took her was because I said no to his stupid brother. So what if Bala dies? Jah is stronger than that. If they are both gone, he'll come back to me. We just need her out of the picture," Moesh finished, and they started moving again.

"We'll find her, baby. If that's what you want, we'll find her."

They scoured the woods, never once looking up. And they'd have moved on and never found me if the branch I was sitting on hadn't creaked dramatically when a gust of wind sang through the trees. When I settled on it, it seemed sturdy, and maybe it was. During a lull from nature's full song, it groaned under my weight loud enough to draw their attention. They did what humans rarely do; they looked up.

"There she is!" The sharp-eyed omega caught sight of the pink tank I'd thrown on this morning and started shouting and pointing.

The man nearest my position shouldered a shotgun, and I jumped to another tree as he fired the first shot. The branch that had held me exploded in a spray of bark and leaves. I jumped trees again, this one was larger, and I got on the backside of the trunk before the shotgun blasted again. Pieces of birdshot dug into my skin, and I suppressed a scream as blood spilled down my arm.

I heard the shotgun rack and knew I needed to do something. The men had walked around the truck and were below me, looking up. The shotgun raised again, and I did the only thing I could. Grabbing a knife from the belt on my hip, I threw it.

Blood bloomed from the man's throat as the knife landed where I'd aimed. He dropped the shotgun and clutched at it before going to his knees. Bright red blood flowed from between his fingers, and his choking gasps could be heard from my perch above.

"Daddy!" Moesh sank to her knees, grabbing at her father as he fell. His eyes stared up at me, vacant but no less accusatory.

Moesh grabbed the shotgun and screamed as she reloaded and pulled the trigger. Her aim was off, but not so far off that some of the metal balls didn't nail me in the thigh. She racked the slide again, and I pulled another knife.

I felt Jah and Bala's utter terror through the bond, and that distraction made my throw go wide. Moesh pulled the trigger again, hitting me in the other shoulder. Grabbing another knife, I threw it with deadly precision. The knife landed between the fifth and sixth ribs, and she dropped instantly, pulling the knife out. The first rule of knife play is to always leave it in, not that it would have saved her, as my strike was true. Blood splattered with each beat of her heart until she lay still on the forest floor. The uncle ran. He abandoned the shotgun and ran screaming through the trees.

I didn't cry. I didn't even want to. These weren't my first kills, not by a long shot. It was them or me, and under that premise, I chose me every time. I sat down on a big limb, leaning back against the trunk to catch my breath. Blood flowed freely down my leg, and I wondered if the shot to my thigh had hit an artery. Lacking my usual grace, I slipped down the tree, falling the last several feet onto my back. I lay for a long time, looking at the sun filtering through the treetops. It was beautiful, it was, but I didn't want it to be the last thing I saw.

The sound of heavy rotors broke the silence in the small grove of trees. I'd only heard that sound one time before, and it was immediately jarring. During the troubles in the Seventh, The Marines had deployed some heavy hitters like the old but still fearsome Apache helicopter. I'd never seen anything move so quickly across the skies. The sound was so unmistakable and innately frightening that I took cover whenever I heard it, regardless that I knew they were on our side.

A shadow of the thing danced over me as it approached the beach, and I forced myself to stand. The wind the blades generated whipped the trees from side to side, and I swayed under the force of it. Picking one knife out of the dead man's throat and the other from where Moesh dropped it, I limped toward the sound of it landing instead of away.

Chapter Thirteen

Bala

My heart raced faster than the helicopter whisking us back to Cope. We'd felt the adrenaline racing in Tosh's blood through her bond with us. We'd felt pain more intense than any we'd known, and we knew she was in serious trouble. The funny thing is, we'd never felt her fear. Whatever was happening, our omega faced it with determination so fierce it left no room for that useless emotion. And she faced it alone.

Jah had stood up in the middle of the meeting with The Alpha and announced that something was very wrong with Tosh. Initially, I had thought he was being dramatic until the same feeling of dread filtered to me. The Alpha, seeing our distress and having been there before himself, commandeered one of the fastest helos in his fleet, and here we were. Not leaving the matter to one of his subordinates, Lukas came too.

The feeling had gotten worse the closer we got to Cope. That useless emotion stabbed me in the gut, leaving me to bleed out. I'd never felt more helpless in my life. Jah sat across from me, looking out the window in silent determination. Lukas was next to the piolet, who had completed a supply run and hoped to be home in time for supper until The Alpha screwed up his plans.

We flew low over the town, noting nothing amiss, but the streets were empty, so maybe something was. It was the supper hour, and people should be out and about. The Apache buzzed our house, and nothing looked out of place there either. I craned my neck, noting that the curtains blew out the open deck slider caused by the blades' downwash.

The helo continued to lower as it approached the beach, and I was glad to have had access to it. The lumbering shuttle would've taken over an hour to land there instead of the mere thirty minutes the Apache needed. The beach was empty, and again, nothing looked out of sorts.

Jah and I were out of the bird before the blades could stop, ducking to avoid them and the sandstorm they made. We ran in circles, trying to pinpoint where she was using the bond, but we were frantic by then and unable to focus.

"Stop!" Lukas demanded, placing a hand on both our shoulders. His tone brokered no argument, and that is why he is The Alpha. He had a way of speaking that did not allow disobedience. "Look there," he finished.

Tosh limped toward us, covered in blood. Sun glinted off a blade in each hand. Her arms were limp, and one leg dragged behind her. Still, she felt no fear. We would know. A deep sense of exhaustion vibrated through the bond, but nothing more.

"Tosh!" I yelled as she approached. I saw the knife belt on her hips and the tightness with which she gripped the bloodied blades in her hands, and my pride in her soared. After an initial moment in which time was frozen, I sprinted to her side, screaming and unable to hold back the tide of emotions swirling through me. Jah ran beside me, and we reached for her together. She collapsed into my arms, the knives never falling from her grip.

When she went limp, I turned in my tracks, racing back to the Apache and laying her body on its floor. The pilot tossed the first-aid pack at me, and I ripped it open, grabbing gauze pads. I held pressure to a wound on her thigh that was bleeding freely. Jah climbed in next to me, his eyes glassy with unshed tears.

"What the fuck?" he said, smoothing Tosh's hair from her face.

Her shoulder was a ruined mess, and blood spatter marked every part of her skin. Jah grabbed a bottle of saline. Cracking it open, he soaked more gauze pads and began the careful work of washing her skin to find her injuries.

"She's been fucking shot," he said, growling and glaring up at me like I'd shot her myself.

"We'll find out who did this," I growled back. "And then they die."

Jah cleaned around my hand and found more penetrating wounds. She'd been shot with a shotgun, and she was filled with birdshot. Her pulse was strong and steady beneath my hand, and I was glad for that, but the wound on her leg continued to bleed.

"Use combat gauze," Jah said, rifling through the pack. "Here," he said, opening a package and handing the special gauze to me. "It'll stop the bleeding. Even if it's arterial, it'll buy us time."

I held it on the bleeder and watched as Jah stuck an IV in her arm. We'd both taken first aid, but he'd gone further and gotten his medic certification. He was much better at the medical stuff than I was, which I was grateful for. He hung a bag of saline before continuing to clean the blood from her.

"There must be a hundred fucking pellets in her. They have to come out." He dug further into the pack, pulling out sterile hemostats and disinfectant. "I'm going to do it while she's out. I'm not waiting on a fucking doctor, Bal. This is terrible. What the fuck," he said again, echoing my sentiments exactly.

"What the fuck, indeed," Lukas demanded from the doors to the bird. "I followed her tracks to the woods beyond the shoreline. There're two bodies: one male and one female. Both with knife wounds." Lukas gave Tosh's hands a pointed glance. "There is a single shotgun on the ground between them."

I looked up at Jah, holding his eyes. I didn't mean for the look to be accusatory, but it was.

"She wouldn't," he said, but the tone of his voice told me he knew that she would've. She definitely would have. Moesh had always been fucking crazy. Her family too. Jah never should've

135

messed with her, but he'd hoped she'd be crazy enough to accept us both.

We never should've left Tosh alone. We hadn't taken Moesh seriously, and that was a mistake we wouldn't make again.

"I'll go, Jah." The combat gauze had worked, and the most significant wound on her leg had stopped bleeding. "I'll be right back."

I left Jah pulling metal out of my unconscious wife and followed The Alpha to the treeline. Not thirty feet in, I saw the bodies of Moesh and Jamil White laying on blood-stained sand. Pieces of torn leaves and wood littered the ground around them, and I looked up. "Our girl is a climber," I said, following Tosh's progression through the trees. Chunks of the tree trunk were missing, and branches and leaves were torn from it.

"They fucking shot her, Lukas," I said, my voice shaking. I was talking more to myself than him, but he glanced my way, anyway.

"She's deadly with a knife. These omegas catch more bodies than most marines," he added as he turned back to the helo. "We need to look into this. It looks justified, but I need to have enough information to be sure."

The growl started in my soul, ripping from my mouth before I could stop it. The Alpha grabbed me by the neck, not putting enough pressure to do anything but catch my attention. "Under the circumstances, I will give you leeway, but continue growling at your own risk."

From the roof of a building hundreds of yards away, I could take him out, but that would be the only way. Lukas was the strongest alpha the New South had ever seen, and I'd never beat him in a fight. I choked the growl off and forced my eyes down.

We caught sight of Jah carrying Tosh through the dunes, so we followed to our house. He was far enough ahead of us that when he uttered "Motherfuckers" under his breath, it took me a minute to see why. They'd broken our door down. Wood splinters and chunks of it lay scattered across the carport, and my fury only built. There was no way one man and an omega could've broken it. I had an idea who else was involved, but I held my tongue.

Upstairs, Jah laid our wife on our bed, arranging her limbs so that she appeared comfortable. "She lost a lot of blood," he said. "She may sleep for a while; she probably needs a transfusion."

Scrubbing my hands down my face, I said, "Fuck," because it was all I could think of to say.

Lukas walked around the room, noting the chaotic state of things. It looked like they had chased her through the house or maybe just trashed the place. The slider to the deck was open, and a glass of tea sat beside a chair that would've faced the sun at one point.

"They waited for us to leave," Jah said from beside me. "And then they chased her through the fucking dunes. They would've killed her," he said, his quiet steel in the silence of the room.

"We need to find the uncle. What's his name?" I asked, glaring at my brother for the first time in my life that I meant it. This was his fault. But then I knew it wasn't. It was Cope's fault. This fucking small town was wired for this shit, and I'd known it, which made it my fault too.

"George," he answered. "George White. Fuck." He sat on the bed beside Tosh. Her golden skin was so pale that it was almost translucent in the dying sun. Her mouth was open and slack, and her head turned to the side as if she was unable to hold it up.

"She needs a hospital," Lukas said, his eyes never leaving her face. "I can see the pulse in her throat. We need to take her to Columbia; it's a short flight from here."

"She should've woken up," Jah said. "I pulled all that lead from her, and she never moved. Maybe she fell from the tree and has a head injury. Lukas is right; we need to take her."

Pushing him aside, I picked Tosh up and carried her back through the house. It didn't feel right to stay. We'd thought she was safe in our home. We thought our reputation would protect her, but not even that could protect her from Jah's scorned omega plaything. Hell hath no fury is right. "I'll go with the pilot. You stay and take care of George. I'll burn Cope to the ground if that

138

task is left to me." I didn't look back as I walked through the house, jogging the distance to the waiting helo.

As fierce as Tosh was, she weighed nothing. I'd carried takeout bags larger than her. I'd left my mate alone when I'd known better. We should have insisted she went with us. She could've trained in the gym at the capital or drank on the streets of Greenville for all I cared, but I should never have left her alone.

Yes, the south has a reputation for hospitality, but there are some places filled with darkness, and I'd known Cope was one of them. More a part of Southern Gothic culture than most, superstition, bias, old hatreds, and creole voodoo fed the roots of it, and I'd discounted that. I'd shoulder the blame for this. Jah would too.

I barked an order to the pilot, who didn't question me. The blades started on the Apache, and I slammed the door closed, cradling Tosh to my chest as it took off. He radioed ahead, alerting the hospital to an incoming trauma, and within minutes we were on the roof, and Tosh ripped from my arms.

I growled at an old beta nurse who growled back, her finger planted deep in my chest. "Stand down, marine," she said. "She's ours now; we have her." And then they were gone.

Chapter Fourteen

Jah

I watched until the helicopter was out of sight. I knew it needed to go, but I hated that I wasn't with them. I'd known Tosh should be in a hospital the minute I saw her, but I'm a selfish fucker and thought I was enough. I'd thought I could fix her, and I had, partially, but I underestimated how much blood she lost. She could've died. She still might. I refused to entertain that idea as I followed Lukas through the house and down the stairs. Bala and I had taken the truck to Greenville, and the only mode of transport left to us was two new Harleys we'd barely ridden.

Running back, I grabbed the keys off the hook and handed one set to Lukas. He arched a brow at me before glancing at the beautiful bikes. Shrugging one shoulder, he picked Bal's and kicked it to life.

The day was perfect for the ride, and it would've been great had it been Bal and me cruising through town and looking for something to do. As it was, people saw us turned quickly away, and shop doors closed, locking as fast as they could. Maybe they knew, and maybe they didn't. I tried not to blame them, but word gets around in a small town, and it was hard to believe that they'd heard nothing of Moesh's plans. They'd done nothing. Let them lock their doors. If I found out they were involved, it wouldn't stop me.

The bikes' modified designs made them far louder than they should be, and their growl reached every corner of Cope. Curtains closed as we cruised through the town, looking for any sign of George White on our way to their tarpaper shack on its outskirts.

While we lived on one end of town by the beach, the Whites lived in a low-slung ruin on the other. Passed down through the generations, as most places were, it was poorly maintained and barely inhabitable. Moesh lived there with five other people, and if any were involved in Tosh's shooting, I would kill them.

We rolled through the front yard and up to the door. Though the house was in shambles, the yard was tidy. Chickens pecked the ground at my feet and landscaped flower beds were beginning to bloom.

"I ain't had nothing to do with it, Jah. I swear." Old Aunt Char ambled across the porch, avoiding the sagging center that threatened to collapse under her weight. "I swear," she said again, cutting her eyes to The Alpha. Her toffee-colored skin went pale when she recognized him.

"What do you know?" he asked, kicking the stand down and crossing his arms.

"They know I liked you more than them," she chuckled, looking at me, the sound coming out strangled. "I'm not partial to that girl and knew you could do better. She's always been trouble. They didn't tell me nothing."

"They wouldn't, Alpha. She's right about that," I sighed, scrubbing my face and feeling the long growth of my facial hair catch in my wedding ring. It was a reminder of my failure. Tosh had been mine for a few days, and now she was gone, her life hanging in the balance.

"George?" The Alpha asked, pinning her with a glare.

"Gone. Didn't even pack a bag. He just took our only vehicle and left. He didn't give no explanation."

"Moesh and Ty are dead," I said. "They attacked mine and Bala's new wife. They shot her." My shoulders heaved, and I choked on the words.

"She all right?" Aunt Char asked, her voice low with concern.

"She will be," The Alpha said, starting the bike up kicking up the stand.

"You deserved better, Jah. Always did. You take care, now. Hear?" She walked into the house, leaving us in the yard. Aunt Char was good people and one of my Gran'maamy's friends. She wouldn't lie about George being there. If anything, she'd kill him herself if he was.

"We'll find him," The Alpha said, and I laughed. I threw my head back and laughed so hard tears rolled because he was right. We'd find him. There was nowhere that George White could hide from us. Had he managed to kill our mate? Maybe, just maybe, he would have destroyed us too. But all he'd managed to do was infuriate the two best trackers the New South had. Not even luck could help him now.

Lukas turned his bike towards the road leading to Columbia. It was less maintained than Greenville's two lanes, but the bikes easily navigated potholes and the rare abandoned vehicle. We made good time and parked right in front of the hospital. I followed as he strode through the door, demanding to know where Tosh was. The greeter took one look at him and personally escorted us to a waiting room, where a nurse told us she was in surgery.

I scanned the room, looking for my brother, but he wasn't there. "Another man should be here for her. Have you seen him?" I asked.

"Her mate?" she answered.

"They're both her mates," Lukas answered. The nurse's eyes snapped up, meeting mine and glancing away.

"What did he do?" I sighed.

"He bullied the doctor. He threatened to kill him if he wasn't allowed into the operating room with her. He dropped The Alpha's name, and the doctor allowed it," she rushed, looking at The Alpha with terrified eyes.

Lukas tipped his head back, pinching the bridge of his nose. He inhaled like he were trying to calm himself. "It's fine," he growled, prowling to a chair and sitting down.

I'd heard rumors that Lukas destroyed a hospital brick by brick when his mate was injured during the conflict up north. Maybe they were exaggerations and maybe not, but I doubted it. I'd seen them together, and there is no omega more loved. And their daughter? He'd burn the world for them both.

A nurse came not long after I poured a cup of wretched coffee thick enough to float a nail in. He led us to a room with glass doors. Bala sat in the corner, scrubbing his hands over his face. His red eyes were tired when they met mine, but he sat a little straighter at the sight of Lukas.

Tosh lay in the middle of a bed that dwarfed her. A breathing tube went down her throat, and her hands were tied down to keep her from pulling at it. Pumps pushed medicine into her body, and monitors watched every beat of her heart.

"She'll be fine," a man in light blue scrubs and a surgical hat over his hair said as he pushed off the wall. "She had internal bleeding from the shot to her thigh. One of the projectiles entered the large vessel, ripping through it and partially blocking blood flow. Thankfully, it didn't move into her heart. We removed the remaining projectiles, washed the wounds with antibiotics, and repaired the vascular damage. She needed a massive transfusion of blood products due to the internal bleeding, so we will keep her intubated and sedated overnight. We'll reassess in the morning, but she should be home within a few days. We'll move into the ICU as soon as a bed is available." He gave Bala a pointed look before leaving the room.

Bala dropped his head into his hands, making me wonder what happened between the two men. The surgeon was an alpha, and I can only imagine the fight in the OR. It would have been difficult for Bal to bully him, so they must have made some kind of agreement.

Lukas walked to the bed, looking at our little mate with a closed expression. "I'll pay the bill," he said before turning to us.

"We can pay the bill, Alpha," Bal said, not looking up from the floor.

"I know you can, but I insist anyway. This wouldn't have happened if I hadn't encouraged you to leave her in Cope. As per our earlier conversation, Tosh can go on all missions except those that are blacklist confidential. You will bring her to my house and let her babysit my wife and child in those cases. She's more than proven her fighting skills, and she'll need them." And with that, Lukas walked out, leaving us alone.

"Never again." Bala looked up. His eyes were as hard as I'd ever seen them, telling me that we'd be taking Tosh on those blacklist confidential assignments, regardless. I nodded my agreement and approached the bed.

Tosh looked peaceful. Her skin was dull, and the golden hue to it buried under a pale shade of grey. She hadn't so much as twitched since I walked into the room, and I worried that her sedation dose was too high. She was a tiny thing, attitude aside. I untied her wrist, sitting on the edge of the bed to hold her hand.

Bala was right. Never again. Heavy bandages covered her left shoulder. She wore a gown and was clean. Someone had pulled her mass of hair back, braiding it so as not to get into her wound. I hated that someone else provided her care when that was our job, but I understood. Bala rose, walking to the door. "I'll grab something from the cafeteria and be right back. Don't leave her alone."

Like I would.

I smoothed my hands over Tosh's face and down her neck. The pulse there was steady and strong.

"We gave her enough medicine to knock down a horse. She fought like a dragon. I don't think she realized she was making it worse; she just felt the need to fight."

I looked from my wife's face to see another nurse at the door; his expression was friendly as he glanced at Tosh. My eyebrows narrowed on him, and I felt my alpha asshole gene kick in.

"Omegas are something else, aren't they?" he said with a wink.

I took in his stature and features and thought he was an omega too. I took a tentative sniff to confirm. I smiled at him, glancing down at Tosh. "Yes, I suppose they are."

"I'm going to move her to the ICU now; we were waiting on a bigger room since we figured you'll both want to stay."

"You figured right." I rose from the bed, retying Tosh's wrist so she couldn't go for the tube.

I followed him onto an elevator and to a much larger room in a noisy area. Staff rushed from room to room, and the ICU looked busy. They situated Tosh, adjusting lines and pumps to their liking. I went to one of the oversized recliners against the wall and watched everything closely. During all of this, Tosh never moved. They changed her position, retying her hands, then covered her up. Staff kept a wary eye on me and I them. My instincts demanded that I intervene, but I knew they were doing what was best for her and forced myself to let them.

Bala strode through the door, his jaw carved in an angry line. He carried a tray of coffee and burgers. "They didn't say they were moving her," he growled before setting the tray on a table. "They should've told me."

I ignored him, knowing that nothing I said would ease the tension he felt. The bond between Tosh and me hummed faintly like she was asleep. On the other end, she must feel terrible, and I tried to calm myself and send her better feelings. Bal looked my way, sighed, and did the same.

It was a miserable night, certainly the worst in my life. While they were doing their job, nurses came and went from the room every few minutes. They adjusted pumps and emptied her catheter. They checked vital signs and listened to her lungs. In the early hours of the morning, they started weaning her sedation, and her limbs began to move. She was more vocal through our bond by shift change, letting us know exactly how unhappy she was with the situation. Her body may have looked listless, but her mind was awake and pissed the fuck off. Right after shift change, a large group of doctors came in, and one of them pulled the breathing tube.

Tosh took deep, angry breaths on her own, canted her head my way, and glared before promptly falling asleep. Bal sat beside me, fingers steepled and expression fierce. We watched her breathe for hours. I would have laughed if the situation weren't so dire, but she slowly and surely breathed on her own, and I was never happier to see a chest rise and fall in my life.

"Your scowl will become permanent if you don't stop," she muttered. Her voice was pained but held an edge of steel that was common for her.

"Little squirrel." Bal stood, striding to the bed and scooping her into his arms. "You've terrified us. Don't do it again."

She tried for a laugh, but it came out as a croak. "I'll try to remember that," she added, her voice filled with false sincerity.

He nuzzled the top of her head, purring for her. The vibration shook the covers. I waited all of three minutes before snatching her away and curling her to my chest. It was my turn, goddamnit. I added my purr to his, and the sound was obnoxious in the small space. I peppered her cheeks with kisses, and Bal pulled the tips of her hair, dropping her heart rate on the monitors.

"Don't overwhelm the poor girl." The surgeon stood in the doorway, his arms and expression cross. "Everything looks good today. Her labs are better, and her repeat X-rays are fine. If she eats and walks down the hall a few times, we'll let her go tomorrow."

"Thank you," I said. I handed Tosh to Bal and rose to shake the man's hand. "For everything," I added. He smiled and left us alone with our wife.

"I'm fine," Tosh sighed, struggling to free herself from Bal's tight grip.

"You're not fine," he growled, holding her tighter.

"You're hurting me," she said, and he released his tight grip, nearly dropping her on the floor. With a laugh, she said, "Just relax; everything is okay."

"Everything isn't okay," I started. "But it will be. What happened?" I needed to know. I thought I had it worked out in my head, but didn't want to miss a detail.

She told us how she had been attacked, and I fought to keep my anger from filtering through our bond, though no doubt it did. She didn't embellish or show emotion as she spoke, but I could tell she was upset. She was probably trying to soothe her two meat-headed mates instead of herself, in true omega fashion.

"You're very good with a knife," I told her when she finished. It was the only thing I could think of to say that wouldn't topple the conversation over a cliff, but that didn't make it any less true.

"Thanks, babe." She winked at me, picking at the meal placed in front of her by an assistant. "Can we go home now?" she asked, moving her food around so it looked like she had eaten.

"You have to eat," Bal said, his voice husky with worry and tempered steel. He hadn't said a word during her recounting of events, but I knew him. Even without the mating bond, I could feel his anger simmering. Cope would be lucky to escape it still standing.

"Tomorrow, mink. Eat your supper. Afterward, we'll go for a walk down the hall, as the doctor said. Tomorrow, we'll go home." I made a mental note to call our Gran'maamy and ask her to set the house to rights. We'd have no problem fixing the door once we were there. Under the circumstances, no one else would go near our place. Lukas was switching out our bikes and leaving the truck to take Tosh home more comfortably.

Shoulders slumped, she did as I said. I took note of it, as it was possibly the first and only time it would happen.

We walked the unit two times, her small hands in our giant. We kept her in the middle, and curious eyes followed us everywhere. Some smiled, and some frowned, but no one was overtly unkind. I suppose we were a polygamous marriage, which was uncommon enough in the New South proper, regardless of what happened in the Seventh, to be noteworthy. Not that I'd ever thought of it that way, and not that anyone would challenge two oversized alphas and their relationship with anyone.

The walk exhausted her, and she was asleep before I pulled the covers over her shoulders. She looked so small that it made my heart stop. We'd almost lost her. The attack could have easily led to her death, and the only reason it didn't was that she trained to fight.

I'd known that our hometown would be challenging for Tosh, but I never dreamed they would go so far as to hurt her. I expected words said behind her back, maybe even to her face. I'd known that she would get long stares and cold shoulders at a minimum, but I never dreamed anyone would touch her. It was all my fault. I'd known that Moesh was going to cause trouble. Now Moesh was dead, and my mate was injured. I'd carry that burden forever. What happened was on me, and I'd own it. Bal might blame Cope, but I knew where the real culpability lay.

Now that the tubes and wires were off of Tosh, we took turns curling around her. She lay in my arms, and I purred so that only she could hear. Bal slept in the corner until he couldn't take it anymore and shooed me away for his turn. It was a long night, but when the first light of dawn cracked over the blackened horizon without Tosh waking, it was worth it.

Chapter Fifteen

Tosh

I woke up under a wall of muscle and surrounded by the rich scent of sandalwood and citrus. Pulled from a hair tie, one of Bala's tightly woven curls lay across my arm. His amber eyes were closed, and the room silent as a snowy winter night. My body hurt. There was no getting around it. I felt like I'd fallen from a tree, been shot at, and operated on simply because I had.

Jah's soft breathing from across the room pulled my eyes his way. He was tilted back on a large recliner, arms crossed, and eyes closed. His face pinched with worry in the way having nightmares can cause. His natural scent was stronger than usual, calming the anxiety his absence from my bed gave. I missed his warmth beside me.

I lifted my head, and Bala startled, pulling himself off of me. He took a deep breath as he reared back, his eyes snapping to mine. "Will you ask the nurse for a pain pill and my discharge papers?" I asked, pulling my legs to my core. My right thigh hurt to the point of distraction, and I needed to pee. Bala nodded once before rising and walking into the hallway.

I pushed the blankets off, and Jah woke, rushing to stand when he saw me sliding off the bed. "Let me," he said, scooping me into his arms.

"I can walk, you know. The doctor said I should."

"I don't care what he said, hush your mouth," he mumbled, his voice sleepy and hard to understand. His accent was thick enough that I deciphered his words post-utterance. "You can walk later. I need this."

I shook my head, smiling a little. They were good alphas; what can I say? He put me on my feet then leaned against the door, waiting.

"Uh. You can go now," I laughed, making shooing motions with my hand. He scowled at me, his brows closing together and lips tightening. "I'm fine. Off you go." His frown deepened, but he kissed the top of my head and left anyway.

I cleaned up as best I could, brushing my teeth and washing my face in the small porcelain sink. The mirror was too high for me to see anything beyond my forehead, but even that looked terrible. I tried wetting my fingers and tapping the braid to tame it, but it was all snarls of loose hair. I couldn't wait to take a shower, and at the moment, I'd have sold my soul for one. I took care of the rest of my needs and changed into the sweats and tee-shirt left in the room. I still had two IVs that needed to come out, but then I was ready.

Back in my room, the doctor waited, a team of students and residents behind him. "You look better," he said to me, pointedly ignoring my alphas. Bala growled, and Jah's lips tightened.

It really was a miracle that they shared so well. Most alphas couldn't stand to be in a room together, as evidenced by my duo's reaction to the alphas mixed into the medical crowd. Jah slid behind me, wrapping his long arm around my shoulders. Shaking my head, I stepped into him, hoping to chill him out.

"I'm sending you with a few days' worth of pain medicine and instructions to care for your wounds. The stitches will absorb, but you need to follow up with your doctor to have them checked. No baths, but showers are okay. Limit physical activity and don't overexert yourself," he said to Bal, arching an eyebrow.

It was funny because most doctors were Betas, but the more demanding fields, like surgery, attracted alphas. I'd volunteered as a candy striper in high school, and it was fun to watch the interactions between them. This was no exception. Bala growled low enough to raise the hair on my arms. Chuckling, I said, "Boys. Do you want to go home or not?"

Bal stopped growling. The doctor smiled, and Jah's arm loosened. "The nurse will bring your papers," the surgeon said before leaving the room.

I was picked up and placed in the middle of the truck's front seat. I wanted to take a helicopter ride home and was disappointed. I didn't remember much of the ride to the hospital, which sucked because I'd always wanted to ride in one. They took the rutted roads as slowly as possible, but by the time we made it, I was exhausted and in pain. A three-wheeled, bright-yellow bicycle sat in the driveway when we got home, its wire basket in front filled with bags.

Before Jah could open his door, Beulah Dawn O'Day marched down the steps and to her bike, glaring our way before grabbing her bags and stomping up them again. My heart sank. I'd hoped to fit in this little town, but it was painfully, no pun intended, obvious now that I wouldn't. Jah opened his door with a sigh.

Bala followed, picking me up and kicking the door closed. I kept the groan to myself. My body hurt to the point of distraction, and I fought it not to show.

"Come, little warrior; let's get you inside and on the couch," Bala hummed, purring as he carried me up the stairs.

Pieces of the broken door lay scattered around the carport. Jah growled, the sound warning of deadly things to come as he turned on his heel, heading toward the truck. "I'll find a door while you get her settled," he snapped. I felt his irritation filter my way. I knew it wasn't me he was irritated with; it was the situation, but I hated it nonetheless. The bond demanded peace, and none of us felt peaceful at the moment.

"I told him not to mess with that girl," Ms. Beulah said, bearing down on her grandson with a wilting scowl. She smacked Bala on the shoulder with a rolled-up magazine like an errant puppy. "I knew that bitch was trouble, and I can't say I'm sorry she's dead," she finished, clearing up my confusion as to who she referenced.

"I told him too, Gran'maamy," Bala said, shuffling away from her blows.

"Don't you Gran'maamy me. I'm the head of this family, and you better listen." She moved through the house, whacking him as he shielded me, her steps swift and sure for someone of her size and age. "You done had your omega a few days, and she already hurt. Come to Gran'maamy, baby, and let me look at you," she said, plucking me from Bala, eliciting a growl. She leveled him with a death glare, and it stopped.

She put me on my feet like I was a doll, turning me this way and that. She clucked over my injuries, her glare growing sharper as she went. "Now, you go on in there and climb into the bed. Gran'maamy gonna have a talk with this young alpha and set him to rights. I made you some chicken soup; I'll bring you a cup." She stood to her full height and placed her hands on her meaty hips. I didn't think twice about doing what she said.

Bala took a step toward me, and she made a sharp sound reminiscent of a game show buzzer, halting his progress. "She needs pain medicine, Ma'am," he tried, looking at his feet.

"I'll get it. I can't believe you boys left little Tosh by herself. You shoulda done called me to stay with her. What were you thinking? You weren't; that's the problem. You know better'n that." She stomped to the kitchen, and I heard dishes clatter.

"But," he tried, only to be stopped immediately.

"No buts. You boys wanted a mate, and you got one. You found one that took on both of your dumb asses and got her hurt immediately. Do better, or you'll answer to me. Now, you go on and get the rest of the bags from my bike and clean up the mess downstairs," she said, and I heard Bala walk away as I climbed into bed.

"I can't believe dem boys," she muttered, slamming cabinet doors and knocking silverware around.

I heard her coming my way long before I saw her. "Here, baby," she said, her voice utterly empty of the venom she'd shot at her grandson. "Chicken soup and a pain pill. You'll be right as rain in no time. Now, where's your ComLink so I can put in my number? I may be old, but I'm mean," she said, sounding like fluffy bunnies and the opposite of mean. "You call me if those chuckleheads leave you again, and Gran'maamy will come keep you company while they're gone." She sat on the corner of the bed, her face lit by her smile.

"I don't have a ComLink, Ma'am. Uh, Miss Beulah." I melted at the first sip of the chicken noodle soup, a tiny groan escaping before I could stop it.

The smile fell from her face, despite my enjoyment of her soup. "You don't have a link?" she asked sweetly, her eyes hardening despite the sugary tone she used. "And my boys didn't give you one?"

I shook my head, declining to use my words. I shoved homemade noodles into my mouth in place of them. I'd never had better soup in my life. When they say chicken noodle soup fixed everything, they mean that Gran'maamy's chicken soup fixed everything.

"Gran'maamy be right back, sugar," she added, smiling sweetly at me, then her head whipped in the general direction of Bala, and she stormed away.

The cup of soup she'd given me was oversized, but I was starved. Hospital food sucks, and I'd eaten as little of it as possible just to get out of there. I had the small chunks of chicken mixed with noodles in a thick broth gone in no time. I swallowed the pill she'd brought with the dregs of the broth and lay down, enjoying the feeling of being almost comfortable. I took in the room from my spot as I listened to Beulah berate her grandson again, enjoying it. She was right. I'd told them to take me, and they hadn't listened.

I snuggled in, waiting on the pain medicine to work. Soon the angry words were replaced by the sound of hammers banging on nails and the hushed whispers of conversations in the other room. It was nice to be left alone, if I was honest. My body ached so badly that the overbearing, concerned alpha behavior my men showed was too much for me.

Gran'maamy brought another cup of soup and stood with her hands on her hips until I finished it. Then, she brought me a slice of pie and only left me alone when it, too, was gone. The pill finally kicked in, and I drifted into a dreamless sleep, comforted by the sounds of home around me. I only awoke when the sky was midnight black, and the bed dipped under the weight of two men.

They didn't fight to cuddle me, only eased their bodies close so I could soak up their warmth. I stayed awake long enough to fall asleep again to the sound of their deep, even breathing and was glad to be surrounded by them.

Chapter Sixteen

Jah

Gran'maamy was right. One hundred percent. After nearly beating us to death, I got it. I was surprised she didn't make us find a switch to wail on us, but she chose whatever else was handy instead. I'm pretty sure she lost a shoe to the cause. Once Tosh fell asleep, Beulah Dawn sat us down and gave us a stern talking to and an education on what was what. The thing is, I'd known she was right before it got that far. My instincts screamed at me to take Tosh with us, and I'd ignored them. Never again.

"Just because an omega is strong," she'd said. "Doesn't mean they are ever going to be stronger than a group of anything. A group of any dynamic could take out an alpha, let alone an omega. She married you boys for a reason, and you failed her. You can trust her to fight, but never on her own," she'd argued. "You do it again, and you'll answer to me, hear?" She'd left us after that, and we'd stewed on her words the rest of the night.

Despite her harsh lecture, Grandmother had left a lasagna and a passel of groceries behind, Southern Justice delivered with love. And she wasn't wrong. We'd thought we were ready for a mate and enjoyed the fact that Tosh could handle herself, and she could. We'd been the problem. Any other omega would've been dead at the hands of her enemies, and I was grateful to have another chance with her.

Bal and I sat in the living room long after Gran'maamy left, talking about our next steps. We'd always been better together, and that is how we came to understand our new roles as Tosh's mates. She needed to be our focus. Yes, we had jobs that were critical to the safety of every citizen in the New South, but only one citizen really mattered. We'd find a way to do what needed doing, but she'd play a part too. As dangerous as that might be, it didn't compare to the danger of leaving her behind.

With a plan nailed down, we'd curled as close to her as we dared, not wanting to wake her. She's not had a good day since coming to us, and that needed to change. I smiled at the feel of her body next to mine, loving the way the bond hummed between us. Part of me wished Tosh was angrier about what happened and that the bond could punish us more than we punished ourselves. That's not how it goes, though, and happiness at being together made the bond sing.

During the night, Tosh got up, limping into the bathroom. One leg dragged behind her a little, and I hated that. On cue, Bala and I sat up as the pain she felt leaked into us. The shower turned on, and it took everything I had not to follow her. Bala got out of bed, and I heard ice clink into a glass. The sound of her pain pills falling into his palm hurt more than a hard punch to the gut.

The shower ran for a long time, and steam floating from behind the closed door carried her scent mixed with the smell of misery. As soon as the door opened, Bala handed her the pill and a glass of water to chase it with. We lay down, giving Tosh room to fight her body into a comfortable position. Funny how in the days leading up to her attack, we'd made love constantly. With her discomfort palpable, sex was the furthest thing from our minds. I reached out, unable to help myself, and pulled the wet tips of her hair as I purred. In the moonlight, I saw her smile, and her face go slack as she fell back asleep.

Sun streamed through the windows, and the smell of coffee drifted in the air. Bala was still asleep, and the tiny space between us empty. I looked around the room, catching sight of Tosh on the deck. She sat with her back to the slider and a cup in her hand. Morning sun glinted off the hidden highlights in her hair, making her look like an angel, and I enjoyed the vision before I hopped up to grab a coffee and join her.

"I was sitting out here when they came," she said instead of a good morning. "It's rather foolish to have only one entrance to your house. What if there's a fire?" she asked.

What if you're attacked, I thought. I'd known she'd scurried over the deck railing and down the post like the squirrel she was, but she was right. It wasn't a brilliant design.

"You're right," I said, taking a seat next to her and loving the feel of the sun on my face. "We'll build some steps from the deck and maybe add a locking gate at the bottom."

"It's not like I had trouble getting down, but still."

"I have no doubt you had trouble doing none of it, little mink." I tried for levity, but all I could envision was her fighting for her life. "It shouldn't have happened," I added. Gripping her hand where it lay on the armrest.

"No. It shouldn't have. But it isn't anyone's fault but theirs, so let it go." She looked my way, her face serious. "Let it go, Jah," she said again.

Sighing, I tipped my head against the chair so that the sun hit my face. "I don't think I can, Tosh. I'm so sorry."

"Apology accepted; now let's move on."

I met her eyes, and she held them. Her color was much better today. Her cheeks had a bit of pink in them, and gone was the sallow look she'd had yesterday. Her violet eyes were darker, though, and there was an edge of pain to them as they demanded I do as she asked.

"Okay," I sighed, squeezing her hand tighter. She winced, and I dropped her fingers, seeing the scrapes and bruising on her hands and knuckles for the first time. How could I let that go? I couldn't, and knowing I'd just lied to her didn't sit well, but there was no way around it.

"What did The Alpha want?" she asked, drawing my attention away from her mangled fingers.

I sighed again, closing my eyes to compose myself. "He wants us to go after a couple accused of child trafficking."

"Selling children?" she asked, laying her hand on mine.

"Yeah. Lukas suspected that they sold Darrian Battle's wife when she was a kid. She was one of the women rescued in the Seventh at that compound."

"Oh my God, I remember that. Those women were in terrible shape." It had been awful to see them, and the resolve to change things in The New South had hardened in all of us at the sight of them. "Most didn't survive."

"Well, proof surfaced that the women came from the same couple. Darrian found evidence that they sold children, too, and had an arrest warrant issued for them. He probably wouldn't have looked as hard if they hadn't kept bothering Grace, but they wouldn't leave her alone. Darrian thinks they were looking to worm their way into her life to take their kid when it's born. Fat chance of that happening." I laughed, thinking of Darrian Battle. He was as savage an alpha as I'd ever met. All the Battle Alphas were.

"Isn't Grace the one they were going to put down? I thought she was too far gone to save." Tosh looked my way and raised one neat brow at me.

"She was, I guess, but Darrian managed to do it."

"Huh," she said, pursing her lips and nodding her head. "Good for her. You see it sometimes in the panhandle. Women escape from the New North or The Middle West, and most don't come back from the damage done to them. So, what do we need to do?" she asked, like she could slip that one little word by me.

I took a deep breath and let it out, deciding to alpha up for once. "The Alpha tracked them to The Second District and lost them. They may have slipped into The Middle West, but regardless, Lukas lost their paper trail. He wants us to find them and bring them in. Darrian wants them dead."

"I see. What do the O'Day brothers want?" she asked.

"We get paid either way. Personally, I don't think either one of them deserves to live, but Lukas wants to make an example of them," I explained as we watched the sun creep higher. Behind us, we heard Bala rise and walk into the kitchen. Cups rattled as he took one and filled it.

"Maybe if he did make an example of them, people would think twice," she said with a shrug.

"Maybe. People are terrible, though, so maybe not, but Lukas is determined to make The New South better."

"Thanks to Eve," she chuckled.

"Mostly." Tosh wasn't wrong. Lukas was always a good leader, but after Eve, he was definitely a better one. Funny how a group of omegas changed the landscape of the world.

Bala walked onto the deck, stood at the railing, and looked at the ground. "We need to put in stairs," he growled.

Tosh and I shared a smile. "We were discussing that, among other things," I said, ruffling Tosh's hair, as that might be the only place on her that didn't ache. Still, she flinched, trying to cover it with a stretch.

"I could use another cup of coffee while we figure out how to go after this couple The Alpha wants," she said. "And then breakfast needs to happen."

She went to get up, but Bala stopped her, saying, "I'll get it; stay where you are." The last came out as a growl, but he meant well.

"The sun's getting too hot anyway." She pushed up from her chair with a sigh. She looked uncomfortable, but I doubted she'd ever complain.

Tosh settled at the island while Bala pulled out eggs, bacon, and sausage from the fridge. I grabbed bread from the cabinet and popped it into the toaster. I wished we thought to make grits, but it was too late.

In the middle of flipping eggs, Bala let his head drop back and took a deep, ragged breath. He turned, holding the spatula in from of him like a weapon. He stared at Tosh, his eyes skimming her face and snagging on his bite mark before continuing. Decision made, he said, "I think they are slipping over the border between the northern part of the Second into the Middle West. The border wall there is more of a suggestion than anything. Reports coming from the area suggest that patrols turn a blind eye if the price is right. We need to go and investigate for ourselves."

"We're hoping there isn't a more significant problem. Best-case scenario, there are one or two bad eggs. Worst case, there is a situation similar to the Seventh, and we'll have another battle on our hands," I added, laying it all out. "The New South can't afford another insurrection. The Alpha wants us to determine what's going on and the best way to handle it."

"We can do things that he can't." Bala jumped in as he plated breakfast for Tosh and slid it in front of her before refreshing her coffee. "He has to use official channels, where we can use stealth and misdirection to get answers. Getting answers and solving problems is what we're best at."

"We can also make sure his targets never reach the Capital, should it not be in The New South's best interests," I finished.

"I see," she said before digging into her meal. "So, where do we start?"

I shared a look with my brother over our wife's head. "Where do we start, indeed?" I asked in the way we've always communicated. It's almost like talking to one another with words, and either we had some weird form of ESP, or we're both crazy.

He blinked, saying, "I don't know," to me. We've always been able to do this; it freaked most people out when they realized our silent communication was more detailed than their verbal one.

Tosh ignored us, eating with a gusto that'd been absent the last few days.

Unable to ignore the silence any longer, Tosh looked up from her plate. "Where?" she asked again, brokering no argument.

"In a few days, we'll go to the Second and see what we can dig up," I offered, buying us some time.

She quirked an eyebrow, only half satisfied with my response. "Do you have a computer of any kind?" she asked, scooping more eggs into her mouth as she waited for an answer.

"There's one in the second guest room that doubles as an office. But it's old and slow," I added as I wondered what she was up to.

"And what is this couple's name?" she asked, finishing her plate. Her eyes had a light in them I hadn't seen before, making me wonder all the more.

"Brandon and Joy Farmington," Bala answered, watching the conversation between Tosh and me with avid interest. He picked up her empty plate, waving it. "More?" he asked.

"Nah, I'm good." She rose slowly, stretching her arms over her head and bending at the waist to loosen up. "I can do the dishes," she said as she walked to the sink.

"I'll get them," I said, watching to see what the little mink would do.

"Then I'm just going to go check out that computer." A grin drifted across her lips, crinkling the corners of her eyes as she walked away from us.

I lowered my eyebrows at Bala, who stood frozen as she walked away. He shrugged, and I quirked my lip down, wanting to follow her. Instead, I filled the sink and washed the dishes. We had a dishwasher, but seldom used it. Gran'maamy preached against them our whole lives, calling them the germ spreaders and the devil's tool for laziness. After, I put grits in the slow cooker for supper tonight, adding a dollop of cream and some butter from the fridge.

An hour later, when we still hadn't seen or heard from Tosh, we walked down the hall to make sure she was okay. We found her bent over a notepad, with three open screens in front of her. One screen displayed a photo of a couple in the middle of what appeared to be a street fair. A map displayed roads and towns between the Sixth and Second districts on the second screen, while on the third screen, images from traffic cameras and a facial recognition program flashed so quickly that I couldn't catch them. Tosh made notes, glancing up only occasionally. The old computer hummed from the effort, but it kept up with whatever she'd asked.

She didn't notice us, and we crept toward the living room, leaving her in peace.

"What is all that?" I asked as Bala poured himself a few fingers of bourbon.

He didn't answer, just shot the drink and walked to the bedroom, returning with a manila folder I knew well. I watched as he read and reread the file we had on Tosh.

All the omegas from the Seventh had made one. Once NS304 became law and the omegas in hiding came forward to find mates, they created files detailing their skills, hobbies, characteristics, and mate preferences to make the matching process more successful. I knew that file backward and forward. Tosh had left out the minor detail about being a computer whiz and possibly a hacker, probably because hacking was a crime unless you worked for The New South. I mean, people did it, but an omega doing it was unheard of. The slower, gentler dynamic, my ass.

"It's not in there because she didn't declare it," I said, unable to watch Bala look for a paragraph that didn't exist.

Tosh was uneducated as far as we knew. We hadn't cared about a lack of formal education when she'd agreed to take us both as mates; it was a small and insignificant detail. But the devil is in the details, as they say, and we'd have to be careful that this particular one never became common knowledge.

Lukas would trap her into doing work for him in a heartbeat, and she'd become more his than ours. That was unacceptable. Little mink, indeed. No doubt, The Alpha's wife knew and had chosen to keep it to herself as well. I'd bet my life that Tosh had a hand in finding the insurgents' compound. It was buried in the mountains and vigorously protected by isolation. I'd always wondered how they'd been located. Now I thought I knew.

"We say nothing," Bala growled, pouring himself another glass. He sipped it as he flipped the papers in his hand over, looking for something hidden on the back. Why he'd be surprised by Tosh's nondisclosure, I can't say. I knew from the glint in her eyes seen on her official picture that she was a fox. There was a deviousness there the camera wouldn't have caught if it didn't run deep. I loved it.

"This makes her even more of an asset, brother. We're both shit with computers. Imagine if we had an expert on our side." I walked to him, patting him on the back.

"They have trackers for this sort of thing. They'll catch her," he worried.

"Hmmm. I bet she's nailed that down, Bal. She didn't look like an amateur in there." Grabbing a glass, I stood shoulder to shoulder with him and poured us both a drink. "Let's see what she finds before you worry too much. Maybe she's looking up directions to the Second, and we're overestimating what we saw.

Bala barked a laugh, saying, "Right. Because facial recognition is part of a map app." Sighing, he rubbed a scarred hand over his face. "It's my job to worry," he added as he stared at the ceiling like it held the answer.

"And it's my job to tell you not to. The little squirrel is ours. Are there any other alphas more qualified to protect her?" I asked, knowing the answer.

He growled, rattling the glasses on the counter. "No," he said.

And he's right. There may be bigger alphas, like Lukas. There may even be stronger alphas out there somewhere, but there damn sure weren't more vicious alphas than Bal and me. We were wicked fighters who used stealth as a weapon, and most of The New South feared our name. No one except for some newly dead idiots in the town of Cope would dare square up to us.

I let a cold smile spread across my lips. "She'll be fine, brother. She'll be fine. I will enjoy ripping anyone to shreds who tries to take our fox from us."

And that is how Tosh found us, sipping bourbon and sharing cold smiles.

Chapter Seventeen

Tosh

I walked into the kitchen, carrying notes from my search. Jah and Bala were holding glasses of some dark liquor and sharing feral smiles. "Uh, boys?" I asked, interrupting their moment of bro-bonding or some shit. I looked between them as they held each other's eyes a moment longer, engaging in silent conversation as they tended to do. "I've got some information," I added when they broke their stare-off.

Their heads swung to me in an eerily identical move. I cleared my throat. I'd never seen a more predatory look than the one they shared as they looked my way. My heart rate ratcheted up a notch, and my instinct to fight or flee was demanding I flee. But I am not prey, so I stood my ground.

Jah and Bala had been nothing but kind to me. They'd been attentive to my needs and conscientious of my desires. They'd shown me none of the viciousness they were known for, but I saw it in their glance. It would serve as a reminder that some things are better left hidden. And a better reminder that one should never confuse what someone shows you versus who they are at heart. These men were violent. They were brutal and vicious examples of the true alpha dynamic, and I'd do well to remember that. They would never hurt me; I knew that. On a fundamental level, they'd be incapable of harming me. But what would they do in my name? I saw the answer on their faces.

And just like that, the looks were gone.

"What have you found, little squirrel?" Jah said, his smile turning friendly as his face opened up. His eyes twinkled with delight, and I marveled at the dramatic change.

"I, uh," I started, looking between them one more time. I took a deep breath before restarting. "Brandon and Joy Farmington are in Union City, Second District. Three days ago, traffic cams caught them driving through Memphis, first on Route 40, then 51 to Union City. There appears to be a minor in the back seat, but the pictures are grainy." I handed a copy of the picture I'd taken off the cameras in the area. Their printer was older than the computer and used only black-and-white ink, but I believed my assessment was correct. "I caught them again on street cams along the main routes heading toward the outskirts of town where the wall between The Middle West and The New South is the least guarded. Also," I continued, watching them absorb the information with expressionless faces.

I'd had a knack for computers from an early age, and I'd taught myself to hack into just about everywhere there were firewalls. It was something I kept to myself, and only Eve Jennings and my father knew about my ability. Eve because she'd asked for information on insurgents, and my father because he'd killed a local official who'd caught me hacking into government files. I was only thirteen at the time, and his form of blackmail payment had offended my father endlessly. I'd learned to cover my tracks and never gotten caught again.

"I looked through the camera footage from the last month. They've made this same trip multiple times. The cameras delete footage every thirty days, so I couldn't go beyond that." I flicked my gaze between them, unsure of how to say this next part. The smiles had already dipped to frowns, and what I had to say might cause them to explode. "In every town I've tracked them to, there are bonded, unbonded, or omega children missing. Some as young as eight. They don't seem to care who they take. I, uh, accessed."

"Hacked," Jah interrupted, his frown slipping up for a beat.

"I, uh, okay. Yeah. I hacked into missing persons reports. Two of the omegas were happily mated, one was unbonded, and two were children. There are no suspects in their disappearances." I watched as my mates straightened their spines, going stiff. Instinct made Bala growl, and I knew what was coming next.

"You're not going." He glared at me from under brows crunched Cromagnon tight.

I folded my arms across my chest, arching a brow. They'd left me alone once, and it hadn't turned out well.

"Brother," Jah tried.

"No."

"Bala." Using his name pulled Bal's glare from me to Jah.

"They are taking any omega they find, and you want to take our omega wife to hunt them? Do you know what they do to break bonded omegas in The Middle West?"

"I know," Jah answered, cutting his eyes my way, "but we can't leave her. Not again."

I didn't know what they did to break bonded omegas in The Middle West, and I didn't think I wanted to. The New South had never been as cruel to their omegas as the New North and Middle West. At least, that's what our leaders say, but who knows how things actually were beyond those walls?

Bala sighed, scrubbing his hands down his face and staring at the ceiling again like he sometimes did to calm himself. "Okay," he said. "She's safer with us than she is on her own."

I smiled inwardly, not letting my excitement show. They needed me. They might not know it yet, but they would. "I can take care of myself, but with you there, I won't have to," I added. "It'll be fine."

Jah nodded to himself, and Bal continued to scowl. "Listen, let's walk down to the beach. The sun will help loosen me up, and maybe the water is flat enough to go for a swim. The sooner I'm up and moving, the sooner we can go. I don't want to hold us back."

"Little squirrel," Jah said, wrapping me in his arms and silencing me with a blistering kiss. He pulled away reluctantly, saying, "You aren't holding us back. It would have taken us days to find the Farmingtons. You did that in a few hours. We have time to wait until you're one hundred percent. It's a long drive to the Second, and Union City is at the furthest reaches of the district. You'd be miserable if we tried to leave right away. We'll take our time and do it right," he finished, releasing me to stand on my own. That kiss had started a fire, though I'm sure he hadn't intended it. A slow smile spread across my lips as I thought of all the physical therapy they could provide to help me heal faster.

"Let's take that walk, mink," Bala said, pulling my thoughts from the naughty direction they'd traveled.

"Right. Okay."

I'd been right. The sun was warm and the ocean flat when we rounded the last corner to the beach. It was almost too hot, as no breeze blew. Pampas grass stood still and straight under the bright sky, edged in pink as it sometimes was post-war. Gulls flew overhead, their cries breaking the silence the absence of waves made.

"There are still creatures in the deep waters, little fox," Bala warned as I sped to the waterline at a brisk walk.

"Then you must be the bigger monsters," I said, shucking my shirt off and pulling my pants down my legs. "I'm going swimming." I let the sun's rays touch my bare skin before I walked just far enough into the water to dive safely under the surface. I felt Jah's groan in my soul when my ass breached the surface as it followed my shoulders down. The walk, the sun, and the water worked to loosen my muscles, and knowing I shouldn't stay submerged too long lest my stitches pull, I stood knee-high, letting the slow flow of water and gentle waves cool the heat between my legs.

Bal walked to me, smoothing his hands over my shoulders. "The sun is strong today. It'll burn if we're not careful," he said as he rubbed the knots from my shoulders and neck.

"I know. It just feels so good. I already feel ten times better." I let my chin drift to my chest so he could rub the base of my skull.

I heard a loud splash and watched Jah sail through the water like a fish. Tiny bubbles surfaced as he swam further and further out. He popped up, breathed once, then submerged again, swimming our way like a seal.

"A half an hour or so won't hurt," I said, my eyes glued to the water running down Jah's chest from where he stood in front of me.

"Had I known you'd get naked and swim, I'd have brought sunscreen," Bal sighed.

I grinned as Jah rolled his eyes. These men. While violent and vicious with others, worried I would get a sunburn. I suppose, on top of my other injuries, I shouldn't want a sunburn either. Bala pulled the tips of my hair, and his purr sent shivers down my skin, causing goosebumps to rise. I reached behind me, hoping to rest my arms around Bala's hips as I watched Jah swim, but he was so far behind me that his arms must've stretched to reach the muscles he rubbed. Instead of his hips, my hand brushed the tip of his hard cock as he tried to keep me from feeling his discomfort. I wasn't the only one feeling needy. I knew they were trying to take care of me, but I'd broken some ribs, not my pussy.

Jah walked forward, a warning in his eyes. "Tosh," he said, using my real name.

"Come hold me, Jah," I demanded.

He quirked his head to the side, unsure of what I was asking. I stepped back, stroking Bala's hard length. His hips jerked forward, and his groan made my pussy drip. My skin was hot from more than the sun, and I needed him. I can't say why when my body hurt so badly, but I did.

Jah's arms came around me, and I leaned into him, resting my cheek on his chest. His citrus spice smell washed over me, weakening my knees, and I had to calculate in my head to make sure this wasn't estrous striking me. It was just Jah, though. His natural scent enhanced the need I'd been feeling all day, not some dynamic-driven cycle. "I need you," I said, looking up at him. His toffee skin and hazel eyes caught and reflected the sun, and it took my breath.

"Squirrel," he said. "We'll hurt you."

I stroked Bal faster, wanting him inside of me. I pushed my ass out, presenting him with the evidence of that need, and heard his rough groan and deep inhales as he scented me.

"Put my cock inside of you, little fox," Bal whispered his breath hot on my neck.

"Bala," Jah said, trying to ease me forward and away from his brother.

"Please," I said, feeling Jah's arms tighten as I guided Bala to my entrance and sank onto him with a groan. I looked up at Jah, but he was watching Bala, giving him a hard look.

"Make her come, brother," Bal said as he stroked carefully into me. My core fluttered, and between the warm water, hot sun, and hard cock, it wouldn't take much to push me over.

Jah leaned down, capturing my mouth with his. He kissed me like cracked glass threatening to break, and I let him. I was horny, not nuts. My body hurt, but I needed them too. I sank into Jah's kiss, letting him support my weight and take my mouth as Bala fucked me slowly. We'd never fucked like this, and I liked it. Slow and easy like a southern Sunday, he pushed in and pulled out. It was delicious and desperate. Jah dropped his hand, strumming my clit once, twice, three times, and I fell apart in one of the strongest orgasms I'd ever had. It took my breath, and pain shot through my ribs as my muscles clamped on Bal's cock, trying to force him deeper. I forced myself to ignore it as I crested, groaning into Jah's mouth but unable to kiss him anymore. Bala continued his slow fucking of my body for only a few more moments before he gripped his base and pulled out enough so as not to knot me. Hot cum streamed from his tip, bathing my core and dripping out as nothing held it in. His body shuddered, and he placed a hand on my back to steady himself as he continued to unload days of frustration into me.

A larger wave rolled over us, washing Bal's cum away and making me growl at the nerve of it. I wanted knotted. I wanted all of him, but I understood. We were in the ocean under the sun. Thirty minutes to an hour bound together might be dangerous to all of us. I let the growl taper off into a purr as another wave came, washing the evidence of Bala's orgasm away. He shuddered once more before stepping back and turning me to face him.

I held Bala's mouth, resting my hands on his chest and letting him take my weight. His kiss was gentle, and his tongue probing. My muscles were jello, and I felt almost sated. Almost. Who knew that a soft fucking could accomplish as much as a hard one? Still, I reached behind me, knowing what I'd find. Jah whined a protest when I stroked his cock. It wasn't an actual refusal as his hips bounced forward, and I took advantage of the movement and sank onto him.

His groan vibrated his entire body, and he held my hips still while his cock twitched so deep inside of me that I was painfully full. I wouldn't have been upset if he'd come immediately as I think that's what I wanted anyway. If he cared about fucking me after his brother, it didn't show, and if they'd cared, they'd have not chosen this lifestyle.

Bala cupped my breasts, his lips never leaving mine. He held on as his brother pushed into me, driving me insane with his slow thrusts. It gave the tip of Jah's long cock time to hit and hold the pressure point behind my cervix, causing stars to explode behind my eyes. My breath caught and held as I grunted through the long orgasm that rolled slower than Jah's hips. I broke contact with Bal's lips, laying my head on his chest and wrapping my arms around his waist. It was too much, and when my knees threatened to buckle, Bala supported me until his brother slid halfway out, emptying himself into me with a long sigh.

"You're fucking perfect," Jah said, laying his forehead on my back as his body continued to twitch in mine as he gripped his knot to keep it from expanding.

"Hardly," I laughed, smiling into the water as the waves rose again. Using Bala, I pulled myself up. "I needed that." I sighed as I ran my hands over the smooth planes of his chest. "I really needed that," I added, laughing.

"You're welcome. It's our job to satisfy you." Bal's chuckle was dark and amused as he used the ocean to rinse my skin. I slapped at him while he laughed. I mean, technically, it was their job, but it's not like they didn't get anything out of it.

"Yeah, it's a real hardship, babe," Jah joined in the laughter at my expense, but it was well-meaning, and I didn't mind.

The sun, sea, and sex loosened my sore muscles, and I walked without pain to the beach. Omegas were weird in that they really did need their mate. A mated omega healed twice as fast as a single one, and with two mates, I'd be good as new in no time. At least, that's what I told myself as we finished the long walk to the house.

I'd missed lunch and was starving. Despite the season, it was hot inside. The windows were open, but no breeze offered to cool the room. I pulled sandwich fixings from the fridge and piled them on bread for the boys before making my own. I pulled the pitcher of sweet tea from the fridge and poured it over the ice in three glasses. When Jah and Bala walked in from their respective showers, I finished my sandwich and went to clean the salt and sand from my skin.

When I returned, I found them huddled over a ComLink on speaker.

"Where?" Jah growled, his eyes roaming over me as he assessed my gait. I was feeling better, but there was a hitch in my step that wouldn't straighten. I'd worn a loose-fitting dress as my skin had burned during our trip to the beach. Fucking alphas are always right. You can't tell them, though; it adds to their ego issues.

"Orangeburg. He's at his cousin's house, 711 Amelia Street." I heard a voice I didn't recognize and wondered who it was. "He didn't go very far, dumb son of a bitch."

Bal looked at me, and his low chuckle and glittering eyes took my breath. I met his eyes and saw nothing but the predator staring back. "Thank you, Jameson. I appreciate this more than you know."

"You've been tied up with your mate, and helping you helps me. Lukas wants the Farmingtons gone, and if George White is in the way of that, it's my job to help," Lorelie's mate said.

Jameson was The Alpha's second and mate to one of my few friends. I'd never met him in person and had only seen Lorelei a few times since they were forced by circumstances to mate. Lorelei had come around to the idea of Jameson, and hearing his voice on the phone gave a hint as to why. It was magnificent. Typically, a mated omega would be unaffected by another alpha, but Jameson's voice sent a shiver down my spine. He was that strong. Lukas better watch that one like a hawk. Still, I'd heard Jameson had no desire to be The Alpha and only wanted his wife and their new baby.

Jah noticed my shiver, saying, "Jameson, we've got to go. You just made my wife shiver with your cultured Upcountry bullshit. Don't make me hunt you next." He gave me a wink to let me know the threat meant nothing.

"I can't help it that you Lowcountry alphas don't have the swagger your brothers upstate enjoy." Jameson's chuckle came through the line, making me shiver again and dart my eyes between my men. The reaction was out of my hands, fucking dynamics, and I stared at the ceiling, looking for deliverance. Fuck my life. "That being said, your mate is more than safe, and I want no beef with the O'Day brothers."

"Damn right you don't," Bala growled. He narrowed his eyes at me, and the glint of his teeth through his feral smile had me backing away from them.

"Don't forget I'm injured," I whimpered, heading toward our bed with an exaggerated limp. "I think I'll take a nap. Or maybe go for a walk. Yeah, I'm going for a walk." I limp-scurried toward the door only to be blocked by a mountain of dark brown skin and flashing amber eyes.

"You're ours," the wall of muscle said.

"I know. I'm yours. Only yours," I tried, backing away from him only to run into a concrete wall that inhaled my scent.

"If you were well, you'd be getting your ass tanned for that reaction, little squirrel." Thick arms banded around me, holding me tight, but not too tight. "He's strong, and I know you can't help it, but I'd mark your bare ass all the same. I still might, just not today." Jah's lips traced the shell of my ear, and I shivered so hard I hurt myself. I groaned, sinking into him.

"I'm going to make you come now; I have to. You only have yourself to blame. I need to mark you. You can't help your reaction, but neither can I." Bala pushed into me, forcing me to walk back through the door of our bedroom. "Lay down," he ordered.

I stifled a cry and did as he said.

"Pull your dress up and bare yourself," his growl caused slick to flow. I tried to remember if he'd done that before, and after our initial mating, I didn't think he had.

I whimpered again, my back arching off the bed when Jah's growl added to the rich sound of testosterone rattling the windows of the room. Their scent overwhelmed me, proving that I was well and truly theirs despite my natural reaction to Jameson. I slid my dress over my hips to reveal my bare pussy to them. "Beautiful," Bala ground out as he watched me writhe and gush slick at his growled command.

"Ours," Jah added, sliding his hand under my dress to tweak my nipple. "Lift it higher and bare your breasts. I would do it for you, but you've been a naughty girl."

I whined as I pulled the dress up. My shoulder stung, and I could go no higher. Jah took it, easing it over my head and slinging it to the side.

Bala pushed my knees wider, sinking between them to nip at my clit. Pulling away, he slapped my pussy, making me suck in a breath. "This is ours, little one."

"I know!" I cried. "I couldn't help it."

They knew that. No one else could call my slick or make sex anything other than rape, but a stronger alpha dynamically could elicit a slight reaction from anyone: alpha, beta, or omega. It was natural and couldn't be helped. That's how The Alpha led so many and how all alphas led in general.

"And we can't help this," Jah said, gently tugging my head to the side using my hair. "Open," he demanded, feeding me his cock as soon as my lips parted.

I had no doubt that, were I whole, their punishment would've been much worse. As it was, Bala attacked my clit with nips and growls, gorging himself on the slick he called forth. Jah, unmoved by my whines and whimpers, pushed himself between my lips and down my throat as he held my head still. He used my mouth as he would've my pussy, and I couldn't help but hum for him when the first taste of pre-cum hit my tongue. Encouraged, he moved his hips faster.

I came apart for Bala, my cries muffled by Jah's cock. Yet neither stopped, and my body went limp until Bala made me come a second time. He swallowed audibly with every contraction of my core, and I wanted nothing more than to be filled by him. I bucked my hips against his mouth, stilling when pain shot through me from the movement.

"Be still," Jah groaned, increasing the pace of his thrusts. He pulled out, gripped his base, and released a stream of his cum on my chest, splattering my face and hair. His grip on my chin was tight, and he kept me from avoiding the hot streams. "Take it," he growled, and I relaxed in his grip. When the last stream of cum finished, he let me go to rub it on my skin, making me whimper louder. I had wanted to taste him, but this was a punishment, not a reward.

When my orgasm finished, Bal rose on his knees, pumped his cock twice, then released his cum on my belly. It ran between my legs, and I groaned as Bala rubbed it in, singing words of praise as he went. He coated my thighs, dipping his coated fingers into me. "I love you, little squirrel. Your pussy is incredible. Nothing has ever tasted so sweet. Your cries make me want to claim you again and again. You're mine. You're ours. Let us mark you."

I lay as they rubbed their cum into my soul, closing my eyes and luxuriating in the feeling of them claiming my body in this primal way. It was instinct. I didn't need an education in dynamics to understand. I let them use me to calm their jealousy, and it didn't hurt that it felt amazing. I was all for an omega's right to choose their mate, but I wasn't one of those omegas who wished they were an alpha. My bras were safe from the flames.

But that didn't mean I was going to sit on the sidelines while they crept around The New South saving the world, no. That wasn't me either. I'd be a true partner to them, and with my skills, their jobs would be safer and easier.

Like a doll, Bala pulled me to his lap when he was satisfied with his paint job. He arranged my legs on either side of his hips and wrapped his arms around me as he tugged at the tips of my hair where they brushed my hips. His purr was loud and didn't stop when he asked, "Did we hurt you?"

"No, love," I answered. "I'm fine. I feel amazing, actually."

He went still beneath me, his hands pausing where they buried in my hair. His purr resumed, and he nuzzled into my neck, breathing me in and out. His cock twitched where it rested between my legs, and he laid me down carefully. "No more for you, little mink. Rest. Brother, comfort our mate while I make supper, but don't keep her from resting."

Bala slipped off the bed and pulled his pants over his hips, covering his growing erection. Jah snuggled into my side, his purr deep and soothing. My eyes felt heavy, and I knew I'd overdone it when I fell into sleep with the feel of him tugging on my hair.

Chapter Eighteen

Bala

Tosh's eyes were closed before I left our bedroom to start supper. We'd been hard on her, but not too hard. I knew she couldn't help the involuntary shiver Jameson's voice caused, but that didn't mean we could stop our reaction either. I would've happily tanned her ass had she been feeling better. Another time, I'm sure. I looked forward to it.

She was so tough. Strong-willed, sexy, intelligent, and glorious in bed, Tosh was the best thing I'd had in my life. Ever. I was grateful for her. She'd called me love. My lips quirked upward at the thought. I'd fallen in love with her as I'd chased her through the wild Lowcountry landscape. I'd never been bested in the way she bested me, and that is how she wrapped me around her finger. I'd hoped one day she'd love me too, but I hadn't expected it. The mating bond would make us happy with or without love, and feeling the emotion itself had been a dream I hoped she'd one day share. And maybe she did. I let it lie there.

I had other things to think about; George White was in Orangeburg. The dumbass. Cope was almost a suburb of the larger town, and fourteen miles isn't nearly far enough to think he was safe from me. From us. A cold smile spread across my face, and I let it. Pulling chicken from the fridge, I set about breading it while

I thought of all the ways I'd like to kill him. I'd only get one, though, and I needed to get it right. Dunk, roll, dunk, roll, dunk, roll; I placed the heavily seasoned and breaded chicken pieces in hot bacon grease with a bit of butter melted in for good measure and watched the chicken brown on contact. I flipped it to brown the other side, then turned the burner down to let it simmer until done.

While it cooked, I put a stick of butter and browned some onions, adding bacon until it was almost cooked. Then I drained and dumped a jar of Gran'maamy's string beans into the pot, putting a lid on and letting it cook. I'd have made biscuits, but Gran'maamy had left some, so I just heated them. I checked the grits and found them done. Adding more butter, I stirred them to creaminess while I waited for the chicken and beans.

While everything finished, I straightened the house. You'd think that it would stay clean, but with three people in and out, it didn't. I peaked in on Jah and Tosh, finding them tangled together. Her cheek lay against his chest, and both their chests rose and fell in sleep. His arms wrapped tightly around her, and it was honestly the most beautiful thing I've ever seen. Her wild honey hair fell over the skin of his arms, and the contrast was striking. I'd never been more terrified, satisfied, happy, and anxious in my life now that I had a mate.

Funny how it all came down to a woman. Seeing my brother with her made my heart flip. I'd known I wouldn't be jealous of him and Tosh, but I hadn't known it would make me love him even more. She was ours, and together we would give her the best life.

The timer on the stove sounded, and I pulled the chicken off, placing it on a baking rack to drain and rest while I stirred the beans and grits one more time. I hated to wake Tosh and Jah, but neither had eaten enough today and would feel better with full bellies. Then we could plan our trip to Orangeburg. It didn't make a difference that Uncle George had fled, not causing Tosh any harm himself. No, that didn't matter at all. He'd been there. He had to die because no one could go against our mate and live; that would encourage others to become bolder against us. Nope. Dying was going to be the easiest thing he did when I got my hands on him.

I eased to the side of the bed, placing my hand on Jah's bare back to alert him of my presence before kissing Tosh on the cheek. "Hey, baby. Supper's ready." I placed another kiss on her temple before nuzzling her hair.

"Is that fried chicken?" she asked, her nose tipping up to scent the air.

"Mmmhmm."

"Homemade?" she asked, her eyes popping open.

"Ain't no dirty chicken in this house, mink. Of course, it's homemade," I scoffed. She looked confused for a minute like she didn't know what I said or maybe what dirty chicken was, but then she shrugged her shoulder and pushed off Jah's chest.

I held my hand out, and she took it so I could help her up. Jah growled before opening his eyes and catching the smell of chicken in the air. "Mmm, chicken." He jumped up, following Tosh to the kitchen, leaving me to shake my head and smile.

Tosh had her plate piled high in record time. She had half a chicken to go with the pound of grits and beans. I'd made a ton, and she could eat that and more before making a dent in it. We'd made her hungry and hadn't fed her, and I felt terrible about that. Yes, orgasms were my job, but so were full bellies, and I'd slacked on that last part. I was doing okay on the first part, though. Hopefully, it evened out.

Tosh gave a satisfied hum when she tasted my chicken, and I couldn't look away as she devoured what I'd made for her. When she got to the grits, she growled, attacking them like they'd offended her. "Shoulda started with these," she mumbled around a full mouth. "They're better than Miss Beulah's. Don't tell her I said that," she added, giving me a fear-tinged cut of her eyes. Funny how she was more afraid of Gran'maamy than she was of Jah and me. She wasn't wrong, though. We learned from the best.

Jah got up, spooning more food onto her plate as he licked his fingers. Then he picked through the chicken, looking for a fat breast that he laid next to the grits he'd given her. Before he sat, he finished his plate and grabbed more. We'd all worked up an appetite, and by the time we were satisfied, all the food was gone. Tosh wobbled to the couch, her hand over the obscene swell of her belly from the food baby I'd put there. It was an adorable nod to what the future hopefully held for us.

I didn't want kids now; I wanted to enjoy us. Learn to be us. Maybe that was un-alphalike of me, but it's how I felt. I'd heard there were shots and things for that, but wasn't sure how Tosh felt about it. I didn't want to wait forever, maybe just a few estrous cycles. We had some details to iron out with our jobs and obviously with the town of Cope. I wanted our kids to ride their bikes up the street safely, without fear of angry exes.

Still, the sight of her hand resting on a rounded belly I'd caused arrested my heart in my chest. Her head tilted back, and the quiet purr from her lips had me rethinking my position. I'd never seen her more satisfied, and that satisfied me.

Jah rose to clean up, his movements lithe and efficient. The house was comfortably quiet as I cleared the table, placing dishes in the sink for him to wash.

"I can do that, you know," Tosh said, her voice heavy.

"That's unnecessary, little squirrel. We can do it faster, so we can get to bed sooner." I smiled at the top of her head from where it showed over the back of the couch.

"What's the plan for tomorrow? How do you want to play Orangeburg?" she said, her voice clearer this time.

"Orangeburg is our concern, Tosh," Jah interrupted, making me go still.

"Uh, what?" she said. "I think I may not have understood your words under that thick accent of yours." Her voice had a razor's edge to it, and I felt fairly certain she'd understood him perfectly. She was just showing her Southern woman's soul and giving him a chance to repent before she killed him.

"Uncle George is our problem, squirrel. He hurt you," he tried, softening his words but not backing down from the original statement. "You need another day or so, and the bigger issue is the Farmingtons. We'll handle George so you can be ready to go on to bigger things."

Her head turned, and she clambered around to lean over the back of the couch and face him. Her eyebrow arched as she glared, giving him one last warning of what was to come, but Jah was stubborn and possibly stupid as he missed it.

"You've got to be fucking kidding me, Jah. After everything that man put me through, you are not leaving me out of this. The entire reason," she hissed, "that I am on house arrest right now is because of him and that family. You are not shutting me out of this." She glanced at me, hoping for support, but I had backed away from the fight, leaving Jah to clean up this mess, too. I agreed with him, but I'd be damned if I said that out loud.

He let the pan he was washing clatter into the sink and stalked to her, his finger pointed in her direction, and I knew then that he'd lost his mind. I'd never known Jah to be suicidal, but here he was, committing suicide. I leaned against the wall to watch, ready to step in when it turned violent.

"George belongs to Bal and me. He's ours. They attacked you, almost killing you. You are our mate. Our life. You stole two kills from me by saving yourself, but that was *my* job. *Our* job. I need this, and I won't let you take it from me. Not only do we need this, but Cope does as well. Maybe they needed to know that you could take care of yourself, but they need to know we can take care of you more. This isn't a job, Tosh. It's personal. I love you, but I'm not backing down from this," he finished, and I thought maybe he wasn't as dumb as I'd thought when the fight went out of her.

Tosh sagged on the couch, reaching for him. He collected her in his arms, the back of the couch between them, and held her while he pulled the tips of her hair. "I love you," he whispered again into her hair. "I need to do this."

She sighed, nuzzling her head into his chest, making my heart go tight. "I know, baby. I know. Okay." And just like that, it was over.

"We'll go tomorrow and probably only be gone a few hours, maybe less," I said. "Gran'maamy will come to stay for a bit while we're gone. I'll have her bring more chicken soup, and you'll be on your feet the day after. Her soup is curative." I laughed, knowing it was true. The only reason she hadn't already brought more is that we'd asked her for some space.

"Okay," Tosh said, sliding out of Jah's arms and onto the couch. I knew she wouldn't always be this easy, but Jah was right, and she understood that. Cope needed a reminder that it wasn't just our omega that was brutal. "I'll get on the computer and have things lined up for Union City," she said, almost as an afterthought.

I didn't want her to do that, either, but it was the lesser of the two evils. We'd known she wouldn't lie in bed and eat cookies all day when we'd asked for her. Jah and I had to learn to find a balance between her strength and our admitted weaknesses. "Sounds great," I lied, and was rewarded with her bright smile, and I thought maybe it wasn't a lie at all.

Chapter Nineteen

Bala

We crawled into bed, holding Tosh between us. She was pliant as we arranged her limbs, purring as we did so. I'd never heard of an omega purring before her and wondered about it. I'd heard stories. I guess I knew it was a possibility. In school, some guy would brag about it, but I'd always doubted it was true. It was a throwback to when omegas were truly happy: the purr. Broken and chained omegas didn't do it, and if the crashing birthrate over the last few decades was a clue, so was pregnancy.

Then these new omegas came along with their highfalutin' ideas about an omega's *choice* of all things, and here I was, listening to the sweet song of an omega in my arms. What the fuck. They were right, all of them, and the ripples of that were spreading far and wide. Things were changing. Lukas's omega was a lawyer of all things and a damn good one. Jameson's mate shared an office with her, doing something, and most of the omegas from the Seventh worked in some capacity, so I'd heard.

I'd be proud of the little computer genius, knife-throwing, deadly hacker in my arms, and support her in whatever ways I could. I wondered. "Do you want children?" I asked, my voice careful.

She sighed against me, and I felt Jah stiffen. His anxiety leaked through our bond, and I urged him to tamp it down so we'd get an honest answer. "I do," she said, her voice barely above a whisper. "Just maybe," she paused, taking a deep breath. "Just maybe not now. I don't know," she added fast. "I just want to…be together for a little while." She leaned back, meeting my eyes with a worried look.

I smiled, leaning down and capturing her lips in a gentle kiss. "That sounds perfect. We'll figure it out." Jah relaxed against her back, and we settled into the deep, soft bed for the night.

The sound of the smoke detector woke me. "Fire!" I shouted as I smelled smoke, and the thick haze of it clouded the air. Jah jumped up, got tangled in the blankets, and fell to the ground. I went to grab Tosh and carry her out of the house, only to find she was gone. Whispered curses came from behind the closed door, and I rushed to open it, hoping the fire hadn't gotten to her already.

Slamming the door open, I ran into a nightmare. Tosh stood on the couch, waving a dishtowel under the smoke detector, hoping to silence it. The windows were wide open, and cold spring air streamed into the house, making swirls in the thick smoke. "I made breakfast," she said happily as she continued to wave the towel. "The toast might be a little burned, but it's on the counter for you."

The smoke detectors stopped wailing as I walked deeper into the horror show that was our kitchen. My hand flew to my mouth at the carnage. Gran'maamy's ancient cast-iron pans sat soaking in soapy water in the sink. They were submerged, only their handles sticking out. I let out a startled gasp, rushing forward, but it was too late. Behind me, Jah stifled a horrified shriek. "Baby," he managed. Piles of browned eggs were on plates at the table, alongside burned bacon and blackened toast. "It looks great," he croaked.

My heart pounded in my chest, and a frisson of genuine fear went down my spine. Gran'maamy was coming today. Her two-hundred-year-old cast iron skillets were soaking in soapy water, and she. Was. Coming. We'd had a good run. We really had. Too bad it was over. Death would be better than what she'd do.

Tosh beamed with pride as she poured thick, black coffee into cups and set them on the table. The fluid moved unnaturally, like gravy in a boat, and I looked at Jah, meeting his horrified eyes with my own as we learned something vital about our wife. She could not cook. Not even a little bit. Her file hadn't mentioned it, but of course, we had assumed. Assumptions are deadly, and Gran'maamy was going to kill us today.

I didn't care, not even a little bit, about the cooking part. Jah, and I liked to cook and had always done it, but the skillets. Oh, God, the skillets. I sighed as I picked up the coffee and grimaced when it slid down my throat like motor oil. Forcing myself not to cough, I took a spoon and tried the eggs.

Tosh beamed while we ate, loving the savage growls we made. It wasn't on purpose. Our bodies were fighting the urge to vomit and screaming at us to stop eating what was on the table, but what could we do? Hurt her feelings over burned bacon? How can someone ruin bacon? You'd have to ask, Tosh, because I didn't know. But we ate anyway. Watching her happy smiles as she dug into her breakfast like it was the best thing she'd ever eaten. "Needs more salt," she said, shaking a handful onto her blackened eggs.

I couldn't tell her that no amount of salt was fixing this.

Jah rose, surreptitiously dumping the rest of his eggs in the trash before covering it with a napkin. He rushed around the kitchen, cleaning up the skeletal remains of breakfast while Tosh cleaned her plate, and I pushed things around so it looked eaten.

"I'll help." I jumped up, grabbed my dish, and placed a kiss on Tosh's cheek. "Thanks, baby," I said, handing Jah my plate and picking up the plate of eggs off the counter to walk them to the trash.

"Ooh, I'll take those," Tosh said. "If you're full, that is," she added. "I'm starving."

"All yours, little squirrel," I said, wondering how in the hell she could eat them.

"I don't get much of an opportunity to cook," she said, sighing as she shoved another bite into her mouth. "But I enjoy doing it when I can." Her bright eyes and happy smile made me feel like an ass for dumping her breakfast in the trash, but honestly, it was inedible.

"This batch is a little overdone," she added as she cleared her plate. "But still pretty good."

I wondered what they ate in whatever little town of the Seventh she came from, that this was acceptable. Gran'maamy would've died of a heart attack at the first bite.

"We appreciate that you cooked for us, little fox, but Bala and I love cooking too. It makes us feel like better mates than we are. You know we're driven to care for you. You give us so much, and we give nothing; let us do this one thing. At least most of the time, okay, baby?" And just like that, Jah solved the problem. That's why he was a better mate than I was.

"Ah," she said, her hand going to her chest. "Well, I guess when you put it that way. That's the nicest thing I've ever heard."

I went around, kissing her temple and taking her empty plate. "Why don't you clean up before Grandmother gets here. Jah and I can finish this."

Tosh blinked up at me, smiling. "Okay."

As soon as she disappeared into the bedroom, I shut the door, turning on Jah. "Do we have time?" I screeched, looking frantically at the clock.

"Fuck. Hand me the lard," he growled, his movements quick as he pulled the cast-iron pans from the sink. I pulled lard from the pantry while he used a metal spatula to scrape burned eggs from the first pan.

The second pan wasn't as bad, so I rinsed it and dried the cast iron before using a paper towel to smear a layer of lard onto its surface. I did my best to make the lard even, then put it on the oven rack to bake. She would know. She would absolutely know. Our only hope was that she would take pity on our new wife and us. Oh, she'd never harm a hair on Tosh's head, but us? Oh, us, she'd harm. There was a precedent for it.

I watched as Jah dug his hands into the lard before massaging it into the now dull skillet. Gone was the shining black surface, and I hoped it could be saved. Generations of meals had been scrubbed clean, and it may never be the same. It would take months for the food cooked in it to be flavorful again. Part of the magic of cast iron is that those flavors are never really washed away. Well, until Tosh. She'd washed them away all right.

The oven dinged when it reached temp in record time, and the second pan went in. It was a rush job, but it would have to do. Gran'maamy would be here in a few minutes.

Tosh walked through the bedroom door in a light blue sundress with long, loose sleeves. It flowed from her breasts, moving as she walked and hiding the curves beneath. Her white teeth shone when she smiled, a contrast to the lipstick she'd applied. A light dusting of makeup covered her cheeks, and her lashes were darkened. "You look beautiful." I walked to her, picking up the skirt and running it through my fingers. The blush on her cheeks made my heart trip.

The thing about Tosh was that at first glance, she might not be as striking as her omega sisters. Their colorations were so unusual that they took your breath immediately when you saw them. Tosh is different. Her beauty involves layers that take time to see. You don't look at her once and think, wow. It takes two glances to see it and three to be floored by it. Her hair flows into her skin, flows into her features, flows into her shape, and then she raises her eyes to you, and there is no more beautiful woman in the room, maybe even the planet. Her hair was almost molasses-colored this morning, the wild honey muted by the indoor lighting, yet the warm highlights shone and deepened the mass of it into untamable glory. She was incredible.

She smiled when she caught my slack-jawed stare. "I'm feeling good today. Hurry home," she added with a wink. "I'll work on the Farmingtons and be ready for you. We can go at any time."

With that, she moved away, her eyes sweeping the kitchen. With nothing left to do, she took a cup of coffee and went out the doors to the deck.

Jah looked at me, shaking his head. "They said she was plain," he sighed. "They must have never looked at her." He shook his head, turning the oven off to let the skillets cure. If we were lucky, we'd get away with it.

Chapter Twenty

Tosh

I sat in the late-morning sun, enjoying how it felt on my skin and on my sore muscles. I heard a knock at the door and knew Miss Beulah was here, so I got up, moving more slowly than expected but better than the day before. It amazed me how quickly I healed, but then happy omegas do crazy things, and I was very happy. That's one of the reasons Eve fought for us to have a choice, and the New South as a whole benefited from her win.

I stretched like a cat, reaching high above my head to ease the ache in my ribs before walking into the house to find Miss Beulah with her hands on her hips and nose in the air.

"What's dat smell?" she asked, looking around.

The boys were in the kitchen, looking guilty of something. I didn't blame them; Miss Beulah could make anyone feel guilty. She was nearly as wide as tall, and as an alpha herself, she wasn't short. She was intimidating as hell. The boys shuffled from foot to foot, looking around.

"What'd you burn up?" she asked.

"Oh, I overcooked the eggs a little, Miss Beulah," I said, breathing a sigh of relief. She had a good nose; the eggs weren't that overcooked. "It could be the toast I burned too."

"I smell lard and cast iron." Her growl followed her as she walked to the oven and opened the door. Jah and Bala looked everywhere but at me.

Miss Beulah let out a low whistle when she stuck her head in the oven, and I got an image of an old Grimm fairy tale in my head. "D'ose pans is mighty clean," she said, her voice high-pitched and sweet.

"I washed them this morning!" I smiled, walking up to her and grinning ear to ear, happy that she noticed.

She rose to her full height, looking down at me with her hands on her hips. Her brows were narrowed, and her expression darker than her eyes. I got worried when, just like that, she deflated and smiled at me. "Dey look real clean, sweetie. Bless your heart," she said, glancing over my shoulder at one of the boys.

One of them whimpered, and I wondered what was the matter. "You okay, love?" I asked, turning around to find both of them pale as parchment paper.

"Yep," Jah squeaked, patting my arm weakly and watching his grandmother like a hawk. My eyebrows met in the middle, and I wondered if he was okay.

"You boys did a decent job curing them, but dey gonna need another coat," she said, steering me away from them. "Now go on, git outta here."

"Yes, ma'am," they said together, rushing toward the door.

"Love you, babe. Bye," Jah said, his feet pounding down the stairs.

"We'll be back before dark," Bal said, glancing between Miss Beulah and me before bolting out the door. I shrugged my shoulder at them. They must really want to come home to rush off without even a kiss.

"Stone cold killers, pshhh," Miss Beulah said under her breath. "I'll bust dey ass for dis. Ain't nobody bigger dan Miss Beulah Dawn O'Day." She turned, her smile wide and eyes curiously murderous. "What do you want to do today, sugar?"

"Oh, uh." I stopped, scratching my head.

"How you feeling?" she asked, scanning me from head to toe.

"Much better. Your boys have taken excellent care of me." I couldn't help the easy smile that crept across my face. They really had; there was no denying it.

She sighed, pinching the bridge of her nose and looking at the ceiling, showing me we Bala got that look. "Dey are good boys," she said. "Feel like going into town? I brought my car so you wouldn't have to walk."

I didn't think the boys would be happy about it, but the look on her face didn't broker an argument, so I simply said, "Yes."

I eased down the stairs behind Miss Beulah, moving almost as slowly as she did. She had a giant boat of a car, with curves and fins like a sea creature, that looked like it had definitely seen a century or more, yet somehow looked new and timeless. Sun glinted off the white finish, and I wasn't sure I'd seen anything prettier in my life. "I love it," I said, rubbing the dash and inhaling the scent of old car and sunshine.

The entire car rocked when Miss Beulah lowered herself into the driver's seat with a huff. "Ah, sugar, thank you. Us two old girls have been through a lot together." She shut the door and turned the key, and the car started with a throaty growl.

I smiled at the sound, snuggling into the seat. The sun hit me just right, and I couldn't help the purr of satisfaction that started deep in my chest.

Miss Beulah's head turned my way in the slow way a snake might when it sees a mouse. The purr stuttered in my throat and silenced. I blinked at her, waiting. "You love my boys, don't you, little sugar."

"I do. I'm very happy they asked for me." I didn't smile or show my teeth, feeling suddenly more like prey than I had when my husbands chased me through the Carolina wilds. "I got lucky with them."

"I think maybe, dat they are the lucky ones, little Miss. Cast iron pans aside." She seemed to make a decision, nodded once, and off we went.

When I say the trip into town was slow. I mean, I've seen unmotivated box turtles move faster. Miss Beulah drove her boat down Main Street at an obnoxious pace. She'd wave as she went, and no one went un-greeted by her. She'd pull over to the side of the road and talk with this person and that one, and I wondered if this was what she meant by 'go to town.'

Admittedly, we were one United New South, but there is the South, and then there is the Deep South. It really does make a difference. My hometown of Cameron is sandwiched between three countries, and it shows. Despite being in The New South, it doesn't share the southern flair the rest of the country has.

I was smiled at, fawned over, and given the careful side-eye by the town's people, but what Jah and Bala failed to do, Miss Beulah did amazingly well. She introduced me to everyone, and by the time we made it to her diner, I was feeling a little better about the town of Cope. There was also no question as to whom I belonged. Miss Beulah. I belonged to Miss Beulah. Jah and Bala might think they were the most fearsome people in this town, but they had it all wrong. Their grandmother was, and there'd never be a hair on my head harmed again because of it. Age had its privileges in Cope.

At the diner, she tucked me into the family booth and shuffled away to the kitchen to get us a glass of tea. She returned with a menu and the skinny girl I'd met the other day. "Shenay, this is Miss Tosha. She's Jah and Bala's mate. I don't think dey introduced y'all proper the other day. Tosh, dis is they little cousin Shenay. She's an omega too. She's young but seems like she gets into more trouble dan you, even. Maybe." She gave the girl a look, and Shenay dropped the tea and scurried away. "Had to get her dat shot. She won't take no man. She's too young anyway, but she always been precocious. She only seventeen, don't need no babies until she mated.

My eyebrows shot to my hairline, and my mouth dropped open.

"You gonna catch flies in there."

"Yes, ma'am," I said, dropping my eyes and closing my mouth. I looked at the menu and felt Miss Beulah's gaze heavy on my head.

"Do you want babies?" she asked, looking carefully at the menu. The tone of her voice gave away the undercurrent of the question, and I thought, just maybe, that I was getting to learn the nuances of Miss Beulah.

I sighed. "I do. Someday. The boys too. We just want to be a little bit. There's no rush. I want to know them and have time to focus on them before everything changes. I haven't told them, but my estrous is coming. We've talked about kids, and they want to wait too, but with birth control illegal, we don't have much choice."

She chuckled. "Choice is a funny word," she said, looking my way. "I don't think I heard that word much at all until you omegas from up north took over the place, but you know what? You're not wrong. You're not wrong, and nothing is illegal if the price is right."

I nodded, not sure of what to say except, "We only have a few weeks."

She pulled an old ComLink from the folds of her dress and shot off a quick text before signaling for Shenay. "Let's order," she said, tucking the ComLink away.

Lunch was fantastic. I had country-fried steak with all the fixings, washed down with a few pitchers of water and some sweet tea. Miss Beulah used her ComLink on and off, and by the time we were stuffed full, she seemed satisfied and put it away.

We held court in the back of the diner until I could fit a piece of sweet potato pie in between the cracks left by lunch. People came and went, and the atmosphere was decidedly different from the last time I was here. The people were open and friendly, or curious and polite, but no one was snide, and no one made a harsh comment or gave a harsh glance.

With the pie gone, Miss Beulah rose, ambling to the door. "Come on, girl. One more stop, then home. Dem boys are gonna beat us back and flip out when you're not there," she chuckled, and I knew that was her plan all along. She was a wily one, to be sure.

We pulled in front of a nondescript house. The paint on the side was white, and the only noticeable thing about it was that it wasn't peeling like so many other homes along this stretch of street. Giant, old oak trees dripping with Spanish moss hovered across the road like architecture. This section of town must be original to Cope, holdovers from days long gone by. They were sprawling and oh-so-southern in design, and their beauty ran deeper than peeling paint and sagging porches. These old homes were the graceful bones upon which southern societies were built.

"Miss Beulah Dawn O'Day, to what do I owe the pleasure?" A stately man whose bones were no less old and graceful than the wrap-around porch he stood on smiled down at us. His skin was dark against his stark white hair and the white suit he wore like some tribute to gentler days. A crisp black bow tie stood out against the rest, making the overall picture one I'd remember for all time. All I needed was a mint julep and a hoop skirt, and I'd be transported far, far into the past.

"Dr. Sampson, I do declare," Miss Beulah said, causing me to do a slow turn of shock in her direction. Not only had her accent deepened, but her back had straightened by several inches. The smile she gave him was unlike any I had seen on her face before. The Nuances of Beulah Dawn O'Day were varied and broad.

"This here is my daughter-in-law, Tosha O'Day, suh. She's married to those boys o'mine and all them looking after that shot, you know the one."

"Now Beulah Dawn, she's pretty as a peach, rare as one too. Aren't you ready for more babies, young lady," he said, addressing her, not me. I watched the interaction raptly, unable to take my eyes from either of them as they performed a skit of pure southern charm unlike any I'd ever seen.

"Aren't you kind, Dr. Sampson," Beulah said, blushing as she turned her head shyly, causing my mouth to drop open at the sight.

"But her and the boys just got married, you know, and want a little, uh, time before commencing to have youngins." She swept up the grand stairs, taking the arm he offered with a gentlemanly bow.

"Come along then, little miss. We'll get taken care of and on your way in no time," he said, smiling brightly over his shoulder.

What the actual fuck?

How is it in small-town Cope that a doctor older than the South itself could have something so illicit as a birth control shot? Morgantown was dripping in affluence and influence, and that shot was only a rumor someone had heard from someone else. Free omegas everywhere would give their eye teeth for one, and here this proper southern doctor acted like he had a fridge full of them.

"Come along, young lady," Dr. Sampson tutted, holding the door for me.

The house was no less grand on the inside than it was on the out. Oiled wood floors and railings shone in the light of the afternoon, and furniture as old as the house decorated ornate woven rugs. It was breathtaking.

"Tea, Miss Tosh, Miss O'Day?" Dr. Sampson helped Beulah sit as if she were made of glass rather than a towering alpha female.

"That would be delightful," she answered.

I leaned back on the couch, taking in the old-world charm the house offered. It was like nothing I'd ever seen before. It's funny how some things never change, and others don't stand the test of time. This place was a museum of a time before the old USA fell. It was a time capsule of ornate beauty and charm.

"You have a beautiful home, Doctor," I said formally when he handed me a chilled glass full of sweet tea.

"Why, thank you, miss." He leaned back in his chair, crossing his ankle over his knee. His eyes turned serious as he took me in. "You married both those boys, did you?"

"Yes, sir. I did."

He nodded, watching me from under thick lashes. He rubbed a hand across his chin in a thoughtful way. "Those boys always were different. Real close, like. You doing all right with them?" he asked, tilting his head as he waited for an answer.

"They're very good boys," I answered, knowing it wasn't untrue. They were good to me, that they were off murdering someone who tried to hurt me aside. Actually, that little tidbit made them better boys. My hands weren't clean and hadn't been for years, but that didn't make me a bad person. "And excellent mates, sir," I added, watching Miss Beulah smile at my answer.

"And they're not unkind to you?" He leaned forward, looking me in the eye.

Miss Beulah huffed like she was offended, but held her tongue.

"No, Sir. Never unkind to me."

"Okay, then, I understand. Being a newlywed to two alphas like those boys is going to be a big job. I understand if you want to hold off a spell on having babies. Makes sense. Jah and Bala have demanding jobs, and adding a baby in the mix might topple the apple cart, and we can't have that. Is your time close?" he asked, and now it was my turn to tilt my head.

"Oh," I answered. Yes, of course, he meant my estrous, but as frank as one could be with a southern doctor, there were still some things that weren't overtly discussed. "Within three weeks, I'd say. More like two."

"Perfect!" He rose from his chair and took a syringe from the serving tray that held the tea. "If you're sure?" he asked again.

I nodded my head, pulling up the sleeve of my dress. The shot went in smoothly, but the sting as the thick liquid pushed into my muscle made my eyes water.

"All set. Now, side effects are rare, but you could have some cramping, a low-grade fever, and possibly some muscle aches. It might feel like you have a virus. You'll need one every three months before each cycle if you want more time with your boys. Once the day comes that you're ready for little ones, I'll be seeing you. Start taking some vitamins, and we'll make sure everything goes smooth and easy for you."

"Thank you, Doctor." I rose to my feet, following Miss Beulah's lead.

"You're mighty welcome. Miss Beulah, let's have some lunch next week when things settle around here."

"I'd love that," she answered. "The boys will tear up the town looking for her soon enough if I don't get her home to them. Thank you again," she finished, offering him her hand.

He kissed the back of it, bowing at the waist, then walked us to the door. "Until then," he said, watching as we walked to the car and drove away.

It was getting late, and I knew without a doubt that Jah and Bala would be home before us. Despite the setting sun, Miss Beulah took her time, winding through town and stopping to talk to folks along the way. I shook my head, wondering at the way she borrowed trouble with her grandsons. There was no doubt in my mind who held the title of queen of this town, though, and I can assure you, it wasn't me.

Once we finally reached the last house between theirs and the town, she finally hit the gas pedal and drove me home.

Chapter Twenty-One

Bala

The trip to Orangeburg was quick. I still couldn't get over the fact that Uncle George had run there. I suppose it shouldn't surprise me, as that family was not known for its intelligence.

Jah speared BBQ pork from a paper bowl with a fork, gleefully watching the little brick house with closed curtains and barred windows. There were toys in the yard, and as much as we wanted George dead, we wouldn't involve children. "That shit looks old," he said. "That layer of green says the kids are long gone."

He was probably right, but we stayed a while longer, casing the house for signs of innocent bystanders. The curtains never moved, and the doors stayed closed. After another hour with no movement, it was time to go. Families are busy, and if there was one in this house, they weren't home.

We slid out of the truck, closing the doors soundlessly and sliding through the overgrowth to the corners of the place Uncle George holed up in. With a tip of his chin, Jah cut toward the back, and I rounded the side. Easing to the side door, I pulled a set of picks from my pocket and worked the lock. In seconds the tumblers moved, and the door creaked open.

Pulling my gun, I opened it enough to slip through, closing it behind me, so it didn't make a noise. I was in a kitchen that was more than lived in. Dishes lay dirty in the sink, and flies buzzed above the mess. The air was still and fetid, making me doubt the tip leading here. After clearing the kitchen, I ghosted through the hall, knowing Jah would meet me from the other direction.

He crept around the corner, his gun out and pointed at the floor. With one shake of his head, he let me know the lower level was clear. I tipped my head toward the stairs, and we ascended them together.

We were big men, and the house was old. The creaks the stairs made sounded like gunshots, and any hope we had of slipping in undetected vanished. Footsteps running over our head alerted us, and we exchanged stealth for speed. At the top of the stairs, we split, each taking one side of the second floor.

"Got him," Jah said, and I heard the crunch of bone on bone. "Oops. He slipped and fell on my fist. Clumsy fucker. Uncle George, you are one clumsy fucker," Jah laughed.

I couldn't stop the smile that spread across my face, and I didn't want to. I slipped the gun into my waistband, my hands itching for blood.

"I didn't do nothing, boys. Nothing. I didn't touch a hair on her head."

"You fucking shot at her!" I said, snatching him from Jah's grasp and shaking him like an errant puppy.

"Not me!" he cried, trying to peddle away from me.

"Whether that's true or not doesn't matter, George. You were there. You fucking knew," I emphasized that word with my fist, "that we would not let it stand."

"Moesh is my niece, man. I gotta look after her," he whimpered.

"And Tosh is our mate. What did you think would happen? How did you imagine this ending?" Jah snarled, landing a punch to George's kidney and another to the base of his spine that cracked with a loud crunch.

I smelled urine and knew that if the punch didn't sever George's spinal cord, it was damn sure bruised. His bowels let loose, and I went back to my theory that it was severed.

George whimpered, begging for mercy, but they hadn't shown any to Tosh, and he would find none in me. "Moesh and Ty are dead," I said, hitting him solidly in the chest. I didn't want to kill him yet, but there was no way I could hold back. "The best part of that is that our wife killed them. Not me. Not my brother. My omega wife. It would almost be worth it to let you live to tell that tale, but my pride won't let me. Sorry. Not sorry." I punched him in the chest again, and this time, I knew I had landed it right when his eyes rolled back in his head. The hit had changed the rhythm of his heart, and I hit him again to change it back and keep him alive a little longer.

Jah landed a hit to the other kidney, and the dull thud of the sound let me know he'd ruptured it. This was almost over, but I wasn't satisfied and never would be. The Whites had almost taken my wife from me, and one man's blood wasn't enough to assuage my anger. I wanted the whole bloodline dead. They needed purged from the ranks of polite society after what they'd done to Tosh. But I settled for hitting Uncle George in the chest again. The last punch must've broken his sternum because my hand sank into his chest, and I felt his heart beat erratically against my hand. It stuttered and stopped before starting again.

I met Jah's eyes over the dead man's shoulder, and after one more hit to his kidney, he dropped between us.

"Well, fuck," he said. "I was hoping the fucker had more stamina than that. Well, let's clean up and head home." He shook his head in disappointment as we trudged down the stairs.

There was a spring in our steps as we left the house, though. We didn't care that everyone would know we'd killed him. The Alpha sanctioned it, and people needed to know. Should our viciousness be in doubt, others would suffer. Jah and I were the threat that grandmothers everywhere used. 'Eat your peas, or the O'Days will come for you' was uttered a hundred times a day in The New South, and we couldn't afford to look weak.

We wiped ourselves down with the wet wipes we kept for just this reason, then changed our shirts and dumped them on the floorboard. After pulling clean tees over our heads, we climbed into the truck and headed home. There was still plenty of daylight left, and I was hoping we would get there in time to take our wife to supper.

Now that Uncle George was dealt with, we needed to put together a solid plan for the Farmingtons and settle in for Tosh's heat cycle. We knew it was coming. Subtle changes in her body told us we had a few weeks, maybe a month, and we wanted to be home for that. The Alpha be damned, I wasn't serving my wife in a hotel. We made quick work of the drive home, anticipation making my foot heavy. Jah couldn't sit still, and I knew his shifting and fidgeting meant the same as mine.

A few hours was too long: we needed Tosh, and we needed her now.

Chapter Twenty-Two

Tosh

"Where the fuck is she?" The words were so forceful that the windows rattled, and Miss Beulah chuckled. I knew then this was her plan all along. Where I'm more of a go along to get along person, Miss Beulah was an alpha, and she was flexing her muscles. Gran'maamy my ass.

Something heavy crashed, and I sped up, taking the stairs as fast as my little legs would take me.

"Boys!" I said, slamming the door open. I was ripped off my feet and crushed to a chest before I could make any protest but a muffled gasp.

"Put her down, you big gorilla," Miss Beulah said as she swept in the room. She dropped her pocketbook on the couch and tutted over the state of the kitchen table. Upended, it lay askew in the dining area, and chairs scattered throughout the kitchen.

"Pick this mess up, boys. You need to learn restraint," she said, meeting their glares.

I smiled inwardly as they backed down, righting chairs and fixing the table. "You should have let us know," Bala chimed in, not backing down.

"You left her with me. Are you saying that you don't trust me to keep her safe?" she asked, her voice sweeter than the first sip of tea on a hot summer day.

"He's not saying that," Jah tried, but Bala answered immediately with a "Yes, I am."

"Stop." I stepped in the middle of the alphas, giving my best glare. "It's fine. We've been out all day. It ended with a trip to the doctor for that shot we talked about. I was having a good time until I walked in the door, so calm the fuck down," I finished, using my meditation skills to their fullest.

Bala scrubbed his hands down his face, then shook like a dog, his tight curls bouncing on his cheeks. "You're right. Gran'maamy, I'm sorry. This is all very new."

"Of course, dear," she said, patting his cheek and moving deeper into the house.

Jah wrapped his arms around me, pulling my scent into his lungs. His heart rate slowed, and I could physically feel him getting his shit together. I laid my head back on his chest, scowling at Bala until he exhaled, taking a few inches off his height.

Tiny drops of blood speckled his face. It looked arterial, and I surmised their mission had been successful. "All finished up?" I asked.

"Yeah. We're good to go."

I nodded my head, glad to hear it.

Miss Beulah began telling the boys about our day, down to every detail. Included in the litany was every person she spoke to and also spoke to me. Every word was repeated, and inflection of tone shared. Then began the speculation as to what it all meant. I chuckled because I knew what she was doing, but she'd done more to induct me into life in Cope in a few hours than they had done since I'd been here, so I let her do her thing.

She sat at the kitchen table once Bala had righted it and talked long after sunset. I moved around the house, checking computer searches that I'd set to run and finalizing a few plans I had for our trip to Union City. Bala and Jah sat with their Grandmother, clearly anxious for her to leave. Blood still spattered their skin, and it was a hilarious mockery of southern hospitality that they didn't ask her to go so they could clean up.

I packed a bag and set it by the door. That got the boys' attention, and they finally rose to usher Miss Beulah out the door. They muttered goodbyes in the proper Southern way, and when finally she left, they sighed behind the closed door.

"Clean up," I ordered as I unstacked the dishwasher, feeling them closing in on me, wondering why they never used it.

Their petulant grumbles followed them out of the room, and I couldn't help but smile. I didn't mind them covered in blood, especially if it belonged to my enemies, but a dank smell clung to them, and I had to draw a line somewhere. I followed to the bedroom, tugging back the blankets and stripping naked. I rubbed the blankets over my skin, my hands twitching with the desire to build a nest. I didn't build daily, but I wanted one now.

I twisted the blankets quickly, making a little nest that would have to do. It wouldn't hold two alphas, but it would cradle me through what I planned next. I pulled the last blanket over me, snuggling in deeper.

Jah and Bala were good men, following doctor's orders and all that. They'd been a little too good, and I wanted them to be bad.

"I was a bad girl," I said when Bala exited the bathroom with rivulets of water running down his chest and a towel around his hips. His eyes snagged on the little nest I'd thrown together, and he couldn't force his gaze back to me.

"You have, have you?" His dark chuckle sent a shiver up my spine and made gooseflesh rise on my skin. He rubbed his chin as he walked forward, and his tone suggested I should run, but I ignored that instinct. Instead, I focused on the satisfied hum of the bond between us.

"Yes," I answered, wiggling my hips under the blanket.

He ripped it off me and tossed it aside. He hummed when he saw me bared to him. "A very bad girl. You're supposed to be taking it easy."

"I'm just lying here," I said, going for innocent.

"Naked."

"Naked."

"Hmmm."

"What's this?" Jah said from the door. He was using a towel to fluff his dark curls, and the movement dragged my eyes to the vee at his hips.

"Our mink is naughty." Bala advanced on me, dropping the towel and showing how excited that made him.

"Is she?" Jah's feral grin stopped my heart, and if I didn't feel their happiness through the bond, I'd worry.

"We owe her a spanking," Jah said.

"For what?" I asked, faking indignation over the idea.

"You're right, brother. We may owe her more than one, but as she's injured, we'll take it easy." Bala advanced on me, gripping my ankles and flipping me, so my hips rested on my nest's wall.

"What? Why?" I sputtered. I'd been thinking of multiple orgasms, not spankings, but sometimes they aren't mutually exclusive of one another.

"You got shot," Bala offered as he palmed my ass before placing a quick strike on it.

I yelled out, kicking at him.

Jah approached me from the other side, sitting next to me on the bed. His fingers parted my thighs, and he rubbed my core. "You're soaked, Tosh." He growled in the alpha way, causing more slick to flow before bringing his fingers to his lips and sucking them clean.

"You ran from us," Jah said as Bala landed another strike expertly. Jah soothed it away, rubbing my clit and making me arch off the bed.

"I ran from murderers," I panted.

"Hmmm," Jah said. "You were out all day after we asked you to stay in."

"For your safety," Bala added with another crack to my ass. My cheeks were on fire, and I was panting with the need for them.

"For your safety," Jah seconded as his fingers plundered me, and I groaned out my pleasure. "You must listen to your alphas, little squirrel." His breath tickled my ear, and the bed moved as he tossed his towel aside. He slid to the floor, anchoring my legs apart as his mouth sucked the slick from my weeping core.

"You taste like sunshine, Tosh."

Bala landed his final crack to my ass as I came, mixing a little pain with my pleasure. He gave no explanation for it, just rubbed the welt he left behind. Fisting my hair, he pulled my head to the side, crushing my lips with his. I groaned into his mouth as Jah speared me with his tongue before climbing up my body and arcing over me to slip his cock between my folds.

He released a hiss when he hit bottom, then used his powerful body to fuck me into the mattress. Bala kept his lips on mine, and I loved it. He took my cries and moans as I made them, swallowing them down. Jah slipped behind my cervix, hitting that magic spot, and I fell apart around him. His thrusts faltered as my body clamped on his, demanding his knot. Wave after wave of my orgasm forced his, and he shouted as his knot exploded and he filled me up. He rested his forehead against my back, running his hands over my skin with a sigh as he pushed his knot deeper, making my body grip it harder.

"Fuck, baby. You break me down," Jah said.

Bala kept kissing me, and my body kept massaging Jah's knot until it deflated. Hot fluids rushed between us, and he scooped them up and drank greedily. I never knew an alpha to do that outside of estrous, and I watched his throat work as he swallowed us. Bala released my lips, turning me over and slipping into his brother's place.

He entered me in one thrust, and it was almost too much. Jah pulled my nipples into his mouth, licking and sucking them. Hot breath skated across my skin and raised the hair on my arms with pleasure overload. Bala wasted no time. His hips pounded against mine, and the feel of him hitting that spot and Jah's lips on my skin had me crying out again. Bala fought it; he did. It was a valiant effort. But my body won, demanding his release for itself. Sweat dripped from him, decorating me until he gave up. His knot flared behind my pubic bone, filling me impossibly. His pained groan echoed in the room, and he collapsed beside me, pulling me to him.

Jah got up and turned off the lights. He grabbed the blanket from the floor, covered us up, and together we slept.

Bala's alarm sounded early. He groaned as he turned from me to silence it. "We need to retire, brother," he growled as he slapped the thing off.

"Agree." Jah's muffled voice sounded from deep under my hair, and I smiled, seeing him practically buried under me.

"Then who would save The New South from itself?" I asked.

"Someone else," Bala sighed.

"Anyone else?" Jah added helpfully as he disentangled himself from my limbs.

"Marriage is making you soft," I sighed, running my hands over the muscled planes of their backs. God, but they were beautiful. Never had I seen such perfection chiseled and honed into a weapon to be used for pain or pleasure.

My heart hummed happily, filling the bond between us with joy, and I wondered if this was what love felt like. "I'll make breakfast."

"No!" Jah shouted before dialing it back a notch. "I'll get it, little squirrel. Pancakes?" he asked, adding a sweet smile that contradicted the crazy light in his eyes.

"Uh, sure, babe. Pancakes sound great." I rose from the bed, letting the slight soreness from last night's activities roll through me.

With a sigh, Bala rose, following me into the bathroom. I turned the knobs on the shower, sighing when I stepped into its heat. Hands massaged the knots from my back, soothing the last of the stiffness away.

"You're beautiful," he said, his hands skating down my sides and raising gooseflesh.

"I'm many things, Bal. Beautiful is hardly one of them." I chuckled, ducking my head under the hot spray of water.

He turned to me, his lips crashing into mine. His kiss was hard and hot, his tongue chasing mine, catching and claiming it violently. "That's where you're wrong, my wife," he growled. "You are the most beautiful creature I've ever seen, and when the water kisses your skin, it takes my breath."

"You're very sweet," I said, breathing hard when he pulled away.

"I'm many things," he said darkly. "Sweet is hardly one of them." He turned me again, slipping between my thighs and thrusting into me hard. Hands cupped my breasts, tweaking my nipples, and I fought to accommodate his weight as he leaned into me. "You're fucking beautiful, Tosh. I'm proud to call you mine."

He leaned backward, taking the weight from me and sliding himself out before bottoming into me again. "You are the beautiful one," I whimpered as he punished me with his hips for my words.

His thrusts lifted my heels off the floor of the shower, his hands holding my hips steady. "You were made for me. Your body, your mind; you were absolutely made for both of us. Fuck," he ground out, turning his back teeth to dust. He pulled me to him, his chest to my back. I leaned my head to him as he slowed his thrusts, letting me feel every thick inch of him slip in and out.

"Fuck," I seconded.

"You're beautiful. Say it," he growled, strumming my clit like an instrument.

"You're beautiful," I sighed, feeling that truth to my core.

"Tosha O'Day," he growled, then growled again at the sound of my name on his lips. "Fucking say it."

"I'm beautiful," I whimpered, the unstoppable train of my end barreling toward me.

"Fuck yes, you are." He flicked my clit once more, slapping my pussy, and I exploded around him, screaming his name. He roared his release, clamping his teeth into the base of my neck forcing me to come again. He choked as I gripped his knot, demanding what he gave willingly.

I leaned my weight onto him, breathing hard. His chest rose and fell just as fast, and his hands skated my body like he couldn't explore it fast enough. He pressed kisses to the side of my neck and the hollow of my ear. The ties that bound the three of us hummed in satisfaction. I felt Jah's happiness and my own, knowing I'd made the right choice with them.

Bala's knot released, soaking my legs with the fluids it held back. He soaped his hands, running them over me in a slow show of washing my body. His lips caressed my face and neck as he worked his hands, and I shuddered into him again. "You make me happy, little fox," he whispered into my ear once my body finished trembling.

"You make me happy too," I said, making him take more of my weight. I was wrung out and sleepy from too much pleasure.

"Breakfast," Jah said from the door. He leaned against the wall, a smile playing across his lips. "You have to be starved, baby."

I smiled back. "I am."

Over breakfast, I laid out the most recent surveillance pictures and detailed the route I believed the Farmingtons were using to traffic the people they took. Using CoinCard receipts and pictures from traffic cameras, I thought I had it narrowed down.

"This will save days of hunting, little fox. Maybe weeks," Jah said as he picked up the empty plates we'd left.

"Good, because we don't have weeks. My heat is two, maybe three weeks away. I don't want to be on the road for that."

"We don't either," Bala echoed. "Let's get this done as quickly as possible. You smell too sweet to be out in public."

"Caveman," I grumbled, heading grab my toiletries from the bathroom. But he was right. Changes were happening quickly, and I didn't want to be in Union City when my shit hit the fan. However, the timing was perfect for the plan I had in mind to reel in the Farmingtons.

Chapter Twenty-Three

Jah

"I hope we have two to three weeks, brother," I said, watching Tosh sleep between us. "I'm starting to think we don't."

My wife's skin was flushed, and her breathing heavier than usual. The sweet scent of approaching estrous filled the cab of the truck, and I thought we might be making a mistake in leaving the safety of our house. My instincts were screaming at me to turn around.

"She's got this hunt dialed in," Bala said, rubbing the tousled head in his lap. "One day to travel there, one, two days tops to capture the Farmingtons, and one day home. Even if she's off by a week, we have time. We need to finish this. I never thought we needed someone with her skills, but this proves we do. Those pictures she got are recent. If the Farmingtons move on, we may never find them."

"Call Lukas and ask him to have transport ready, so we don't have to take them in. Because if we do, I'm killing them."

Bala was right; I knew that. I hated taking the chance, though.

"Good idea." Bala picked up his ComLink and typed a quick message. Lukas's response was immediate. "He wants them alive, and he'll have a shuttlecraft or helo on standby."

I nodded once, keeping my eyes on the road. Roads in The New South were tricky. Some of them were great, and you could maintain speeds as fast as your vehicle would travel. Most of the old four lanes had been rebuilt, but not all. In places, chunks of roads were missing, and the skeletons of old vehicles remained.

The further we got from the Sixth, the more true this was. What might have once been a half-day trip stretched into a day. Bala and I took turns driving, only stopping for fuel and bathroom breaks. We'd packed a cooler and kept as brisk a pace as we could. Tosh slept a lot, making me worry more. Either her body was still fighting to heal, or her estrous was coming sooner rather than later. Omegas slept long hours and sometimes days in preparation for five to seven days without.

I caught Bala's worried look as he met my eyes. Ideally, we'd be resting too, as an estrous would force our rut, and we'd need all the energy we could get. "I brought extra food, protein snacks, and water. We'll load up as best we can."

Tosh roused halfway to Union City, her stomach growling violently. She sat up, blinking her eyes to get her bearings.

"Food," she growled, making me laugh out loud.

"Have a sandwich. We'll stop for supper at the next exit."

She grabbed the sandwich from Bala, ripping into it with a cute little growl. Bala handed her a cold bottle of water, and it was gone in two swallows. I whipped the truck off the road, pulling into an all-night diner with a sigh. We should've asked Lukas for a shuttlecraft, but that might arouse suspicion in a place like Union City.

Tosh ordered plate after plate of food, and my worry increased. Omegas can eat a ton, and she was no exception, but this was more than I'd ever seen her eat in one sitting. After her second pitcher of water, she promptly fell asleep. Jah and I hurried to finish our meals, preloading as many calories as we could. The looks the other diners cast our way were not unnoticed, and we paid, hurrying to leave.

The decent roads gave way to paths not fit for travel, and we picked our way along the final leg of the trip, pulling into the parking lot of the hotel Tosh reserved as the sun peeked above the horizon.

Tosh sat up with a groan, looking rested. The edge was gone, and I wondered whether healing, rather than estrous, had changed her behavior during the trip. She stretched with a sigh, looking more like a cat than a fox.

"I'll check us in," Bala said as I pulled luggage from the truck's bed.

Tosh tipped her face to the rising sun, enjoying the feel of it after a long night. She reached into the truck, grabbing some of our bags and the cooler of food. Bala returned with a key, and we followed him through the courtyard and to an interior-facing door. She was smart, our omega.

The hotel was nice, old but clean. Driving through the outskirts of Union City had shown me that the town was all but forgotten by The New South. The skeletons of old cars and buildings still lingered, and little had been done to repair the damage from the Great War. It was a time capsule of the years since, undisturbed and raw. Sometimes there is beauty in these places, but Union City was not one of those.

The place Tosh chose was nice, probably the nicest in town. The old wrought-iron railings had been lovingly restored, and the building's paint was crisp and clean. An in-ground pool lay in the middle of the courtyard, and the wisps of steam rising from the surface told me it was heated. We climbed to the second floor, then moved to a door and followed Bala through after he unlocked it.

The room was large, with a King bed to one side and a sitting area to the other. A large bathroom opened up, and it seemed Tosh had researched the place well. Usually, on these missions, Bala and I stay in shitholes or hostiles. This was definitely a step up, and since The Alpha was paying, why not? It was another reason we needed her and why we would do our jobs better with her in our lives.

"There's a café a block away," Tosh said, adding, "They have free wifi, and it seems to be in the middle of the nicer part of this town."

"There's a nicer part of this town?" Bala asked, dropping his keys on the dresser.

"This is it," Tosh chuckled.

"Well, this place is nice enough. Nicer than our usual." I hugged Tosh to me, releasing her so she could situate her suitcase.

"According to the most recent photos, the Farmingtons come through this area every few days to a week at the most. The café has outdoor seating and an excellent view of Main Street. While you boys are hunting, I can make use of the Wi-Fi and search for updated information." Tosh threw the phrase out casually, and I got the feeling she was hoping neither of us would see the truth of it.

"You put yourself in the middle of their hunting grounds?" Bala growled, not missing anything. "Knowing they don't care whether an omega is mated or not? Knowing they would snatch you in a heartbeat if they could?"

"I put us in the best, safest part of town," the little mink amended.

"In the middle of their hunting grounds." His eyes were hard when he glanced at her.

"I put you in the best location, hoping to capture them quickly," she said, her sly smile giving away everything.

"You're not using yourself as bait, little mink," I said, my voice dropping to a growl against my will.

"I never said I was," she soothed, patting my arm lightly.

"You never said you weren't either," Bala added, stomping out the door to finish unloading the truck.

"Little squirrel," I groaned, reaching for her.

She side-stepped me gracefully, saying, "I'm going to shower then go eat the complimentary breakfast in the lobby before it's all gone."

I scrubbed my hands down my face, feeling the stubble left from not shaving for a few days. This omega was going to be the death of me. I knew what she was doing. She wasn't as slick as she thought.

The shower turned on, and the sweet smell of wet omega floated with the steam, making my dick half hard. On the one hand, I was willing to use her if that meant we could get this over faster and go home. On the other, absolutely not. But the mink was a fox in the best ways, and her plan was solid.

The shower was short, and Tosh emerged in a white, long-sleeved romper. She had her hair in a long, high ponytail that swung down her back. A dusting of pink lip gloss was the only makeup on her face, and she looked sixteen at the oldest and twelve, if I was honest with myself. "Tosh," I groaned.

"What?" She blinked her eyes at me, rounding them impossibly and looking so innocent it made my teeth hurt.

"No," I said. "Just no."

"Do I look bad or something?" she asked, and I wondered if I'd read the situation wrong.

"I mean, you don't look bad," I said. "You just look really young."

"Are you saying I usually look old?" She cocked her hip, narrowing her eyes on me.

"No, of course not. You just look super innocent. I don't think that's a good idea."

"Wow," she started. "Wooooooooow," she dragged the word out, tossing her hair over her shoulder and walking away. "So I usually look like an old, used-up slut? Got it."

"Tosh, that's not what I said."

"It kinda is." She walked out the door, leaving me standing there with my mouth open.

"What the fuck," Bala asked as he looked over his shoulder, presumably at the retreating omega. "She looks like a little girl. Where the fuck is she going?"

"Uh, maybe don't say that to her. She's mad because I already did. She's going to breakfast. You can clean up, and I'll follow her down. We can trade off."

He growled, his eyes following me as I went out the door to find Tosh. I took the stairs, walking around the pool until a sign directed me to the lobby.

Tosh stood with a plate in her hand, talking excitedly to an older woman over a buffet line. "I just got married." I heard her say. "My husbands and I are heading to Nashville for our honeymoon, but our truck broke down," she added. She'd pulled white socks to her knees, and her white tennis shoes gave her an even more childlike appearance. I was going to kill her. If she thought the spankings she had before were too much, when she got the one she'd earned with this stunt, her ass was going to sing.

"Baby," I said, grinding my back teeth to dust. "Didn't we tell you to be careful of strangers?" I placed a kiss on her temple, pulling her to me.

"You shouldn't leave your omega alone then," the old lady said, swatting me with a pair of tongs.

Tosh blinked wide eyes at me, and I felt my back tooth crack under the pressure in my jaw. She'd set us up with a perfect story, though, and I couldn't back out of it now. Small southern towns had one thing in common. Gossip. Word of our backstory would travel. It was unusual enough for an omega to have more than one mate that it would spread like fire.

"Let's eat, sweetie," I pulled her away, stiffening my back and being as condescending as I could.

Tosh blew through her first plate, going back for more. The empty pitcher of water on the table was replaced, and she worked on downing it too. I ate as much as I could, stuffing myself to discomfort, but Tosh still packed it in, and it didn't go unnoticed. Eyes glanced our way as she ate, and I knew this would add to the Tale of Tosh. The southerners from the Second District would understand this omega behavior and embellish their tale with it.

Bala joined us, his dark curls damp from a shower. His glower raised the tension in the room, adding to the allure of the little omega in his presence. Everyone loved dark, dangerous stories, and hers just got more so when he growled a warning to no one in particular. Tosh was a fucking genius. Damn her, but she was still a genius. She'd be a genius with a sore ass soon enough if this played out.

"Our new wife has explained to the oldest woman in the room that we are newlyweds on our way to Nashville to honeymoon," I whispered, knowing he would understand the implications. Old women were talkers. Maybe not as much so as old southern men, but close enough.

"She did, did she?" he narrowed his eyes on her as she gleefully piled another plate as high as it could go.

"Yep," I popped the p for emphasis.

"Bless her heart," he growled.

The laugh erupted from me like a geyser, and I let it, drawing even more attention to us. Our little omega was in deep shit. But a better story had never been crafted. How else could our behavior be explained? In fact, any other story would arouse so much suspicion as to make it evident that we were up to something. Tosh wasn't technically setting herself up as bait, but the Farmingtons would be hard-pressed to ignore her and not ask questions. Somehow, they were part of this town. Whether they lived here or only trafficked through here, they were a staple. People in Union City knew them and possibly helped them. It was perfect. It didn't mean I wasn't going to spank her, but it was perfect nonetheless.

I showered and met them back in the lobby. Tosh had asked for her backpack, and when she slung it over her shoulder, I knew that her plans far exceeded ours. She looked like a middle schooler, all dressed in white with a backpack over her shoulder, and the vision of me wringing her neck couldn't be removed from my brain when I looked at her.

Bala's continuous growl told me he felt the same, but we were in too deep now. We walked to the café Tosh mentioned, and she positioned herself at a table nearest the road. The only thing between her and capture was a dingy white fence.

"Can you get me a scone, a coffee, and a pitcher of water, love?" Tosh asked, blinking wide doe eyes at Bala. His growl deepened, but he moved to comply.

"What's your plan, little fox?" I whispered when he was far enough away not to hear.

"What plan?" she asked, smiling at me in the midday sun.

"Don't bullshit me," I said, faking a smile but growling to let her know the jig was up.

"I don't have a plan," she said, pulling the beaten-up old laptop we'd given her from her pack. Beside it, she added a notebook, and the overall picture was of a young girl doing homework. Her long ponytail swayed when she moved, drawing your attention to her young features. The romper hid her curves, and I wondered if she bought it specifically for this trip.

I sighed, taking her hand in mine and squeezing it.

242

"There's an automotive store two blocks down. Didn't you and Bala need some doohickey for the truck?" she asked. Her fingers tapped away on the keyboard, and from my angle, I could see she was checking local traffic cams.

"We're not leaving you," Bala said when he got to the table. "And move back from the fence; you are too close to the street." He picked her up, ignoring her indignant squawk as he settled her at another table, not so near the road. Heads turned our way, taking in the innocent, round eyes Tosh used to implore him with.

"You're playing into her hands, brother," I laughed low so that only he could hear.

He grabbed her laptop, notebook, and backpack, settling them beside her before adding her scone and coffee. A waiter sat the pitcher of water down, and the scene was set. The scene was perfected by having two possessive, controlling, and asshole alphas breathing down the fine hairs of Tosh's neck. We refused to leave her alone, and after a few hours, she seemed to give up trying to make us. "Okay, enough for this morning," she said, rising to stretch. "Let's go back. A steakhouse down the road comps your meal if you can eat all thirty-six ounces of T-bone. I could eat a horse, so supper's on me.

We left the café and walked back towards the hotel. Tosh walked ahead of us by a few steps, but no more. Bala's head was on a swivel, and I just tried to keep from blowing this mission, but

243

my constant laughter at her antics was going to be a dead giveaway if I couldn't control it.

Bala and I had a stealthy approach to killing. Most of the time, no one even knew we'd been in town when the body was found. Because of our discretion, our faces weren't widely known, and that was a good thing. But the Farmingtons were careful, or Lukas would have already caught them. Putting us out there was a risk, but Tosh was right. We needed this to be an in-and-out mission. Maybe we'd never be able to run an op like this again, and maybe we would, but it didn't matter. Our goal here was speed, and I had no doubt the Farmingtons had already heard about the too young omega with her overbearing mates.

They'd have also heard that she was eating like a horse and smelling sweet. They might even presume that we hadn't claimed her yet. Tosh's romper covered her bite marks, leaving that in question. An untouched, unbound, teenaged omega would sell for premium money, and as most matings are solidified during estrous, they might take the chance on her being a virgin. The worst-case in their minds would be they could sell her anyway, forcibly break the bond, or use her how they saw fit. Again, genius. Again, dead meat. But I saw the beauty of the plan.

Bala, however, did not. "Take it off," he growled the minute the door shut.

"Wait, what?" Tosh continued trying to use her innocence to shield her, but now that we were alone, Bala dropped his pretense of being indulgent.

"You want to do this your way? That's fine, but you'll pay the price for it first, little mink. Bare your ass to me. Now." Bala's belt clinked as he pulled it through the loops.

"Husband," she tried.

"Don't husband me, Tosha O'Day. Bare. Your. Ass."

He'd used her full name, and I watched as her eyes went wide. Setting her lips in a grim line, she pulled the zipper on the romper and bared her shoulders. Turning away, she slid the fabric over her hips and bared her ass to him. She gripped the edges of the table but said nothing, not making a sound when the first strike of the belt landed on her pale skin, marking it beautifully.

I moved to give her the pleasure that should come with this. "No, brother. Not this time. She needs to understand that she can't put herself in danger. Not like this." He landed the belt again, and the little fox gripped the table until her knuckles went white but otherwise did not acknowledge the spanking. Bala landed three more hard strikes to the globe of her ass, then moved to unbutton his pants so that he could take her, but she ripped the romper up her arms. Stomping away from us and into the bathroom, where she slammed the door. The click of the lock echoed in the room's silence.

"Strong work, brother," I growled, pushing past him and deeper into the room.

He sighed as he put on his belt. "She can't put herself out there like this. It's dangerous."

"And now you're saying that we can't handle the danger?" I asked. "You're saying that we can't protect her? Her plan is brilliant, and you know it. You just showed her that you don't trust her or us. That's all you accomplished." I walked to the bathroom door, lowering my voice. "Let me in, baby. Let me take care of you. It's just me," I added as I knocked.

There was no answer, and I knocked again, a little harder. The sound of tinkling metal and the rush of air under the door had me shouldering the door open; flimsy lock be damned. The hotel was built around the courtyard and pool, meaning that there were no interior walls. The tiny bathroom window was open, and I rushed to it. My head fit through, but not my shoulders, but I could see well enough. Tosh was gone, and the drainpipe still vibrated from her descent.

I turned to walk out and grab Bala, but stopped short when my eyes caught a note on the mirror in lipstick. 'Be ready,' was all it said.

"Fuck. Bala. Call Lukas and have transport on standby. Let's roll out."

"What?"

"She's gone." I checked the holster beneath my loose tee, making sure I had my pistol. It was an automatic gesture that comforted me, if only a little. My hand slid up the strap, checking that the extra magazines were there. My heart slowed at the familiar movement.

I stormed through the hotel door, taking the steps two at a time, hearing Bala pound behind me. The little squirrel had known what she was doing. I had to believe that. Maybe she did understand the danger and trusted us to protect her.

I hoped this was all part of some plan and that she wasn't just running blindly from us because my brother had been too hard on her. That might break me; it might also break us. Our daddy and pappy had both warned us never to deliver pain without the lure of pleasure. Bala shouldn't have taken his anger out on Tosh without reminding her that he loved her. I hoped she understood that we did, and this was all for show.

Chapter Twenty-Four

Tosh

I ran from the hotel, intentionally looking over my shoulder fearfully. I thought about my favorite dog and how he looked after he'd gotten hit by a car in front of our house. It was a surefire way to make me cry, and I fought back my glee as the first few tears ran down my face. Focusing on Sam, I ran to the café, only slowing when it was in sight.

Slumping into the seat Bala put me in earlier, I let my shoulders sag and my head fall into my hands.

"You okay, sugar?" the waitress asked, popping her gum when she approached the table.

"Yeah." I sniffled, letting her see my red-rimmed eyes. "Can I get a water?" I asked, wiping my nose on my arm.

What Bala hadn't noticed earlier, because his anger clouded his instincts, was that a car had circled the block twice while we'd waited for Jah to shower and rejoin us. I knew these men were fantastic hunters. I'd seen them in action. And maybe I was the problem. Maybe we could never try to hunt as a team like this again. I could even admit that I weakened them. They were so focused on me that they hadn't noticed the car, but I had.

I would help with schematics and computer stuff in the future and leave the stalking to them unless needed. But this mission was personal. These people needed to be taken off the streets, and I was the perfect bait to lure them in. They were hunting me, but I was not prey. Not to them. They were the prey; they just didn't know it. My estrous was too close to do this the slow way. That shot had sped up my encroaching heat, and every hour that passed got worse, and the boys knew it. My skin wasn't crawling yet, but in days, maybe even hours, it would be. We needed this done, and we needed it done now.

With me as their target, some other omega was safe. Some poor child was safe. I trusted that my mates would never let anything happen to me, and I had faith in myself, too. I'd tucked the belt with the throwing knives under my romper before I fled and had complete confidence that together we'd end the threat the Farmintons presented.

The waitress set a glass down, and I nodded my thanks.

"Are you hungry?" It wasn't the waitress who spoke. The voice was soft and devoid of any accent a true Southerner would have. Her coloring was off, too, and I got the feeling she might not be indigenous to the area.

I blinked at her, schooling my face into dejected misery. I nodded slowly because, yeah, I was always hungry.

"Bring her the open-faced roast beef sandwich and a pitcher of water." Joy Farmington took the seat next to me. I'd seen pictures of Grace Battle, and this woman was definitely her mother. The kind smile that spread across her face didn't hide the edge of steel behind her gray eyes. She was an omega. It floored me that she could be complicit in this, but there she was. Then I remembered that she'd sold her own daughter, and any questions I had about Joy Farmington were answered. I knew better than most that an omega could be both predator and prey.

"Are you all right?" she asked, hunching over so she could meet my eyes.

"Yeah," I answered simply. "Thanks." I swung my feet, glancing at the street in front of the café.

"Boy troubles?" she asked. "I have a daughter a bit older than you, so I understand.

I shrugged one shoulder, spinning my water glass, knowing what I looked like. "Kinda," I answered.

"Do you want to talk about it?"

I shook my head. I perked up when a plate of hot, steaming beef and gravy appeared in front of me. You couldn't even see the bread; the beef was piled so high. I looked at the waitress, and she wouldn't meet my eyes. She just scurried away, casting a glance at Joy.

Fuck.

This is how they did it. The café was involved.

"You should eat. You look starved." Her voice had an edge to it that a sixteen-year-old wouldn't hear, but I did. I wondered how much of this meal I could eat without losing consciousness. I didn't want to eat any of it, but I couldn't afford to spook her either. The white four-door sedan from earlier circled the block again, driving far slower than was normal, even for Beulah Dawn O'Day.

Picking up the fork, I twirled it in the mashed potatoes and brought it to my lips. "My tummy is so upset," I started, letting sadness fill my voice. "I just don't understand any of it," I sighed, kicking my feet like a child as I cut up the bread with the fork and made a mess of the plate.

"What don't you understand, sweetie?" she asked, taking the bait.

"The boys are okay, but I just want to see my mom. It was fun at first, and I was excited to go to Nashville. But one of them spanked me for no reason, and I don't think it's going to be fun anymore. Now I just want to go home." I sipped the water in the glass, not taking enough to affect me if it was drugged too. I had no idea, but I had to play this the right way.

"I could take you to your mom." Joy glanced over her shoulder, her eyes scanning the street. "Where are they now? Those boys of yours."

"I snuck out. I'm supposed to be napping." I sighed again, stabbing angrily at the meat on my plate. "They said I need to rest, but I don't know why. Nashville won't be any fun if I'm resting all the time. Would you really take me to my mom? I only live a little way from here." I blinked wide, round eyes at her, watching the glint in her own turn savage.

"Of course," she answered, forgetting to ask me where home was.

"Okay." I rose, looking over my shoulder. "We'd better hurry. They'll notice I'm gone soon; I can eat later."

"My car is just over there."

She held her hand out, and we walked quickly through the white fence of the café and into the road. I skipped a little, lulling her into a false sense of calm. Let her think I was a child. Let her think me harmless. We ducked into the alley, and I saw the sedan waiting and apparently empty. Instinct told me I didn't want to get into that car, but I moved forward anyway, trusting that my men were close.

"Climb in the back!" Joy reached for the driver's door, and I took the passenger side, ripping the back door open and jumping out of the reach of the man hiding in the back.

It all went quickly from there. Bala stepped in front of the car, shouldering a high-capacity, semi-automatic shotgun I'd never seen before. Like a mirror, his brother moved in from behind. "By order of The Alpha and The New South Marines, you are under arrest," Bala said, his voice even. He sounded perfectly calm as he looked down the barrel of the rifle at Joy Farmington, but I could feel the anger and turmoil roiling in him through our bond.

Brandon Farmington grabbed for me again, probably thinking I'd make a good shield. I ducked, rolling away and hopping to my feet before running to stand by Jah's left side, leaving the right free to fire the shotgun at will.

"Make my day, asshole," Jah said, glaring through the back glass at the older man sitting there. I rolled my eyes at the cliché, waiting to see how this would go. "Get out of the vehicle with your hands raised." Jah chambered a round, moving his finger to the trigger.

"All right, all right!" Brandon slumped from the vehicle, lying on his stomach beside the car with his hands over his head. Joy Farmington followed suit. "My daughter is Grace Battle; there's been some misunderstanding. We were only trying to help the girl," he tried, his voice shrill and panicked.

"Your daughter's real family wants you dead." I smiled, feeling the cold, feral nature of it as it crossed my face. "You're only alive because The Alpha does not."

My mates moved to cuff them at the same time that the little old woman from the buffet this morning sprinted by me, her speed a grand contradiction to her age. She only had eyes for the men, and I stepped in front of her, taking her to the ground. I used her momentum to go into a roll that landed me on top of her with her arms behind her back. She let out a satisfying squeal, catching the eyes of Bala and Jah. She'd discounted me from the beginning, as most people do, and it cost her.

"Tosh, what the?" Bala started.

"They drug the food," I interrupted. "The waitress knew. I'm assuming the runner did too."

"I'll call for backup." Bala stood from where he'd zip-tied Joy's hands behind her back. "The Alpha is on standby for pickup."

Bala tossed me a pair of ties, and I bound the old woman as she cursed me in a very unladylike manner. "We're just trying to survive," she growled, bucking underneath me.

"Selling children is not survival, and I doubt you will survive that either," I said, pushing off her prone body to stand. It didn't bother me, not one bit. This was one elder who didn't deserve my respect.

Jah jerked Brandon to his feet, and Bala followed with Joy. I nudged the old woman, noting that venom and vitriol had stopped spewing from her mouth. Her chest continued to rise and fall in a ragged manner, telling me that she wasn't dead. I was glad for it because she didn't deserve to die. Not yet. Let The Alpha have her first. How many women and children had she sold into a death sentence? How many lives had she ruined?

I pulled the woman to her feet. She was slight and not much taller than I was. She was probably an omega too, yet she'd sold her own like it meant nothing. Maybe she had a story, and perhaps it was tragic, but tragedy didn't give you the right to ruin others' lives. Everyone's life has tragic elements; it should make you a better person, not a lesser one.

Her shoulders slumped as I followed Bala and Jah, pushing the woman into the diner. Bala swept the room with his shotgun raised. "Everyone, stay nice and still until The Alpha gets here to sort this out. Have a seat. Come on out of the kitchen and sit down. Anyone runs, and I shoot."

Jah pushed Brandon into a booth, freeing his hands to raise the shotgun as he pulled his wallet from his back pocket, flipping it open to reveal a badge. I'd known they were enforcers for The New South, but there must be more than one capacity in which they worked. This was the official one, I assumed. Had The Alpha wanted the Farmingtons dead, I doubted that badge would've made an appearance.

The room remained silent as we waited. Let The Alpha figure this out. With the compulsion of his strength and weight of his office, he had a much better chance than we did of getting it right. The entire town could be involved, but our work was done as we'd only been tasked with finding and detaining the Farmingtons. And it was a good thing too. My skin was flaming hot and beginning to crawl. We were very close to being out of time.

Forty-five minutes later, the sound of a fast-approaching helicopter broke the silence. Old leaves and the trash of a small town whipped against rattling windows as the Apache set down in the middle of the small square across the street. The blades hadn't stopped when The Alpha, flanked by his second in command, Jameson, jumped from the bird and strode towards us in full combat gear. A small number of marines piled out of the helicopter behind them, weapons drawn and at the ready. Lukas's eyes glinted murderously, and he ripped the door off its hinges when he pulled it open.

Those same eyes narrowed on Brandon and Joy Farmington immediately, and one side of his mouth quirked in a smile that was anything but friendly. His nose tipped slightly, and he spared me a glance. "The New South thanks you for your service," he said, shaking Bala and Jah's hands after giving them a salute. "You are relieved of duty. Get your omega home." He cracked his knuckles, turning his attention to the people in the diner. "Start talking." The command in his voice was clear, and no one could refuse it. Voices rose as one, and the Marines in the room took their statements.

Bala and Jah slung their shotguns over their backs, reaching for me. "Let's go home," Bala said when my hand slid into his. "You did a good job, little mink, but the end does not justify the means. There'll be hell to pay for the stunt you pulled."

I knew that. Of course, I knew that.

I looked forward to it.

I hadn't wanted safe men. I'm not even sure I wanted civilized ones. I'd failed to be caught in the mating chase by many a good man, knowing they would never satisfy the desire for something wild that burned in my veins. Jah and Bala satisfied that need. Being their prey wasn't a weakness; it was a strength only I'd had the nerve for. Because I was a predator too, and they knew that better than most. I stalked them now, my eyes taking in the smooth glide of their muscles as we walked toward the truck. I felt

256

compelled to bite them, to take them into my body in any way I could. Our first estrous together would be brutal; I could feel the need for their blood rising like the water in that river where they'd first claimed me.

I waited in the truck while Jah grabbed our bags and cooler from the hotel room we'd barely used. He ran down the stairs, the sense of urgency heavy on us all. We'd have to stop for gas but would push through and get to Cope as fast as we could. He'd emptied the little refrigerator in our room of water, and at our first stop, they'd bought gallons of it. They'd downed several, and I'd drunk almost continually between bites of jerky and bags of cashews. We didn't talk, and finally, the sound of tires on asphalt lulled me into a fevered sleep.

Chapter Twenty-Five

Bala

Tosh's soft growl filled the air, growing deeper by the mile. We were almost out of time, but we were also almost home. We'd pushed the truck to its limits, cutting hours off the trip by going speeds that would get us arrested if caught. Once we got out of the Second and the roads evened out, we flew.

Tosh's flushed cheeks and sweet smell had my cock hard and dripping cum already, and it was only a matter of time before the rut took hold. Jah was no better. The wet spot on his pants spread the closer we got to home, and I was grateful Tosh was asleep for most of the trip. One word, one flash of her eyes, and one smile would've sent us over the edge we balanced on, and it would've been over. The truck would run out of gas soon, but we were so close that we didn't care.

Tosh's growl turned into a snarl, and her lips pulled back to bare sharp white teeth. She sniffed the air, turning her nose to Jah's groin, and he groaned. I put the pedal to the floor, flying through the one stoplight and three stop signs of Cope until we shuddered to a stop in front of the house. It would've been nice to get some sleep in preparation for our mate's estrous, but nature would take over, and we'd survive without it. We'd been eating and drinking nonstop.

Jah grabbed Tosh and ran for the stairs. Her howl shattered the peaceful sound of the distant waves, and her eyes snapped open, snagging on Jah. I took the stairs two at a time, locking the door behind us as he put her down. She swiped her baby claws at him, drawing blood the second she was free of his grasp. There was no violet in her eyes; they were black as night and wild as the sea. Her lips peeled wider, and her snarl grew louder. She tipped her head, scenting the air with flared nostrils before stalking forward, the growl never stopping.

So that's the way of it then.

I'd heard that all omegas approached estrous differently. Some were pliant and sweet, while others were anger-fueled from need. Tosh was violence personified. My guess is that she would never be easy, but we would not want her to be. Yes, the sea might have hours where it is calm, and you can swim into the deep without worry, but those times were few and far between, and you only enjoyed them for a little while. Once you had your fill of the peace, you looked forward to the pounding of the waves and the rip of the current. She swiped at Jah again, and he backpedaled, confused by her actions. But I wasn't.

I took her legs out from under her, and she rolled away from me, popping to her feet and swiping at me with her claws. She tore through my shirt, drawing blood, and we both smiled when it dripped down my chest. She licked her lips, and I ripped my shirt off.

Jah circled, finally understanding, and Tosh's wild grin grew. He reached for her, and she swept sideways, clawing across his back and causing him to howl. Her head tipped back, long honeyed hair brushing her waist. Slick flooded the dirty white romper she'd been wearing since this morning, puddling on the ground beneath her.

I roared, reaching for her as I felt my humanity slipping. She barked a laugh and rounded on me. She launched herself, sinking her teeth into my shoulder, then pulled away, her lips stained in blood. But she was gone before I could latch onto her, racing after Jah with an unhinged gleam in her eyes. I loved it.

Jah and Tosh went down in a tangle of limbs, their growls vicious and their intent questionable. The table went crashing, and a chair shattered. The smell of blood drifted in the air, and my cock pulsed, releasing a spray of cum. I took my pants off, stroking it and making cum drip faster. I'd never had a full rut, and this one was going to be incredible.

Jah's tattered shirt flew from the center of their fight, and another rip of clothing followed. Tosh's throwing knives followed, safely sheathed in their holder. I walked forward, reaching into the writhing mass of skin to pull Tosh out by the back of her neck, adding a little shake to make a point. She barked like the crafty creature we'd nicknamed her and slashed at me again.

Wrestling her to her knees, I changed her focus by shoving my cock deep into her throat. She groaned as I fucked her face, each thrust giving her the nourishment she'd need for the days to come.

She arched into me, wrapping her arms around my ass and holding me close as I pushed until her nose met my skin. Gripping her hair, I fucked her mouth with a roughness she loved if the scratches down my thighs meant anything. Jah's jeans came off in one push, and I saw he was already gone to the rut. But I held on longer. He pulled her hips up, kneeling behind her and sinking his cock in hard enough to push her deeper onto me so that I felt the scrape of teeth.

He lost himself to fucking her, and it was the most fantastic thing I'd ever seen. As destructive as they are, hurricanes are still a thing of beauty. She came almost immediately, her cries muffled by my dick. I let go then, unleashing all the frustration I'd had onto Tosh as I leaned to the side and watched her throat expand as I destroyed it. Jah came with a grunt, knotting Tosh and making her go limp. I thrust two more times, grabbing my knot and filling her stomach with enough calories to get her through a few hours until she needed more.

It was glorious. Tosh was glorious. Sated, for now, she purred as she swallowed me down, her blackened eyes meeting mine. She smiled around my cock, showing something of the omega I knew and loved.

I pulled from her, my cock still hard and dripping. Jah's eyes met mine, and I saw some sentience in them along with a thin line of his iris. I nodded toward the bedroom, moving to grab armfuls of the gallon water jugs from the counter.

Jah's knot had released, and Tosh stood by the bed naked and scowling. She paced, whining and unsatisfied but snarled when I offered to help her remake the bed. She ripped the sheets and the little nest there, tossing them into the corner. She did it herself, taking linens from the basket and arranging them in the way only an omega can. Jah and I watched, riveted by the process. Some things in nature can't be explained. Like snowflakes, no two nests are alike, and no omega makes them in the same way.

Tosh eyed us, adjusting blankets before eyeing us again. She braided, twisted, and wove linens into a deep, wide area that took up the entire bed. I'd seen a picture book detailing the beauty of nests, but I'd never seen one made for three, and that's what Tosh built. I was honored the day she married us and had been humbled the day she'd claimed us, but I was awed by the nest she built for us and wondered that the world didn't know the beauty of a nest woven for more than one alpha. It was delicate and complicated yet stronger than it looked, just like the omega who crafted it.

She stared, her chest heaving. Jah's cum ran down her thighs, and I wanted nothing but to get her into that nest and chase his with my own. But I grabbed her before she could fight me, wrestling her into the shower. Angry, Jah went to pull her from me, and I hoped we would not fight over this. She should be clean. We all should. We had a few more minutes before need would make her wild again, and I wanted to lay in that perfect nest without the scent of Union City and a long drive on our skin. I bared my teeth at him, growling to show my position.

Sometimes we did fight. I was older, though not by much, and it made me want to lead our team of two, now three. Jah usually backed down when I pushed but with an omega in heat between us, he might not. I turned the shower on, soaping Tosh quickly. Her skin was flushed and on fire, her moans turning needy as I washed between her legs and down her thighs.

Catching on, he jumped in, washing the scent of Brandon Farmington and landlocked town from himself. Serving an omega meant more than one thing. Yes, fucking was a significant part of that, but caring for them when they cannot care for themselves is an integral part as well. Tosh needed to be clean, and we could clean her. She needed to be fed, and we would provide that too.

Jah soaped her hair, running his fingers to detangle it before soaking it in conditioner. She hadn't said a word, just basked in being tended as she should. But the growl started as Jah rinsed the conditioner, and I jumped out, grabbing a towel. Wrapping Tosh up, I ran a comb through her wet hair before braiding it tightly down her back. We wouldn't have another shower for days, and she'd kill me if her hair was so matted as to be unfixable.

Tended and dry, I herded Tosh toward our room, handing her a gallon of water she emptied immediately. Jah and I did the same, but a swipe of claws across my back told me that our short-lived break was over. A weight hit the perfect spot on the back of my knees, and I went down in a tumble of omega limbs and fierce need. Rolling, I put Tosh under me, growling until her back arched and she soaked the carpet with slick. Burying my head between her thighs, I drank it in, growling to induce more until I was full. I didn't let her come, and her cries turned angry as I picked her up, tossing her into her nest and following behind.

We fought as much as we fucked. Tosh came at me with teeth bared, and Jah entered her roughly, giving her something else but my blood to think about. I pulled him from her so that I could sink into her in his place. He swiped at me too, but a growl set him right, and he fucked her face instead. He even let his knot expand when he came so she could milk it with her hands and force more cum from him.

I made her scream her orgasm with me deep inside of her in that place made for me, her pussy clenching so tight I couldn't move, forcing me to cum too. I fed her our combined fluids when my knot released, taking some for myself. The taste of us on my tongue was the last thing clear memory before the rut took me.

Chapter Twenty-Six

Tosh

I'd experienced estrous before; of course, I had. I wasn't a teenager anymore, but this one? This one was different. With your gay best friend, you are careful. Yes, instinct is instinct, but you remember that the man in your nest isn't your mate somewhere in the reptilian center of your brain. This estrous? Glorious. Ballads should be written, and stars should be named for it. My mates are perfect in every way. A little bit violent and a whole lot caring, they took care of me like no other ever had.

I remembered it all. Through the haze of a sheer curtain that softened things but didn't hide them, I saw it all. I felt it all. The need to fight them never lessened, and they indulged me in it. My body bruised and delightfully sore, the haze cleared as Bala fucked my ass and Jah my pussy. I grunted my orgasm, my throat sore from screaming and rough use by their cocks. I was glad three mates hadn't been in the cards because I think they'd have killed me. But two? Two was perfect.

They came in tandem, gripping my hips. On our sides, with one in front and one behind, they gave me their knots for the final time of this cycle. Jah's eyes closed immediately, and his soft snores made me smile. Never had an omega been served better, and I'd cut the bitch that challenged me on that. Bala's hand slipped off my hip as he, too, fell into a deep sleep. In their minds, I'd be waking them in ten or fifteen minutes to do it over again, but they could rest now. My first estrous as a claimed omega was over, and what a glorious thing it had been. Sonnets were composed of lesser moments.

I took in a deep breath, letting it out slowly as I cataloged the aches and pains I felt. Bite marks decorated every inch of my shoulders, and I chuckled that their need for violence was as deep as mine. It's what made us perfect together. Long strands escaped from the braid and were trapped in the dried, crusted cum on my back. In fact, dried cum covered every inch of my body, and I smiled at the memory of them massaging it into my skin during one of those fleeting moments of satiation.

Their knots released together, and cum flooded the space between us as they slept on, not noticing. In the clear light of day, my asshole hurt. Like after a whiskey-fueled night of passion, things always hurt the following day. I chuckled at the thought, laughing harder when the boys turned onto their backs and began to take the art of snoring seriously. Let them rest; they'd earned it.

I disentangled myself from them one limb at a time, walking around the room, looking for any remaining water. I hadn't lost any weight, and with two alphas feeding me, I shouldn't have been surprised, but I was. This wasn't some lazy estrous where I languished in the nest getting served like a princess. It had been vicious and brutal, physical and exhausting. Still, they'd done a fantastic job. The breaks in my demands had been short, and none of us had slept more than a few minutes. They looked good, too, I noticed as I watched them sleep. They might have lost a little weight, but not more than a few pounds, and nothing that a meal or two wouldn't fix. They'd prepped well, reinforcing that I'd made the right choice, not that I'd doubted it for a second.

I opened the door, taking in the kitchen and living room. Everything was neat and tidy despite the memory of trashing the place in my haste to taste their blood on my tongue. I cocked my head curiously, walking naked into the kitchen to get a glass of tea.

"Make sure you let dem bathe you, sugar."

I jumped out of my skin, turning to face the threat in my house. Only it was Miss Beulah, lounging on the couch with her feet propped on the coffee table.

I took a deep breath, releasing it and trying to calm my racing heart.

"Most omegas want to shower right away, but dats a mistake. Let dem care for you, even if it's hours before they wake up. It will make them feel better for da things that happened during your estrous." She smiled, her eyes taking in every inch of me in one glance. She nodded her head as if satisfied, rising to her feet with only a little effort.

"They don't have anything to feel bad about," I said, pouring a glass of ice-cold sweet tea and sighing at the first taste of it.

"They'll feel bad about all of it. Ask me how I know," she added with a soft smile. She was an alpha, and I didn't know anything about how female alphas worked, but I'm guessing she knew a thing or two about how the males did.

She glanced at my bare shoulders, taking in all the bites and bruises on my skin. "Trust me, Tosh. Let them clean you."

I nodded my head, knowing she was right. I slipped quickly into the bedroom, grabbing a robe and belting it around my waist before shutting the door softly behind me and walking into the kitchen once again.

"Speaking of cleaning," Miss Beulah said, her voice taking on an edge I hadn't heard directed at me before. "Use oil to clean dos cast iron pans, not water. My ancestors died a second time when you washed dem in the sink."

"How did you?" I stuttered.

"Oh, I know. Don't think I don't." She smiled then, making me relax. "Well, it had probably been a hundred years since dey was washed; they probably needed it. I've checked on you every day since I found the truck abandoned by the road. It's been six days. I was afraid you'd kill them."

I blushed, unable to stop myself. Six days wasn't unheard of, but it was a long estrous. I'd thought that having two mates might shorten the duration; I'd been wrong.

"You know," she said as she moved to the oven and pulled out some biscuits. "I wasn't sure 'bout them taking one omega as a mate. I thought maybe it wasn't the right thing. I can see dat it is now. You fit them perfectly."

"And they fit me."

"I'm glad. Those boys have been all sharp edges and death for far too long. It's nice to see them acting like proper alphas.

I nodded once, agreeing but not. Maybe I softened them, maybe not. I wasn't exactly soft myself, but together we were more balanced, I supposed. Maybe she was right about that.

"I made chicken and dumplings. Dat'll put meat on your bones," she said, sliding another pan out of the oven. "They're in the fridge. Just heat'em on the stove until the sauce is hot, but don't let them boil. Dis here is apple crisp. I added some protein powder to the crust since the boys will need it."

"Thank you," I said.

"No. Thank you. They searched a long time for someone to make them happy, and if there's one thing I know for sure, it's that you do." She turned the oven off before grabbing her purse and making for the door. "Oh. Wake dem up in time to watch The Alpha on TV tonight. He's going to make an announcement." She gave me a wink and shut the door behind her when she left.

I sat on the couch, sipping tea and enjoying the feel of a sore pussy and aching muscles. The feeling of peace was so thick in the air that I almost fell asleep. As tired as I was, I was energized too. I wiped the thin layer of dust that had settled on everything, leaving my mates to sleep a little before putting the pot of chicken and dumplings on to heat. When steam rose from them, I turned the burner off before walking into the bedroom and finding Jah and Bala snuggling each other like they didn't know I was missing.

The room smelled like blood and sex. My nest still stood, and I smiled at the memory of making it. It had withstood six days, two alphas, and one omega. I'd never made a nest for three, and it had taken me a while to work out how but now that I had, I'd never sleep without one.

Bala sighed so deeply in his sleep that my smile fell. I felt bad for waking them, but they needed food, a shower, and a clean nest, and it was my turn to provide for them, so I would. I walked to the edge of the bed, twining my fingers through Jah's loose waves. His lips twitched, pulling into a frown, and I smiled. I bet he was sore, too.

I realized something as I watched them sleep. I loved them. God, did I love them. Wild and brutal, vicious and beautiful, they were mine, and I'd burn the world for them. The smile that spread across my face didn't feel like a nice one.

"Baby," I said, leaning over Jah to place a kiss on his cheek.

"You need me?" Jah mumbled, fighting to open his eyes.

"I'll always need you, but right now, I need you to wake up and eat. Then I need you to shower me so that I can fix our nest and we can sleep until Monday.

He scrubbed his hands over his face, combing out six days of facial hair with his nails. "I'm up, little squirrel."

He rose from the bed, his body covered in bites and scratches, some of them deep. His toffee-colored skin was painted in blood, and my slick, and I'd never seen him look better.

I moved to Bala, cupping his chin in my hand and placing a chaste kiss on his lips. "Come eat, love."

"I'll eat you so good you'll scream my name," he mumbled, rolling on his side to get comfortable and not meaning a word he said at the moment.

"While I know that's true, that's not what I mean, Bala. Wake up and come eat."

He groaned, opening his eyes to find the bed empty. "Are you okay?" he asked.

"Better than okay. Supper is on. Then we'll get cleaned up and sleep for days. Come on, baby." I tugged the covers off him, my eyes snagging on his soft cock. It hadn't been soft in days, and the sight of it moved something in me. They'd served so well. "I love you," I said.

He pulled me down to him, rolling us on our sides and burrowing into my back. His lips found the shell of my ear, and the warmth of his body engulfed me. "I love you too, Tosh."

I smiled at his use of my name. "Thank you for serving me so well. Five stars. Recommend."

"So you'll recommend me to your friends?" he chuckled, his breath in my hair stirring a groan from me.

"Never. I'll kill them for considering it."

"Mmhmm."

I sighed again, wanting nothing more than to lie in bed. "Come on. You need food, and I need a shower." This taking care of an alpha business was hard sometimes.

We ate supper, enjoying the comfortable silence, excellent food, and each other. When the food was gone and the table cleared, we turned on the TV to watch the news conference The Alpha scheduled.

"On this night," he started. Eve stood at his side, looking resplendent in a light blue dress and little pill hat. Her red hair was up in a twist. She was regal, more like a tiny queen than an omega. She and Lukas's daughter stood beside Lorelei and Jameson, whose infant son was in her arms. "We come together to celebrate two very different things. Firstly, the passing of the second amendment to NS304, The Omega Rule. For decades, we struggled with fertility, and our numbers decreased." He paused, smiling at his wife and her best friend. "It's funny how something so simple as a choice can change all that. Since NS304's inception, we've seen a baby boom. It was a mistake not to give omegas a choice in who they mated, and it was another to tell them they had no choice but to conceive. As we've seen, babies will come if their mothers are happy and ready. From this day forward, women will have access to free birth control, making the choice to bear children theirs and their mate's. Though some of you are unhappy about both an omega's right to choose her mate and her right to

272

plan when children come, I challenge you to do better. The proof that it works is in front of you. We are making strides toward a better New South for Alpha, Beta, and Omega alike, and I challenge you to join our efforts to move forward or challenge me for the job." The last sentence ended in a growl, a corner of his lip arching to reveal even, white teeth.

"The second thing we are celebrating is the detection and extinction of a ring of human traffickers whose efforts to undermine the fabric of our society are far-reaching. These people were tried and convicted of selling our most precious resource to the highest bidder, often The Middle West. I stand before you to say that this will not be tolerated. Will. Not. Be." He pounded his fist to accentuate each word, causing Eve to place her hand gently on his arm. "Right," he snarled, calming himself visibly. With a sigh, he continued, "I want to reiterate that human trafficking of any variety is a felony and punishable by immediate death if found guilty.

"So, the third thing we celebrate is the death of fourteen citizens who colluded and conspired to sell children, mated omegas, unmated omegas, and the rare beta to The Middle West.

"Operatives located a pocket of individuals in Union City, Second District, and further investigation uncovered fourteen people working together against The New South and the core values we hold dear. Those individuals, nine men and five women, were put to death by firing squad at oh-eight-thirty this morning.

This is a crime that reverberates through generations. Those lost will never be recovered. Understand that this behavior will not be tolerated. Thank you for your time, and have a lovely evening." The Alpha stared into the camera, daring anyone to argue until the picture faded to commercial. We sat in stunned silence.

Have a lovely evening indeed. Fourteen people lost their lives, but how many hundreds suffered for their actions? It was unfortunate they couldn't be killed twice.

"Wow, birth control. That's crazy," Jah said, and I punched him.

"Bold move, but I think it will work," I said, smiling. "There's been a huge jump in births. All we wanted was to decide for ourselves. I've got maybe thirty years of fertility left if you boys make me happy; maybe more. It isn't unheard of. This is a good thing. Plus, how many babies and mothers lose their lives toward the end of those fertile years due to complications? This is a game-changer." I smiled at the thought.

Never did I dream when I met Eve that her fire and resolution would fuel the change sweeping across The New South. And yes, there were some that weren't happy, but changes can be hard, even the good ones. Lukas had a battle on his hands; I had no doubt. I also had no doubt he'd win.

We moved into the bedroom, stripped the sheets, and placed them in the washer. I stood beside the bed, my hands itching to make another nest for my boys, but I needed a shower first. Bala used his body to push me toward the steaming shower Jah prepared. I sighed as the hot water hit sore muscles, relaxing into Jah's immovable wall of a body behind me. "I'm sorry," he said, trailing his fingers over the myriad bites and bruises like Miss Beulah said he would.

"Don't apologize," I said, purring into his chest and trailing my fingers over his marred chest. "We marked each other. Happily."

He grunted, purring to drown out my purr, making me laugh. I sighed as he soaped his hands, running them over my crusty skin. Bala shampooed my hair, and I let The New South's most dangerous men care for me without complaint. They needed it, and maybe so did I.

Estrous is a time of need. Whether it's violent or gentle, demanding or calm, it's a biological need that must be met, or an omega dies. Eventually anyway. It's also about taking. Yes, an alpha gives; he serves. But the omega takes during this time, and they take it all.

As tired as I was, I wanted them. I couldn't help it. I didn't need to feel them inside of me, but I wanted to. I'd taken so much and given so little that I just wanted them. Jah's hands washed my breasts in the least sexual way imaginable, but I groaned anyway, tilting my lips to his. The kiss was lazy and slow, but no less hot. His cock twitched against my stomach, daring to dream once again. I smiled into our kiss, nipping his lips.

Bala moved closer, his hands running up my hips. He tugged the tips of my hair as he purred, arching my neck to him so he could claim my mouth too. His kiss was harder, more demanding than it usually was. I moaned, feeling the trickle of slick between my legs increase, amazed at myself for being able to still make it.

Jah's hot mouth found my nipple, and his tongue lapped the puckered flesh gently. We'd fucked hard over the last six days, but we hadn't made love in a while, and I wanted them. "I love you," I said again.

"We love you too," Jah said, his voice reverent. "You're a gift."

Bala's cock teased my core, and I arched my back into him, giving him access to enter. He slipped in gently. Slowly. I'd missed this. It was love without the violence my estrous begged for. The delicious feel of him slipping deep inside of me and into that space made for him had stars bursting behind my eyes.

Jah went to his knees as his brother moved in and out of me languidly. His tongue found my clit, and he lapped it with a flat-tongued intensity that had me begging to come.

"Please," I panted.

But neither man was in a hurry, and I wondered if they wanted something too. I stopped begging, moaning as I lay my head on Bala's chest as he twisted his hips and purred softly for me. This was love, too. This was service. But it was also so much more than that. I sighed, saying his name as I came in delicious, crippling waves. My body clenched around his, demanding as it always did. And he gave.

Jah rose, claiming my lips as Bala's knot bound us together, and he filled my body full of cum. He held us together, pulling his brother's body closer, so I was pinned between them. My legs trembled from the force of the orgasm, and the only thing holding me up was them.

Jah kissed me, sweet and searching. Bala's kiss landed on my neck and shoulders, his purr never stopping. My eyes drifted closed, and Jah's finger between my thighs made them open. Bala picked up my leg, and his knot released, allowing his soft cock to slip out. Jah pushed in the space Bal left, kissing me as I moaned. "You wanted us," he whispered. "Take us both."

"Always," I said as he moved inside me. I could feel him so deep it seemed impossible, unnatural even. But there was nothing unnatural about this. Nothing at all.

The position of my leg on Bala's arm and Jah's body inside mine had me coming again, a choked scream coming from my ravaged throat. Bala shushed me with a kiss, his hands rolling my nipples to extend the orgasm. I leaned against him, going limp as Jah increased his pace. Pushing my body into his brother's, who held fast against the force of it. I felt his knot before he grunted. It expanded almost painfully for both of us. We'd used these bodies well and hard lately so that even pleasure caused a hint of something darker.

Bala reached a hand down, rubbing it over the obscene swell of my stomach caused by cum and chicken dumplings. "Someday," he promised. "When you're ready."

"Someday, I'll be ready," I promised too. They washed me again, almost causing a repeat performance none of us could rally for.

While they watched, I sized them up, making a nest fit for two kings and their queen. I made it deep and wide, like the ocean pounding outside our doors. Sometimes wild and sometimes calm, but ever-present like our bond. Like our love. When it was done, I herded them into it, then settled between them and let that love surround us like a favorite blanket.

Tomorrow would come. It would have challenges and failures, wins and losses, choices and battles, but it would come regardless. We'd face it together; stronger for the losses and better for the wins, but more importantly, the love we shared would endure, and the choice we'd made would prove itself the right one until the end of our days.

Epilogue

The Alpha sat at his desk, looking out over the helipad to the trees in the distance. Every day, they seemed further away, and he wondered at the weight of leadership. A knock at his door drew his focus, and after a weary sigh, he said, "Enter." He loved his job; he really did. Things were changing so quickly in The New South that it was hard to keep up with, and there were nights he never made it to bed. Never made it to his mate. Last night had been one of those.

He thought that time would ease the vicious need for his Eve, but it hadn't. If anything, he wanted her more, and he wondered about who had really claimed who. Not that she hadn't claimed him to, but he was lost to her.

Smiling, Lukas thought about the picture she'd make now. Curled around their daughter, her belly rounded with his son. He knew she'd be beautiful. They'd all be beautiful.

Despite the availability of birth control, she'd decided against taking it, wanting as many children as she could birth in as short a time as possible. He worried it would be too much for her tiny body, but his Second's mother had given birth to eight Alpha males in short succession and had assured him that Eve would be fine. These omegas were something else.

Eve Hatfield Justice had demanded a choice for all omegas, promising the moon if he granted it. He'd claimed her very much against her will, making her Eve Jennings, but she'd given him the moon, anyway. Well, after a long fight that she'd finally won. He'd never tell her that, though. He remembered pinning her and taking her while she fought him with fondness, though he'd never admit that either. She was a spitfire and would make him pay if he was anything but apologetic about that night.

In the end, she'd been right, and now that omegas had a choice in their mates, their jobs, and their childbearing, babies were simply crawling out of the woodwork. The funny thing was that not only were omegas getting pregnant at an incredible rate, but betas and even alpha females were giving birth in large numbers, and The New South thrived because of it. The economy was better than ever, and cottage industries centered on pregnancy sprouted everywhere.

And Eve was responsible for it all. Well, maybe not just Eve, but to Lukas, it was only her. It would only ever be her.

All this prosperity came at a price, though, and The Middle West and New North were rattling the bars to get in. The problem was that, if allowed, they would bring their ideas, laws, and politics to his country, making it just like theirs and leaving it a shadow of what it once was. Then the thing they were reaching for would be exactly like the thing they'd fought to flee, and he couldn't allow it. The New South was strong, and its Marines would prevail, but that didn't mean there weren't sleepless nights and long hours.

His secretary cleared her voice, drawing Lukas from his thoughts. Scrubbing his hands down his face, Lukas sat straighter. "What can I do for you?" he asked.

"Your wife sent a woman to speak with you."

The Alpha raised a brow at that, looking at the tall beta secretary Jameson made him hire because Lukas growled at him too much to do things. He'd listened because he relied on him, but rather enjoyed making him do his menial errands. It kept him humble.

Jameson had broken another alpha's forced claim on the omega he'd wanted for himself, and something had happened in the process. Jameson had gotten stronger. Jameson Battle had always been a force of nature, but now he was as strong as Lukas, and he knew it. They both knew it.

Jameson didn't want to lead, and Lukas didn't care that he could. Two strong alphas made The New South better, and Lukas accepted that. Jameson was also Lukas's best friend, and if it ever came to a challenge between them, their wives would bury them in unmarked graves. It was good to know who the real bosses were.

"I'll bring you a coffee," his secretary said, ushering the woman to a chair in front of him before closing the door behind her.

She was a petite thing, and he knew immediately that she was one of the omegas from some remote place in the Seventh. You knew them because they were exotic and foreign, despite being born and raised in The New South. Isolated mountains and cavernous hollows had bred brightly colored people, and they'd made stunningly beautiful omegas. Strange and unique, they were as deadly as they were gorgeous to look at, as most things in nature are.

This one was no exception. With wide, almost almond-shaped eyes that were a shade of green he hadn't seen outside of the fields in the Sixth, she was stunning. Brown hair emblazoned by copper highlights fell to her collar bones, and full lips set in a grim line set off the striking nature of her delicate face.

"How can I help you?" Lukas asked, not looking below those collar bones to what surely curved and flowed like a mountain stream.

"I want a divorce," she said, her tone firm. If she was impressed by being in the presence of the land's strongest alpha, she didn't show it. The omegas from the untamed lands of the Seventh were all that way, and he wondered if even more changes weren't coming because of them.

Lukas sighed, pinching the bridge of his nose and wondering why his wife sent the woman here. "There is no divorce for an omega; you know this."

"I don't care about the mating bond itself. I want out of the legal relationship it entails." Her green eyes glinted with violence, and Lukas wondered what the actual fuck this omega's alpha had done to deserve it. Something, for sure. Lukas had no doubt he'd done something.

"Mrs…?" he started.

"Call me Liliona."

"Liliona, there is no way to reverse the legal relationship between an alpha and his or her bonded omega. It's not done." The Alpha said, letting his authority bleed into the statement, hoping that would be the end of it.

"Your wife disagrees."

"She usually does."

He sighed again, glancing at the treeline leading to his new home, where Eve was. It seemed further away than it had been five minutes ago.

"He violated NS304," Liliona tried.

"How?" Lukas leaned back, crossing his ankle over his knee as he waited for her answer.

The woman fidgeted with her hands, letting some of her nerves show. "Jaxon takes me against my will during my estrous," she said finally.

"Liliona." Lukas wasn't without sympathy, but he understood that wasn't how the dynamics worked. Still, Eve had sent her, and there must be a reason. "When did he claim you? Before or after NS304?"

"Before," she whispered, not meeting his eyes. There was a story here, and it was probably one of the old tales that were common before NS304 had been enacted. His own story was no different, if he was honest.

"The only option is to find a stronger alpha to break the claim, though too much time has passed for that to be a viable plan. A legal divorce does not solve the problem. Death won't either unless you are willing to die too. Is that what you want? Do you want him to die?"

The omega dissolved into tears before running from the room. Lukas shook his head, wondering what cruelty could cause her resolve to fail so utterly. "Did you get her name?" Lukas pressed the button on his ComLink leading to his secretary.

"Yes, she signed in, sir."

"Call the O'Day brothers and have them find the alpha that claims her. I want him brought to me. Alive, preferably."

"Yes, Sir."

The ComLink went silent, but his thoughts did not. Maybe this Jaxon was a problem, and maybe he had violated NS304. One thing he'd learned with these northern omegas is that where there's smoke, there's fire.

Also by Sharilyn:

Trauma: stand-alone contemporary women's fiction

Healer Series: Series Complete

Cerridwen's Tears

Healer

House of Fire

The Scarlet Heron

The Flame Keeper

Goddess Bound

Goddess Rising Series

Goddess Rising

The Eight Series:

Airmed

Ravena

Teagan

Omegas of The New South:

The Omega Rule

The Omega Challenge

An Alpha's Grace

An Omega's Choice: Predators and Prey

An Alpha's Ruin

An Omega's Dance

An Alpha's Price

The WidowMaker trilogy:

Widowmaker

Gravedigger

Queenmaker- coming Summer 2026

Follow Sharilyn on Facebook, Instagram, Goodreads, and her plain old website.

www.sharilynskye.com

About Sharilyn:

Sharilyn spent most of her early years on the Grand Strand of SC, annoying local police officers and pretty much everyone else with her fast cars and loud music. She graduated from the University of South Carolina and now lives on a small farm outside Morgantown, West Virginia, with her family and a menagerie of cats, horses, and visiting wildlife.

Sharilyn writes urban fantasy, fairy tales, Omegaverse romance, and women's fiction. Each title in her Omegaverse series, Omegas of The New South, spent weeks on Amazon's best-sellers list. An Omega's Dance and An Alpha's Price were USA Today and Amazon Best Sellers, and her Healer series has a following that borders on cultish. (She adores you, you crazy Lara Hennessey fans!)

She loves showing Quarter Horses, trail riding, reading, drinking coffee, driving her vintage Corvette, and being annoyed by her kids. If she's missing, check the garage or look for the horse trailer. If one is missing, no worries; she'll be back. Probably.